REBELLION is Book 2 (

After narrowly escaping imprisonment, the greatest of Archang
trying to make his way back to his former stature. Evil surrounds
him, though, and is determined to use him to destroy the entire
Heavens. When he finds out the privilege the Humans have been
given, he can no longer stand idly by.

Welcome to the Rebellion.

Note to Reader:
Start with Book 1, Dawn of Days

In Part Two of this book is the **After Life Journey of Duncan**.

A young boy, close to the heart of his mother, is on the severe
end of the Autism Spectrum. He struggles through his life, unable
to communicate with those he loves most. One day he meets a very
special person who unlocks his mind to his true destiny.

Note to Reader:
All of these After Life Journeys, such as Duncan's, play a
prominent role in the epic last three books of the After Life Series. It
is why they are included in each book alongside the Sagas.
They are also published separately as novellas.

Also by D.P. Conway

Plus
Starry Night, a Magical Tale
Free at the end of this book

Rebellion

The Angel Sagas & the Journey of Duncan

by D. P. Conway

After Life Series
Book 2

Day Lights Publishing House, Inc.
Cleveland, Ohio

Darkness to Light through the Power of Story

What is the After Life Series

This is the start of an epic story of Lords, Angels, Dark Angels, and Humans. There are two types of stories in the series: The Angel Sagas and the After Life Journeys.

THE ANGEL SAGAS tells the story of Creation from the beginning of time to the coming end of time. Long before the earth, or Adam and Eve were created, the Lords created the male and female Angels and the Heavens, where they were supposed to live in harmony.

But when the Dark Lord rises and discontent is sown, the dreams of the Lords begin to fall apart, and everyone must choose a side. The Archangel Sagas spans all 15 books, but in books 1 through 12, the exciting After Life Journeys of our Human characters are also presented.

THE AFTER LIFE JOURNEYS dramatically tell individual tales of 15 modern-day people's lives and journeys to the After Life. There is an autistic young man, a mob lawyer, a girl with Rett's disease, a middle-aged divorcee, a rigid Baptist preacher, a U.S. Senator, a Muslim American soldier, a woman who suffers abuse as a child, and even an avowed atheist who survived the shark-infested waters after the sinking of the U.S.S. Indianapolis.

Each person lives life the best they can, but suddenly, and often unexpectedly, death crashes into their plans. Many never get to say goodbye or attain the hopes and dreams they often desperately desired.

Some are cautionary tales, like the mob lawyer's story. Even the 9/11 hijackers are addressed in book 12, because the series is not only about Heaven but also about Hell, and about a place in between, for those who don't quite fit into Heaven or Hell. The series is about second chances, and life on the other side, a life we all someday want.

All 15 human stories converge in the last three books of the series, as the Angels, the Heavens, and the Earth race toward their destiny, and all are hurled toward the final showdown between good and evil.

Now, I invite you to sit back… and let me tell you a story.

D.P. Conway   All Hallow's Eve, 2020, the year of the pandemic.

Books in the After Life Series

Book 1: Dawn of Days
The Angel Sagas & Journey of Nancy

Book 2: Rebellion
The Angel Sagas & the Journey of Duncan

Book 3: Judgment
The Angel Sagas & the Journey of James

Book 4: Empire
The Angel Sagas & the Journey of Julie

Book 5: The Innocents
The Angel Sagas & the Journey of Laura

Book 6: Revelation
The Angel Sagas & the Journey of Katie

Book 7: Memento Vivere
The Angel Sagas & the Journey of Susan

Book 8: Rise of Legion
The Angel Sagas & the Journey of Brittany

Book 9: Revenge of the Damned
The Angel Sagas & the Journey of Jill

Book 10: Crucible
The Angel Sagas & the Journey of Kyle

Book 11: Deliverance
The Angel Sagas & the Journey of Lena

Book 12 : Title to Be Determined
The Angel Sagas & the Journey of John

Book 13: Title to Be Determined
Series Conclusion Part 1

Book 14: Prophecy
Series Conclusion Part 2

Book 15: Kingdom Come
Series Conclusion Part 3

AFTER LIFE CHARACTERS - HUMANS & THEIR GUARDIAN ANGELS

Julie is a middle age woman who, due to the lack of affections from her husband, becomes discontent in her marriage and is tempted to go outside the boundaries to meet her needs.

JULIE

Angel in the 1st Heavenly Realm.

Julie's Guardian Angel

ANGEL JARIO

Duncan is a young man with severe Autism who one day meets a special visitor who changes his destiny forever.

DUNCAN

Angel in the 5th Heavenly Realm

Duncan's Guardian Angel

ANGEL LINDA

Laura is the principal of an elementary school, who leads the fight in stopping an unprecedented attack on her, her peers, and her innocent young students.

LAURA

Angel of the 4th Heavenly Realm.

Laura's Guardian Angel

ANGEL JOSEPH

Amir, a young American Muslim who is caught up in the tide of resentment after 9/11, goes the extra mile to save his fellow soldiers

AMIR

Host Commander in the 5th Heavenly Realm

Amir's Guardian Angel

ANGEL SADIE

James is a crooked mob lawyer who goes too far in defending his boss against a rival mob family.

JAMES

Host Commander in the 5th Heavenly Realm

James' Guardian Angel

ANGEL MERCIO

Katie, a young girl whose dreams of love and happiness are threatened by a terrible disease, discovers a destiny she never imagined.

KATIE

Host Commander in the 3rd Heavenly Realm

Katie's Guardian Angel

ANGEL ROSIE

AFTER LIFE CHARACTERS - HUMANS & THEIR GUARDIAN ANGELS

Brittany, abandoned by her father, is an emotionally troubled teen who becomes the girlfriend of a gang leader.

BRITTANY

Angel in the 2nd Heavenly Realm

Brittany's Guardian Angel

ANGEL CAROLYN

Nancy, an old woman in a nursing home, is visited by a special person and reminisces back to the days when America was shaped by the Great Depression.

NANCY

Angel in the 4th Heavenly Realm

Nancy's Guardian Angel

ANGEL THOMAS

John is a WWII veteran who loses so much during the war that is sends him on a journey few could imagine taking.

JOHN

Angel in the 7th Heavenly Realm

John's Guardian Angel

ANGEL MARY LEE

Jill and her daughters are faced with an unbelievable nightmare which will ultimately lead to something they never expected.

JILL & GIRLS

Angel in the 6th Heavenly Realm

Jill's Guardian Angel

ANGEL VERIA

April is a young African American girl with special promise who is asaulted at a party and loses sight of all her dreams.

APRIL

Angel in the 1st Heavenly Realm

April's Guardian Angel

ANGEL DARIAN

Rick is an American Baptist preacher who learns that there is more to life than he was taught to believe.

RICK

Angel in the 7th Heavenly Realm

Rick's Guardian Angel

ANGEL INDIRA

AFTER LIFE CHARACTERS - HUMANS & THEIR GUARDIAN ANGELS

Kyle is an American man who was plagued with an addiction that is threatening to dissolve his marriage.

KYLE

Angel in the 3rd Heavenly Realm

Kyle's Guardian Angel

ANGEL RAFIELA

Lina is the daughter of Italian immigrants who faces a private ordeal, as well as circumstances that challenge her will to live.

LINA

Angel in the 6th Heavenly Realm

Lina's Guardian Angel

ANGEL MARCO

Senator Susan Davis is the daughter of a Jewish Rabbi. She becomes a Senator and now must face a personal show down involving her families long held beliefs.

SENATOR SUSAN

Angel in the 3rd Heavenly Realm

Susan's Guardian Angel

ANGEL DAVID

AFTER LIFE CHARACTERS - THE LORDS

Ancient hunter, Lord of the Forest, and Lord of the Heavens and the Earth. Loving, caring, realistic as to what must be done for their plan to work out.

ADON

Lord of the Wind and Sky, and Lord of the Heavens and the Earth. Loved intensely for her soft feminine beauty, and respected for her fierce warrior instincts.

CALLA

Lord of the Sea and Lord of the Heavens and the Earth. The steadying force in the relationship with the other Lords. Tall, athletic, muscular, and closely attuned to the needs of the other Lords.

YESHUA

The mysterious, dark, 4th Lord, created as an opposite reaction by the collective will of the Lords during the act of the 1st Creation.

LEGION

AFTER LIFE CHARACTERS - THE ARCHANGELS

SPLENDORA

1st of the Archangels.

Caught up in an age, old love affair with her first love, Luminé.

LUMINE

The most popular Angel in the Heavens.

Leader of the 2nd Heavenly Realm, and one of the favorites of the Lords.

MICHAEL

3rd of the Archangels.

Tall, muscular, among the greatest warriors in the Heavens.

RAPHAEL

Archangel of the 4th Heavenly Realm.

A charismatic, strong, and brave warrior.

GABRIEL

Archangel of the 5th Heavenly Realm.

Wisest of the Archangels.

Leader of 1st Special Mission Angel Team.

RANA

Archangel of the 6th Heavenly Realm.

Secretly in love with the leader of the Dark forces.

AFTER LIFE CHARACTERS - IRISH ANGEL BIRGADE

DANIEL

Fearless leader of the Irish Brigade who camps atop Slie Mor mountain and are known for their bravery in fighting the forces of Darkness

ANGUS

2nd in command of the Irish Brigade and not always in agreement with his leader.

ANNIE

Fierce warrior for centuries as a member of the Irish Brigade.

AFTER LIFE CHARACTERS - THE DARK ANGELS

Lumine is the leader of the Dark Angels and finds that what he has so desperately sought is not what he was looking for.

LUMINE

Oxana finds her way to the pinnacle of power only to realize she needs more.

OXANA

Antonio is the most trusted commander in Luminare but discontent leads him to do the unthinkable.

ANTONIO

The Dark Fourth Lord is able to transform his appearance at will.

LEGION TRANSFORMED

Sylvia does what she must to survive in Luminare and becomes a servant to Legion.

SYLVIA

Sansa becomes one of Legion's favorite consorts and is forced to do his dark deeds.

SANSA

Tira finds herself caught up in the epic struggle of evil in Luminare.

TIRA

Thomas finds himself trapped in Luminare and faces a day he never dreamed of.

THOMAS

Jasper finds himself trapped under the dome and must decide if he will stay or escape.

JASPER

Sparkis finds himself in partnership with a most unlikely Dark Angel and must decide if he will cooperate till the end.

SPARKIS

Nina is tasked for a special mission she neither wants nor can fail in if she is to survive.

NINA

Thaddus finds himself in the unlucky predicament of keeping a secret that could destroy him forever.

THADDUS

AFTER LIFE CHARACTERS - SPECIAL MISSION ANGEL TEAM

Sadie is the go-to Angel for trouble in the Heavens and is tasked with leading a team in an all important mission.

SADIE

Rosie is chosen to be a member of the Special Mission Angel Team.

ROSIE

Joey, Sadie's 2nd in comand, is chosen to be a member of the Special Mission Angel Team.

JOEY

David is chosen to be a member of the Special Mission Angel Team.

DAVID

Michael, known as the swordsman, is chosen to be a member of the Special Mission Angel Team.

MICHAEL-SWORDSMAN

Dedications

For Marisa
We have deeply shared life's journey.
Cara Femmina, Solo Tu
Io Ti Amo Sempre

For Colleen
my faithful daughter
The years of your encouragement
and help on this series
can never be repaid,
because they carried me
through the darkest of times.

Love, Dad

The Prophecy

In the tree, the secret lies
The ancient seed, bearing life
Whose fruits reveal both dark and light
And opens eyes to the age of strife.

When sea doeth yield the Golden Sword,
Forged and burnished from the fire.
The virgin warrior again will rise.
Bringing hope to listless band.

When armies face eternal doom
And the holy one is lost for good
The feared day has now arrived
Darkness reigns, yet even still…

The fiery column signals time
Seven days, no more may pass
But yea, cannot beyond delay
For sunset yields eternal night

If the fire consumes the host
Unto the end, the dark must go
And Sacrifice will save the day,
And Sacrifice will save the day.

Start Reading

Storm Clouds

Luminé stormed into his living quarters, dazed at all that was unfolding. His sins and carelessness had finally caught up with him, but he needed to find out one thing. He needed to talk to Oxana. He looked inside the bedrooms, then stormed out to the guest quarters. They were empty. *She did this. I know she did this!*

He raced into the office, but she was not there. He then flew up in the air, scouring the area around the headquarters. The gray skies foretold an ominous future. Leaves blown off the trees, still swirled in the air. All seemed to be chaos below him, with his Angels frantically moving around, many pointing to the sky, the landscape ravaged by the storm. He did not see her, so he flew toward the sea. Then he spotted her, standing alone on the beach, looking out at the darkening skies. He raced down and landed in front of her, pointing at her, with an angry look on his face, "You… did you do this?"

"What are you talking about, Luminé?" Her eyes betrayed she was rattled to the core.

Through gritted teeth, his words seethed, "You had something to do with the creature that was stolen from my closet. Did you give it to the Humans?"

"No," she screamed, with an angry look on her face.

Luminé exploded, angrily taking her by the neck, "Tell me the truth! Do you hear me? Tell me the truth!"

Oxana's head fell back in pain, choking, unable to speak.

"Tell me!" he screamed.

Tears began rolling down her face, and Luminé dropped her. She curled up in a ball on the sand, crying.

Luminé looked down at her with disdain. The fear in her eyes when he first arrived had given her away. He was almost certain that she knew more than she was telling him. He yelled, "Don't you know? I needed you! I needed to trust you!"

Shaking, she uttered out the words between sobs, "You... can... Luminé ... you... you can!" Then she raised her head, "I did not do... this... I told you about my dream! That is... all I know." She dropped her head in the sand, emotionally exhausted, unable to speak anymore.

Luminé thought back to the moment she had seen the crate in the Garden, how surprised she had been. She had not deviated from her account at all. Then he thought of his own folly. He was blaming her, and the blame belonged soley to him. All of a sudden, he regretted hurting her. He dropped down onto the sand, cradling her head with his hands, "I'm sorry, Oxana."

She pushed him away, "Leave me alone."

But he persisted, "Oxana, please, I shouldn't have hurt you."

She turned away, "Just leave me alone right now, Luminé."

He stood up slowly and turned to leave.

Oxana lifted her head, "Where are you going?"

"I don't know. I need to get away. I have to... I have to think."

"No!" she exclaimed. "Don't leave. You need to be here, in your realm." She used her arms to push herself up, then stood. "You must not look weak, Luminé. It will hurt you."

Luminé exhaled loudly, nodding. She was right. He took off toward his headquarters with her following. As they neared, they could see hundreds of Angels gathered in the compound looking up at the swirling, darkening skies. No one had ever seen the skies of the Heavens like they were now, and a feeling of fear swept through them all.

Luminé and Oxana landed and started walking into their living quarters. Suddenly an Angel pointed at the sky. Luminé turned, and dread seized him. A group of seven Throne Room guards was flying in formation and headed right for them.

The seven guards landed in his courtyard as hundreds of Angels watched. The seven guards marched over to Luminé. They stopped, and the lead one stepped forward and momentarily stood at attention. He held out a rolled-up sealed scroll and declared, "Luminé, by order of the Lords of Heaven, you are under arrest."

"What?" he scoffed. "Let me see that!" He grabbed the scroll and unfurled it.

By order of the Lords

The Archangel Luminé is to be immediately apprehended, arrested, and brought to the Throne Room to stand trial.

"Trial?" asked Luminé. "What is the charge?"

The lead guard turned to the other guards, "Seize him."

At once, the guards grabbed Luminé and quickly bound his hands. Oxana screamed, "Let him go!" Luminé shook his head, signaling she should stop. He turned to the lead guard and demanded, "I have a right to know the charge!"

The guard clenched his teeth and said, "Treason."

They lifted him into the sky, carrying him to the Throne Room.

Oxana stood stunned, watching them disappear. She snapped into action, yelling at all those standing by idly, watching, "Get back to your duties." The crowd immediately broke up.

Oxana turned and resolutely marched into their quarters, then stumbled, her knees weakened by debilitating fear. The sudden collapse of all of her hopes and dreams had fallen upon her. She went to her room, closed the door, and began to cry.

~ ~ ~ ~

It was late evening as Sadie left the Earth and flew toward her home in the 5th Heavenly Realm. She was exhausted. As she went over the Heavenly Sea, she marveled at the darkening skies, darker than she had ever seen. Whatever happened in the Garden was affecting the Heavens as well, and it scared her.

Suddenly it began to rain. It was not the gentle soft rain she was used to. It was a hard, cold rain that instantly soaked her clothing. She kept flying through, trying to shield her eyes, but then the rain grew stronger and faster, and so did the winds. She found herself floundering in the skies, desperately trying to keep moving forward, but she could not. All at once, she allowed herself to drop down into the sea. She plunged below the surface, then bobbed up and floated, doing her best to shield her face from the pelting raindrops.

Finally, the rain lessened, then stopped. She flew back into the air and soon made it home. Marcellus was on her balcony, waiting for her. "Marcellus, what are you doing here?"

"I have to talk to you." He looked at her drenched clothing, "What happened to you?"

"I was flying over the sea, and the rain and wind, they were terrible, dangerous even. Oh, Marcellus, I'm scared."

He took her in his arms and held her tightly. Sadie closed her eyes, her breath heightening one last time, before slowing. Feeling safe was something that had been taken for granted, almost unnoticed, but to have suddenly been so afraid, magnified what had been taken for granted. It felt uncomfortably profound.

Marcellus said, "They've arrested Luminé. There is to be a trial."

"Why did they arrest him?"

"I don't know. The rumor is he had something to do with what happened in the Garden."

"When is the trial?"

"In three days."

Sadie lowered her glance, thinking, feeling bewildered at yet another situation. It seemed like everything was spinning out of control.

"But there is something else," Marcellus said, "Oxana knew something."

Sadie's eyes widened, "What do you mean?"

"I was there with her and Luminé when they visited Adam and Eve in the Garden. There was a crate in the bushes, not far from the forbidden tree. The exact size crate a creature like that could be put in. Oxana acted very strangely when she saw it. I am telling you, she knew something."

"Where is the crate now?"

"It's in the Garden."

"Take me there now. I need to see it."

"But, it is already dark."

"I don't care. We will light the torches. I need to see that crate."

~ ~ ~ ~

The following day, Sadie and three Angels under her command raced through the skies toward the 2nd Heavenly Realm. When they reached the frontier, they were stopped by two guards.

"Halt, no one is allowed in or out of the 2nd Heavenly Realm." They were both large Angels, the kind Luminé preferred for his frontier guards, and they did not look happy.

Sadie went up to one of them, and put on her game face and put it within inches of his. "I Commander Sadie from the 5th Realm, and I am here on official business from the Throne Room."

"That does not matter," he shot back. "Luminé said there are no exceptions."

"Luminé has been arrested. He is no longer in charge. Now move out of the way."

The guard did not back down but stiffened and said, "Oxana has told everyone his orders are to be upheld."

Sadie drew her sword and placed the point of it on the guard's chest. Those with her drew their swords too. Sadie demanded, "Get out of our way right now."

The guard drew his sword, but Sadie's companions rushed him as Sadie turned to the other, daring him to reach for his sword. He did, and she slashed his arm as the others tied up his companion.

"Let's go," Sadie said, as she and her companions raced to the headquarters and went up the stairs and down the hall.

Luminé's secretary stood in their way, "May I help you?"

"Where is Oxana?" demanded Sadie.

"In there," replied the secretary with a worried look.

Sadie tightened her lips, brushed past her, and stormed into Luminé's office. Oxana was seated at Luminé's desk, nervously pretending to be going over paperwork. Sadie went around the desk. "Get up, Oxana."

Oxana coolly glanced up, "Why should I listen to you?"

"Because you're under arrest. And you will stand trial in the morning."

Oxana's face grew white as she tried to remain calm, "for... for what?"

"For conspiracy to commit treason. Does a wooden box mean anything to you, Oxana?"

"It's not mine!" she yelled, her eyes now widening with dread.

"Oh, don't worry, we know everything. Now get up."

Shadows

After arresting Oxana, Sadie headed to see Splendora. She took her time flying over the sea, and she was glad to be alone. She needed time to process it all. She was worried about what was going to happen, not to Luminé or Oxana, as they would get what they deserved, but to herself, to the rest of the Angels. The sudden onset of the terrible storm yesterday had downright scared her.

It was by far the worst storm she had ever been through. In the past, the thunder and lightning were gentle and things to be marveled at. Usually, storms were accompanied by wind and rain, but not like yesterday. Yesterday's storm was downright frightening, sending Angels everywhere running in fear for cover. The swirling dark clouds had never before been part of their world, and each enormous clap of the thunder seemed to shake the surrounding sky and possess anger that made one think of approaching doom. The lightning, too, was no longer something to marvel at, but rather something to cringe from and shield one's eyes from.

It was more than the storm, though. It was the animals too. They had become wild, no longer subject to the Heavens, but rather subject to themselves, and suddenly vicious. Gentle lions, tigers, elephants, large fish that swam in the sea, and every single kind of animal was now something to be feared, not only by the Angels but by the other animals as well. While flying over the sea with Oxana in chains, Sadie and her guards had witnessed the black and white whales attacking one of the larger whales that Michael had designed. It was still alive, moaning in the beautiful waters, but its flesh was torn in a hundred places, and dark blood surrounded it, floating on top of the blue waters.

Reports of terrible injuries were also coming in. A lion had mauled an Angel in the Sixth Realm, and she was badly wounded. Animals were eating other animals too, both in Heaven and on Earth. In the Second Realm, there were stories of wild boar roaming in packs and ravaging Angels homes. Something had to be done.

Sadie knew that all of this represented a permanent shift in her world, in everyone's world. Whatever happened at that tree in the Garden of Eden had changed everything for the worst and forever.

Fear had become a dominant emotion inside her. Everywhere she looked, she found threats and danger. She was worried about the animal attacks and the sudden chaos that seemed to surround her. She feared that at any second someone—or something—might charge from the bushes and drag her off to be violently mauled.

But that was only part of it. There was fear within too, the fear she had failed, fear she would be judged for her part in this cataclysmic failure. She had been in charge of guarding the Garden of Eden. The fact this occurred under her watch made her feel extremely vulnerable. What if she were demoted? What if she were punished or even sent away.

She needed to speak to Splendora to understand just how much at risk she was. Splendora was there when it happened and she had alluded to the fact she knew something. Sadie remembered her exact words, 'Luminé made a talking animal. I saw it, and he told me he destroyed it, but he lied.'

Sadie would get to the bottom of it. It might be the only way to save herself.

When Splendora opened, her arm was bandaged, and a sullen look was glued to her face. Her normally open-air villa on the sea was dark and closed up. The curtains were drawn, and an air of dim stillness hung over all that Sadie had never before seen.

"Come in, Sadie."

"How are you doing?"

"Not good," Splendora said, glancing down at the blood seeping through her bandage. She looked up, eyes searching for understanding. She needed to unburden herself, "Sadie, I've been going over and over all the things Luminé had said to me leading up to this." Her eyes looked away and drifted out the window, for a moment, unwilling to face Sadie. "I should have seen it was coming, Sadie, and... I had a duty to tell the Lords."

Neither said a word for a moment, as a tense heaviness held sway. Both of them contemplating the entirety of the mess. Sadie broke the silence, "Oxana was just arrested."

"What!"

"Marcellus told me that when he, Luminé, and Oxana visited the garden, there was a wooden crate 3 feet by 2 feet. It was the exact size to have carried a creature of Serpe's stature in. He was certain Oxana had seen it before."

Splendora slowly put her hand over her mouth, as if a sudden revelation had come, "Sadie, wait." She closed her eyes for a moment, nodding, remembering something, then looked up, "How could I have forgotten? I just realized something. Oxana was not only there with Luminé; she was there by herself the day before yesterday."

"Where!" Sadie exclaimed her face in defiant disbelief.

"In the Garden of Eden. When I talked to Adam, he told me that Oxana had visited Eve the day before."

"Adam told you that?"

"Yes! Oxana was in the Garden, and later that night, Serpe showed up at their door. The next day, they ate from the Tree of Knowledge of Good and Evil."

"Are you sure Adam said that?"

"Absolutely. Sadie, too much has happened. I don't know how I forgot."

Sadie's eyes widened, "Marcellus said they had seen the crate over a week ago. Her being there the same day Serpe showed up practically proves she is the culprit."

"It sure seems to."

"There's more!" Sadie exclaimed, with her mouth hanging open, "I examined the logbook at the garden entrance this morning. Oxana's name was only listed from when she was there with Marcellus. She must have snuck in somehow."

Splendora said nothing, thinking, still worried about her own failings.

Sadie said, "You have to testify to what Adam told you. Oxana cannot get away with this."

"I can't!"

"Why not?" Sadie said in an alarmed tone.

Splendora turned away, ashamed, "Because I knew about Serpe!"

"Splendora, no! Look, Luminé lied to you… and no one else knows what you told me yesterday. As far as I am concerned, you had nothing to do with this. You have to testify in Oxana's trial. What Adam told you must be stated."

"Fine, I will, but I will also tell the Lords that I knew about Serpe and did not tell them."

"No!" Sadie exclaimed forcefully, "Splendora, snap out of it! You cannot implicate yourself! There is enough trouble right now without you being tarnished. It would distract from what they did! You cannot!"

Splendora's shoulders slumped further and she folded her head into her hands. "Alright!" she moaned, keeping her face buried.

Sadie knew she had pushed enough. She got up, "I will see you tomorrow."

Splendora said nothing but listened for the door to close, then looked up. Yes, she would be witnessing against Oxana, but she would not lie just to spare herself or even Luminé from what he deserved.

Oxana

An air of intense uncertainty hovered over all of Holy Mountain, as Heaven's 700,000 Angels waited in the cloud-covered skies above the Throne Room. They were arrayed in a wide arc so all could clearly see down to the Throne Room floor. There was a loud buzzing of conversations filled with both excitement and dread. Many were nervously wringing their hands, their world suddenly thrown into chaos by the recent events.

Within a short time, the Lords would take their places, and the Angels would all witness something never before imagined in the Heavens: the trials of two of their own, the trials of Luminé and Oxana.

Many in the crowd felt Luminé would finally be held accountable for recklessly breaking the rules for so long. They felt that his decision to create a talking animal was an intentional one. He knew what he was doing when he committed blasphemy, and for that, he must be punished.

But even more felt he was being made a scapegoat and that it was Adam and Eve who should be on trial. After all, Luminé hadn't forced them to eat the forbidden fruit. He shouldn't have to suffer for their sins.

As far as Oxana, no one felt she was to blame for anything.

The Throne Room attendants blew loud trumpets, signaling it was time. All grew quiet as the doors at the back of the Throne Room opened, and the six Archangels walked in across the marble floor and took their places on the left side of the Lord's thrones. They would soon decide the fate of their own Luminé, fallen archangel.

Moments later, the three Lords walked in and took their seats. Calla scanned the massive gathering in the sky. The Lords knew there would be a large crowd, but it was clear that every single Angel had come to witness this fateful day.

Underneath the Throne Room, two massive iron cages had been set up to hold Luminé and Oxana. They were at the end of a long hall that led to the stairs that went to the Throne Room. Each had a plain wooden bench and a blanket within, where Luminé and Oxana had slept the past two nights since their arrest.

Oxana sat quietly, holding her hands tightly, shaking. She had never been so afraid in her life. "What is going to happen to us, Luminé?" Her voice was weak and shaken, devoid of the vigor Luminé was used to hearing.

Luminé turned. He had been chained at his feet and his hands. His chains clanked against the iron bars, and he grimaced, "I don't know, but if there is anything you haven't told me, you need to. Perhaps we can still get out of this unscathed." Luminé's face showed the determination and cunning it always held. He was not giving up.

Oxana screamed, "I told you I don't know anything!"

Luminé snapped, "Oxana, get hold of yourself." He felt bad for a moment, for even saying what he'd said. She was his lover and his confidant, and there was nothing he could do to help her.

Suddenly the door opened, and two guards marched down the hall. Both of them had stone-cold faces, signaling to Luminé what he and Oxana would face during the trial. They passed his cage and stopped in front of Oxana's. The guard peered in at her with disdain for a long uncomfortable moment, then said in a monotone voice, "It's time!"

Oxana's eyes suddenly widened, and her chest heaved. In a panicked voice, she cried out, "I didn't do this! I am innocent!"

The guards smirked and opened the door. Oxana tried to run past them, but they caught her. She clung to the iron bars, "No, I can't. I am innocent!"

"Leave her alone!" Luminé shouted, but they ignored him and forcefully pried her hands loose and bound her hands and feet with chains, then marched her down the hall.

Luminé shouted, "Oxana!"

She stopped and turned, staring back at him, her fingers clenched tightly together. He had never seen her afraid like this, and now he began to worry. "Be strong, Oxana. You can do this."

She swallowed and turned as the guards nudged her forward, down the hall, and up the steps, and had her stop in front of the enormous wooden doors. Suddenly the large wooden doors slowly opened, and Oxana stood between them, with her hands and feet bound in chains. A loud gasp shot through the crowd. No one had imagined seeing her in chains.

Oxana looked out at the epic scene. Every inch of the surrounding sky was filled with Angels. The skies were not blue, but a pale gray and a heaviness, almost dampness filled the air, remnants of the previous day's storms. The Throne Room floor held hundreds of Angels too, mostly commanders, some whom Oxana recognized. Sadie was there too, standing with some of them. At the far end was the Thrones with the Lords already seated upon them, and to their right stood the Archangels.

Oxana felt the shame and the fear of what was to come, but then it hit her. She was the center of the show, and she could use this to her advantage. She stayed still for a moment, considering her move.

The guards pressed her, but she shook them off and walked forward slowly, dramatically dragging her chains across the marble floor, letting the sound shatter the silence. Finally, she reached the Lords and stood resolutely in front of them. It took a long time until finally, she stood in front of the three Lords. All three of the Lords looked different to her. They looked tired, burdened, even worried. She had never seen them like this, and it added to the fear of what was going to happen to her.

The other six Archangels stood at attention to the side of the Thrones. Each was dressed in their white and gold uniform, each carrying their daggers and swords, with their golden boots laced to below the knee. They did not look as burdened, but they were not happy. Grim looks adorned all their faces, except Splendora's. Her face betrayed a worry that Oxana understood full well. She would be called upon to condemn someone she loved, and by the looks of it, she was ready to do it.

Calla stood up, dressed in her maroon robe, and wearing a gold laurel on her head. She raised her hand and shouted in a loud, commanding tone, "Angels of Heaven, Oxana is accused of conspiracy to commit treason. Her trial will begin now."

A long and loud rumbling noise arose from the crowd. The tone was mixed with wonder but also disapproval. Calla sat down, glancing at the other Lords, her eyes conveying the surprise at the reaction of the crowd.

Yeshua then signaled to the Throne Room to bring the evidence forward. The guard carried over a covered item, set it down in front of Oxana, and removed the cover. It was the wooden crate found in the Garden of Eden, the one Sadie and Marcellus had retrieved.

Oxana looked down at the box, then calmly looked back up.

Yeshua asked, "Oxana, this is the wooden crate that allegedly carried the creature Luminé created in the Garden of Eden. Marcellus has testified that when you saw this box, you were greatly startled. He said he thought you had seen it before. Is this true?"

"Yes, it is true, Lord Yeshua, but it is not what you think. I saw the box in my dream over a week earlier. That is why I was so startled." Oxana glanced over at the six Archangels who were intently listening. She wanted to gauge their reaction. Some looked like they believed her, but others, especially Michael and Angelica, remained stoic, telling her they did not.

Adon then said, "Oxana, please tell us about the dream."

Oxana calmly nodded, then began, "My Lords, I dreamed I was walking through the Garden, and I saw the box. When I looked up, there was a stream, and across it was the Tree of the Knowledge of Good and Evil. A small green creature climbed out of a small wooden crate in this dream and stood next to the tree. It smiled at me."

Adon leaned forward slightly, looking intently at Oxana, drawing her attention, but pausing as if she needed to carefully consider her next answer. "Tell us, Oxana. What happened then?"

"The dream ended. I completely forgot about it until the day Luminé took Marcellus and me into the Garden. When I saw the stream and the tree, and then the box, I knew it was what I had seen in my dream, and that scared me. That is the only reason I was afraid, my Lords."

Adon questioned her further, "And are you telling us that you never saw this creature for real… that is, outside of your dream?"

"I did not, Lord Adon."

The Lords glanced at one another. Long ago, Calla and Adon both had dreams, dreams of Legion coming to the earth. What Oxana was saying was not outside the realm of possibility.

Calla said, "Splendora, please come forward."

Splendora walked over and stood next to Oxana. She had changed her mind only this morning and had spoken to the Lords about what Adam had told her. But that was all she had told them. She had not told them everything yet. She looked straight ahead, intent on not looking at Oxana even for a moment.

Calla asked, "Splendora, tell us what Adam said to you when you went to visit Eve in the Garden."

"Adam told me that Oxana had been there the day before visiting Eve."

Calla then looked out to the Host Commanders on the Throne Room floor and shouted, "Sadie, please step forward."

Sadie walked out of the crowd and across the empty space between the crowd and the Thrones and stopped a few yards away from Oxana, then stood at attention, facing the Lords.

Calla asked, "Sadie, you are in charge of the guards in the Garden of Eden. Have you examined the entrance logbook to see if Oxana had signed in to visit the day in question?"

"I did, my Lord."

"Did Oxana sign in on the day in question?"

"No, she did not. She only signed ten days earlier when she was with Marcellus and Luminé. Her name was NOT listed for the day in question. She was not authorized to be in the Garden." Sadie turned her head for a moment to make eye contact with Oxana, then looked back to the Lords.

Calla turned to Oxana with her eyes narrowed and her voice stern and said, "Oxana, you were there visiting Eve the very same day that the creature, Serpe, appeared for the first time to Adam and Eve, and you were not authorized to be in the Garden. So, let me ask you, plainly: Did you have anything to do with the creature being given to the Humans?"

"No, my Lord."

"Then, why were you there, unauthorized?"

The entire crowd grew silent, knowing that Oxana must be trapped in a lie.

Oxana paused, feeling the sudden onset of the deafening silence. This was her big moment, and it had played right into her hands. She could see the faces of many in the crowd, many were showed they were poised to see her fail, but more held faces that signaled hope, hope that she would have an answer, wanting her to overcome this hurdle.

She waited one more moment, letting the tension build, then tearfully blurted out, "I was there because I had something to give Eve."

"What did you give Eve?" Calla asked sternly as her eyebrows touched in the center.

"A necklace, my Lord," Oxana replied, wiping the tear from her eye. "Eve had admired it when I visited the first time."

"Then why didn't you sign in as is required?"

Oxana lowered her head again, waiting for a few more tears to come, then looked up, pointed at Sadie, and defiantly yelled, "Because of her! She has had it out for me from day one! I knew she would not let me go in, so I went myself!"

Thousands of murmurs instantly shot through the crowd, and all eyes turned to Sadie.

Sadie was aghast, realizing Oxana was skillfully building a crafty lie.

Calla turned to Sadie with a concerned look on her face, "Sadie, is this true?"

Sadie turned toward Calla, her eyes wide and her mouth open in shock, and said, "It is not, my Lord. She is acting, I assure you."

Calla exhaled loudly and summoned the Throne Room guards. "Bring Adam and Eve here at once."

A short while later, four Angels, two each carrying Adam and Eve, arrived and set them down in front of the Lords. Their faces were dirty, and their hair was unkempt. It seemed as though they had been sleeping in a bed of thorns. Their faces were pale, and their eyes were wide. Their eyes darted about, looking for everything but seeing nothing.

Calla said, "Adam and Eve, you have been brought here to answer a question concerning what happened a few days ago in the Garden of Eden." Her eyes narrowed towards Eve, "Eve, did Oxana visit you the day before you ate from the tree?"

"Yes, Lord Calla, she did," Eve said in a shy and trembling voice.

"Did she give something to you?"

"Yes, she gave me this gold necklace." Eve lifted her chin and reached under the top of her tunic, and lifted out the shiny piece of gold affixed to a brown leather strap that hung around her neck.

Calla looked back at the other Lords. Both Adon and Yeshua gave a subtle nod. Calla said, "Oxana, the charges against you are dismissed." She turned to the guards, "Unchain her."

Suddenly the crowd erupted in a loud roar that seemed to shake Holy Mountain.

Oxana breathed a deep sigh of relief, then smiled, turning to acknowledge the crowd, waving to their adulations. She walked into the crowd on the Throne Room floor to join some of her companions, but before reaching them, she looked back, locking eyes with Sadie, and gave Sadie the small hint of a smile, signaling she had beaten her.

Sadie stood perfectly still, her eyes empty, pretending not to be affected by what had just occurred, but she was fuming. She remembered back to when Rana had cheated her in the games and stole her ability to be one of the Archangels. This felt the same. Oxana had just cheated her, cheated her from getting justice. Now, she felt humiliated, and yet deep down, she knew she was right. Her gut told her Oxana knew more than she had admitted, and she had somehow fooled everyone, including the Lords.

Luminé

Below the Throne Room, Luminé sat in his cell, chained at his ankles and wrists. He could not hear what was happening above, and he was worried about what was going to happen to him. He had gone too far, and now he would pay the consequences, but what consequences. Would they take away his title of Archangel? He would not be able to bear that. Would they admonish him publicly? This, too, would be difficult to bear.

Adam and Eve were the ones who ate of the Tree, not him. He grabbed the cage bars in frustration and shook them, shouting to the ceiling, "They are the ones who should be on trial!"

No one was there to hear him, except himself, and as soon as he said the words, a voice in his head shot back, "But you designed the talking animal, which had swayed them to defy the Lords."

Luminé knew the voice inside him was right. He regretted designing it. He regretted not destroying it when he told Splendora he would. He regretted being blamed and being here in this cage. But he still regarded the Humans with disdain. They were, in his mind still, nothing more than talking animals.

Suddenly, he heard the roar of the crowd, and his countenance sank. He grimaced, saying aloud, "They must have found her guilty."

He pounded his chains into the iron bars, shaking them violently, trying to get himself free, but it was of no use; he was trapped. The doors at the end of the hall opened, and the guards resolutely marched in. The roar of the crowd could still be heard, and Luminé knew his fate was sealed. He yelled to the guards, "What happened?"

Neither guard flinched, but both of them remained cold and stoic, not willing to give Luminé any sense of what had occurred.

"Tell me what happened!" Luminé yelled, angrily.

But the guards only smirked and reached to open the door of his cage to escort him up.

A voice came from the end of the hall. "Hold it. I need to speak to Luminé."

The guards turned. It was the Archangel Gabriel.

Gabriel told the guards, "Go on up. I will escort him."

Gabriel waited for them to leave, then turned to Luminé. "They dropped the charges against Oxana."

Luminé dropped his head back in a moment of deep relief. If Oxana had gotten off, surely he had a chance too. Now he understood the crowd's roar. A surge of confidence re-awakened inside him. The Angels were on his side.

Gabriel watched the wheels turning in Luminé's mind. "Luminé, don't think for a moment that you are not in a great deal of trouble."

Luminé looked up, jarred from his thoughts, and snapped, "I didn't put that creature in the garden, Gabriel."

"Yes, well, I believe you," he quickly added, "but some of the others don't." Gabriel was sullen, he was tired of Luminé's cavalier attitude, and frankly, he had thought coming down here he would find Luminé more repentant or remorseful, but the opposite seemed to be true.

"What's going to happen?" asked Luminé.

Gabriel lowered his glance. He was not happy to deliver bad news, but he was sure that a dose of reality was exactly what Luminé needed right now. "Luminé, because you already admitted to making the design of the creature, the very minimum thing that will happen is your rank as Archangel is being stripped. *And...* you will have to go away for a year of solitude on a remote Island. That's the very least that is going to happen."

"What! That's ridiculous! I didn't do it!"

Gabriel shook his head slowly, "You better hope what I just said does happen because if you are found guilty of a greater crime, the punishment could be up to five years inside a cage."

"Five years... in a... cage?"

"Luminé, what you did was unthinkable! The ability to talk is reserved for the Lords, the Angels, and now the Humans. Animals are lesser creatures, given to us for our enjoyment. To have given one speech was a mockery of the Lords' design."

Luminé stared at the floor, thinking. Gabriel nor anyone knew that he also created Serpe to be his spy. Humans were special for some reason, and Luminé had wanted to know why. He looked up at Gabriel and asked, "Will you be voting?"

"Yes, all six of the Archangels will decide your fate, after, that is, we hear from the witnesses."

"What witnesses?"

"The Lord's plan on calling a number of witnesses in order to gauge your intent. That I am afraid is where the heart of this matter lies, with the proving or disproving of intent."

"Well, I never intended for this to happen."

"Maybe not, but it sure looks like you wanted to create a talking animal that directly defied the Lords who had trusted you to oversee the design of all the animals. I'm afraid those facts alone will be enough to sway some to vote against you."

"But it will not sway you, right, Gabriel?"

Gabriel would not show his hand. His face showed sorrow, sorrow that he felt in knowing Luminé was as bold and proud as ever. He looked down at the ground, saying, "I will decide after hearing from the witnesses."

Luminé grabbed the bars of the cage. "Gabriel, I need you. Do you understand?"

Gabriel did not flinch but unlocked the cage door, "Let's go. It's time."

Luminé held up his hands, signaling Gabriel should remove the chains. Gabriel frowned, "I'm sorry. My orders are that the chains have to stay."

~ ~ ~ ~

The Throne Room and surrounding skies were in turmoil as hundreds of thousands of Angels were still celebrating Oxana's exoneration. Coupled with Luminé's immense popularity, her rise to power from the obscurity of a guard to that of Luminé's right-hand Angel made her a favorite too. Now, turning the tide in the trial as she did cemented her status as a star.

The three Lords sat in their thrones, watching the scene unfold, very surprised at the crowd's rebellious tone. Yeshua leaned over to Calla and whispered, "What has happened to our Angels. It is as if a spirit of rebellion has taken root inside many of them."

Calla looked at him, her eyes stern and narrowed, "I see it, too."

Yeshua paid particular attention to Oxana being treated like a celebrity. He wondered why the Angels were so happy. Would they have been angry, had she been found guilty of treason? Did they care about what happened in the Garden, the fall of everything good that was planned? How had their allegiance suddenly changed?

Yeshua turned and looked to Splendora, his most faithful Angel. She was not standing proud and tall, as she normally did, but rather shrunken, with shoulders forward. Her brow was furrowed, and her face looked tired and burdened. She was worried. He wondered, *Is she also worried about the rebellious behavior being displayed? No... something else is bothering her.*

Suddenly the large doors of the Throne Room began to open, and silence fell upon all. Then, Luminé 's face appeared, and an immense cheer went up into the sky, only to come to a crashing halt as soon as they opened wider, showing their beloved Archangel standing defiantly in his shackles and chains.

Luminé sensed the energy of the crowd was somehow behind him, and he did not understand why, but he would use it. He needed to be careful, though, so as not to overplay his hand. He signaled for Gabriel to go ahead and waited until Gabriel walked across the floor alone and took his place alongside the other Archangels.

Then, Luminé began his step by step, labored, trek across the floor, with his chains dragging across the marble. The loud sound of chains, dragging and stopping, dragging and stopping, continued all the way across.

Calla leaned over and whispered to Yeshua. "I don't care what kind of show is being put on here. If Luminé had the intent to commit treason, he could not simply receive a slap on the wrist."

Yeshua gave her a sideways glance and nodded, leaned over, saying, "I don't like how loudly they cheered for Oxana. It felt like many were against us."

Calla's face grew worried, "Yes, I… I sensed that too." She turned to see Adon's reaction. His face showed a look of disappointment, and she knew why. She had insisted Luminé and Oxana wear chains. Adon had vigorously protested. She now knew he had been right.

Finally, Luminé reached the area in front of the thrones and slowly lifted his head. He tried to look tired, worn out as if a victim.

All three Lords stood up, and Calla spoke, "Luminé, you are charged with Treason. You have already admitted to the design of an animal that could talk, which was a mockery to our laws. For that crime, you will be sentenced to a one year exile and the possible stripping of your title as Archangel. If you are found to be guilty of Treason, however, your punishment will be much more severe. Do you understand all of this?"

"Yes, I do, my Lords," he said in a fawning tone, trying to appear as submissive and cooperative as he could.

Adon turned to the guards, "Call the first witness."

Luminé also turned, suddenly surprised to see one of the guards from his realm nervously came forward.

Adon asked, "You said you saw Luminé in the workshop making the prototype of a creature and speaking to it. Can you tell us more?"

The guard glanced at Luminé, almost afraid to answer in his presence, but he seemed to gather his courage and looked squarely at Adon, "Yes, my Lord. I was asked to find Luminé, and I thought he would be in the back of the building, so I went around to the back door. When I opened the door, he was holding an odd-looking creature over his head. I thought I heard him say, Serpe."

Luminé was stunned. He had thought only Splendora had seen him. He did not know that a guard had also seen him. But he had heard everything. Nothing yet too damning had been said.

Adon asked, "Why didn't you report this?"

"I did not understand what it was. Besides, Luminé is an Archangel. I did not imagine that anything would be wrong."

Murmurings shot through the crowd as Angels in the skies began leaning over to each other, discussing and commenting to each other on what had been said.

Calla raised her eyes, scanning the crowd, worried at the tone. What had become of their beautiful Angels? Had Legion's triumph truly reached into their hearts? How could so many seem to be suddenly loyal to Luminé and Oxana? She stood up and said, "Call the next witness."

The Throne Room guard called out, "Michael the Archangel, please step forward."

Michael straightened up his towering body even taller, pounded his chest with his fist, then marched over and stood next to Luminé. Luminé looked up at him, and Michael looked down, tight-lipped, his face etched in resolve to tell it as he saw it. He turned to face Calla.

Calla asked, "Michael, as you know, the question of Luminé's intent weighs heavily in these proceedings. As a fellow Archangel, you know Luminé very well. What do you have to say about the matter of Luminé's intent?"

Michael did not hesitate to reply. "My Lords," he said in his booming voice, "Luminé exhibited a dangerous and cavalier attitude toward the rules of Heaven and toward your authority for over a year before this event. It is rumored he carried on trysts with various females with no intention of following Heaven's laws."

"But why should this be held against him?" asked Adon. "This does not seem to reveal anything about intent. All Angels have Free Will, do they not?"

"Yes, Lord Adon, we do all possess Free Will. However, I believe it is a sign of his intent, or rather his discontent, which grew, and grew until it caused this act which has shaken the foundations of the Heavens and the Earth."

The crowd began to act boisterous, many standing, some shouting, others pushing others aside in frustration. Arguments were breaking out in the skies, and it was clear to the Lords that the Angel's loyalties were starkly divided. Calla waited for the rumblings to die down. She then questioned Michael, "And what did you say Luminé referred to the Humans as?"

Michael looked at Luminé with a look of deep disappointment, and without turning away, spoke directly at Luminé, loud enough for all to hear, "He said they are nothing more than talking animals."

A loud gasp suddenly arose from all in the Throne Room and surrounding skies. This was damning testimony. There could be no doubt now about Luminé's sin. It had been made clear since the first day, that though animals were sacred, they were not considered to be divine. Only the Lords, the Angels, and the Humans were classified as divine creatures and capable of speech. For Luminé, an Archangel and the one in charge of the design of the animals to have said this could not be brushed aside.

Calla looked casually towards Adon, making sure he heard it and noticed the reaction of the crowd.

Yeshua stood and raised his hand high, quieting the crowd. He turned to the nearby Archangels, "Gabriel, please step forward."

Gabriel had hoped he would not be called, but he resolutely walked up and stood on the other side of Luminé, putting Luminé in the middle of Michael and himself. "Yes, my Lord."

Yeshua asked, "Gabriel, do you still hold to your statement, made to me with Michael from long ago when you both expressed concern about Luminé's disdain for Heaven's laws and rules?"

Gabriel nodded subtly, "I do, my Lord."

The tension in the crowd escalated again but in more whispers this time. If Gabriel, who everyone knew was Luminé's friend, was testifying against him, it could only mean one thing.

Yeshua looked squarely at Luminé, their eyes meeting. He could see Luminé's countenance fall slightly, as Luminé himself understood what Gabriel's testimony did to his chances. Yeshua said, "Michael, Gabriel, you may both return to your places."

Adon watched everything unfold. The entire matter was heading in the wrong direction. Unbeknownst to all, his actions were at the root of this utter collapse of order in the Heavens and Earth. He had insisted on free will at all costs, but he had greatly underestimated Legion, and he had underestimated his ability to win the trust of the Humans. Luminé had always been his favorite. If matters went too far in the wrong direction, if Luminé were going to be put in a cage for years to come, he did not think he could sit idly by.

It was his turn to question the next witness, and that was Splendora Adon had wished he did not have to call her. He knew how much she and Luminé loved each other, and he had hoped her testimony would sway the crowd. She was the most respected Archangel in the Heavens. It was why he put her on the list. But now, seeing her trepidation, he realized perhaps Luminé had confided in her. Perhaps her testimony would sink Luminé. But it was too late to change anything. He reluctantly said, "Splendora, please step forward."

Splendora felt her heart sink; the moment she had dreaded was suddenly upon her. She was deeply divided. She loved Luminé, not as the others did, for his flare, but she loved him for the goodness he had within him. But he had betrayed everything in his pride, and this she could not brush away.

She up walked behind Luminé and stood next to him. Her eyes gravitated to his, hoping to see even a glimmer of remorse in his face, but he would not look directly at her and only stared stoically forward, looking focused and determined. She wondered what was really in his heart. Would Adon ask her the question she dreaded? Could she lie, as

Sadie had begged her to? Would she be better off exposing Luminé and herself?

Adon leaned forward in his chair and proceeded, "Splendora, it has been said that you knew Luminé better than anyone. Did you see this display of disregard for our rules and laws?"

Splendora did not hesitate, "I did my Lords. Luminé was very reckless in following and applying our laws." A feeling of satisfaction swept through her. It was good to tell the truth. It was freeing.

Adon nodded slowly, then leaned forward even more, and asked, "Did Luminé ever give any indication to you that he was going to create this creature? Or that he would design it to be able to talk?" Adon held his breath. All now rode on her answer, and he had no idea what she would say.

Splendora clutched her lips, trying not to give away the terror racing through her veins. "No, he did not."

Adon replied, "It seems he would have confided in you of all Angels. But he did not. He obviously did not intend for all this to happen." Adon looked back to the other Lords, then sat back on his throne.

Splendora turned and saw Sadie give her an ever so subtle nod. It was not a look of judgment nor sadness, but rather, it was a look of solidarity with each other.

The crowd was strangely quiet. What had Splendora's testimony really meant? Did it answer the question of intent, as Adon seemed to imply by his sweeping declaration? Calla and Yeshua said nothing. It was time for the proceedings to end. All that was left was for Luminé to give his own statement, and then the Archangels would vote.

Yeshua was troubled, though. Too little had been offered, too much opinion and not enough facts to sway him either way. He leaned over to Calla, whispered something, then called out, "Please bring Adam and Eve forward again."

The rumblings began again in earnest, as Adam and Eve were escorted back up. They nervously stood before the three Lords. Yeshua asked, "Adam and Eve, how did you know the creature, Serpe, had been given to you by Luminé?"

Adam replied, "It told us. It said it was a gift from the great Archangel Luminé."

Yeshua felt deep frustration. Luminé would not have been so stupid to announce this to Adam and Eve. Yeshua smiled, nodding, "Thank you, Adam and Eve. Guards, take them back to their home."

When they left, Adon said, "Luminé, it is time for you to make your final statement. Then, the Archangels will render their judgment."

Luminé took one small step forward to make his chains rattle, reminding everyone of the humiliation he was already enduring. He paused, allowing the tension to build, then spoke, "My Lords, as you know, I was upset with not being able to design the Humans. In my zeal, I resisted calls from my fellow Archangels to change my ways. My Lords, I was foolish, maybe even a bit arrogant. However, once I realized my mistake in creating the creature, I need to say that I meant to destroy it. I even told..." He stopped, realizing he had said too much.

Splendora's heart lurched within her. Luminé was about to expose her. She held her breath, and her knees started to shake. Yeshua asked, "Even told who?"

Luminé continued, "I told... I told myself, my Lord, that as soon as I returned back to my home from the day of Creation, I was going to destroy it. But... I never got the chance. When I returned, it was gone. My Lords, I do not know how, but I am convinced that Legion had something to do with this."

He paused, watching the reactions on the Lords and Archangels' faces. His statement had resonated with them. Blaming Legion was the one thing no one could refute.

Luminé observed the reactions of everyone, gauging his standing carefully. He decided to go further and turned around, looking up into the skies at the myriad of Angels watching him. "My Lords, these Angels are all here to see me receive my just sentence, and it is fitting, but I only ask two things:" he turned back to face the Lords. "One, as I am now painfully aware of my failings, I ask for mercy. And two, because I had no intent to cause such trouble, I ask that the loss of my title as Archangel only be temporary and that after a year of reflection, it may be possibly restored." This was the thing Luminé needed most. To be removed as an Archangel would be a fall in status he would not know how to live with. He concluded with a slow sweeping bow, "Thank you, my Lords."

Calla was trying not to show the outrage she felt. "Luminé, you dare to tell us what your punishment should be.

Luminé half-smiled, "You are right, Lord Calla. It is only what I hope for.

Yeshua said, "Luminé, the Archangels, your peers, will now cast their verdict."

Judgment

Calla stood to face the six Archangels, saying, "It is time for you to pronounce judgment." She called out the first name. "Cirianna, is Luminé guilty of Treason?"

Silence gripped the skies as now the first vote would be cast. Cirianna stepped forward, clutching her sword sheath, and declared, "Yes, he is guilty."

The silence that held the Throne Room and sky now deepened.

Calla then asked, "Rana, is Luminé guilty of Treason?"

Rana looked over at Luminé and said, "No, he is not."

A loud cheer raced through the crowd.

"Gabriel?" asked Calla.

"No," replied Gabriel

"Raphael?" asked Calla.

"Yes."

They were tied now, with only two left to vote.

Calla paused, then said, "Michael?"

"Guilty."

Finally, all eyes turned to Splendora. Calla asked slowly, "Splendora, is Luminé guilty of Treason?"

Splendora was torn in every way. The lie she had told boiled inside her. Should not Luminé get what he deserved? It was treason, was it not? But could not her love save him, bring him back. Maybe now, he would listen. Maybe this disgrace would pull him away from Oxana. No! No! She had failed in her duty to tell the Lords about Serpe. She could not fail them again. She needed to cast her vote without any regard for Luminé. She stepped forward and said, "Y…" she paused, lowered her glance, then looked up in order to say 'Yes' but she hesitated, and said, "No! He is not."

The crowd went wild with jubilation. Angels everywhere were shouting and jumping, gleefully jostling. Yet no one understood what had just happened. Calla lowered her head, disappointed at the display. She raised her hand, calling for silence. When it finally quieted down, she said, "Since it is a tie, the Lords will now vote."

Adon did not wait. He stood and said immediately, "I say no. Luminé is not guilty of Treason."

Calla was next to him. She said, "I say yes. He is guilty."

Quiet ensued. Yeshua would cast the tie-breaker. He knew what Calla expected of him. He looked at Luminé one more time, thinking. He could see Luminé's heart. He disdained the Humans, but he had not intended for this to happen. He had mocked the Lords, but it was his weakness, the sin of pride. It was terrible, but it was not Treason. Yeshua shouted, "I say No, Luminé is not guilty of Treason."

The roar shook the skies above the Throne Room.

Luminé fell to his knees, holding his head in his hands, a tear running down his cheek. He had narrowly escaped a dire fate.

Calla glanced at Yeshua, unable to hide her disappointment, trying to understand why he had voted to let Luminé go unpunished for the crime of Treason.

Adon raised his hand high, "Quiet, please. Angels, for the crime of designing the talking animal, Luminé will be exiled for a year. As far as his title of Archangel is concerned, it will be stripped for now, and we will see how the year progresses."

He turned to the Throne Room guards, "Unchain him, and take him directly to the island."

Luminé stood and held his hands out. When the chains were removed, he thrust his hands into the air. The cheers of the crowd grew even louder, reaching a fever pitch that their favorite Angel had been spared.

Calla watched him being led away, then turned and walked alone back into the quarters behind the Throne Room. She could not speak and could barely cry, though she wanted to. Legion had defeated them, and he had found his way into the heart of their life. So much had been lost today, and she wondered how she would ever get any of it back.

Sansa

10 Months Later

It was an hour past dusk as Oxana's friend, Sansa, strolled quietly down the dense forest road toward the home of her lover Jonathan. Darkness was upon her and the cool of the night was causing her to feel a chill, but it would not dissuade her from going there. Earlier in the day, Jonathan had told her he was tired from a long week and wanted to turn in early, but she sensed he was lying, and she was going to find out.

Sansa was one of the more petite Angels, slim with short auburn hair and deep green eyes. Jonathan was the only Angel she had ever loved. Earlier, she had seen him talking and laughing with a female guard named Marla, and she now had a sneaking suspicion that there was something going on between them.

As she approached the small house situated in a clearing alongside the forest road, she saw the faint light coming from the main living room. It looked like a dying lantern. She crept up to the window and peered in. There on the floor, rolling with their bodies entwined, were Jonathan and Marla. Sansa gritted her teeth, seething in anger, looking up at the sky, wondering why he would do this to her. They had professed their love for each other only a year earlier, and in accordance with Heaven's Law of Love, they were to be exclusively for each other.

Sansa turned away. A feeling of rejection and of being cheated, emotions she never knew, welled up within her, consuming her to the point that she could not think straight. Her mind began pulsating, and rage began to mount. She looked in again. They were still on the floor, but Jonathan was now on top of her now. Sansa saw her chance.

She crept to the back door and peered in. As she had thought, they were facing away from it, so if she entered quietly, she would catch them off guard. Her rage was boiling now, taking over any reason that remained. How could he have so easily abandoned her? The whole idea made her feel low as if she was not good enough.

She stepped inside the dark room, lit only by the dying lantern light. She could hear them frolicking on the floor, and she hated the sound of their voices urging each other onward.

She swallowed hard, thinking it through. They were no more than 10 feet away. She stepped lightly toward them, coming up from behind, quietly drawing her sword from its sheath. In one swift move, she ran up to them, raising the sword high and thrust it downward into Jonathan's back.

Jonathan wailed in the darkness. Sansa pulled the bloodied sword out and maneuvered to the side to attack Marla. But Marla pushed Jonathan off, toward Sansa, and rolled the other way. She jumped to her feet, grabbed her sword, and stood naked, in a fighting stance, ready to take on Sansa. Sansa looked down at the moaning Jonathan and then heard the commotion outside. She was out of time. She picked up the nearby lantern, hurled it at Marla, then raced out the door.

Outside neighbors who had heard Jonathan's scream were already collecting in the front yard. Sansa ran out the back and flew into the air, as Marla ran onto the porch, yelling, "It was Sansa. She stabbed Jonathan."

Oxana

It was dark of night, and Oxana waited on the bluff at the edge of a forest on Earth. Legion landed and walked out of the forest.

Legion asked, "Is everything going according to plan?"

"Yes, the unrest is profound. I doubt the Lords will want to keep Marcellus as Luminé's replacement."

"But what if they will not allow Luminé back?"

"It will be hard for them to deny him. All over the Heavens, there is a great swell of anger because a majority of Angels feel Luminé was unjustly punished. They believe Adam and Eve should have been punished. When he returns, we will be ready to demand his reinstatement."

"Still, that is no guarantee."

Oxana would not reply. She had plenty of tricks yet to be played to ensure Luminé's return would be as she wanted.

Legion stepped closer, brushing his hand against her cheek, "But what about you, Oxana. Should Luminé be demoted, you could be his replacement. Wouldn't you want that?"

She jerked her cheek away. "No, I do not. I am loyal to Luminé."

Legion breathed deep. He felt like slapping her, but he needed them both for the next step in his plan.

Oxana bowed slightly, then left.

Marcellus

Marcellus lay awake in one of the guest houses at the back of Luminé 's 2nd Realm headquarters. Though he had been put in charge as the Interim Leader of the realm during Luminé 's absence, he dared not take up residence in Luminé 's quarters. Marcellus still had his home some miles away on the coast, and he retreated there often to get away from the chaos of trying to command the 2nd Realm in Luminé's unpopular absence.

Ever since Adam and Eve had eaten from the forbidden tree, it seemed as though discontent and discord had broken out nearly everywhere. Selfishness, greed, anger, arguments, fighting, even lust were all at work in the lives of many. Just this morning, one of his guards had stopped an Angel from nearly choking another. They were arguing over one of the females. But while these problems of behavior seemed widespread, they certainly seemed to be more prevalent in the 2nd Realm.

Marcellus looked up at the wall, where he had been marking the days since his appointment. Luminé would be finished with his year of isolation and repentance in a mere 15 days. Marcellus secretly hoped Luminé would indeed be stripped of his Archangel title. He didn't deserve it. He didn't deserve anything after being at the heart of the greatest disaster ever to befall the Heavens. Were it up to Marcellus, Luminé would have been imprisoned in the cage for five years, the punishment rumored to have been facing him. He knew Luminé very well, and something told him that the year of repentance and reflection would teach Luminé nothing.

Marcellus turned over again, trying to fall asleep, when he heard horses charging into the courtyard. Three Angels on horseback riding in at full speed shouting. Everywhere others came running, startling the horses. The three leaped from their horses and raced up the steps and knocked loudly on the door.

Keeping his eyes closed, he sighed. He hated his role as the Interim Leader. None of the Angels wanted him, nor anyone else for that matter, to be over them; they wanted Luminé. Marcellus was not respected as he deserved to be or needed to be in such a command position. Every day was a battle against the unspoken defiance. He had held firm though and had dealt out plenty of punishments, including imprisoning more than 70 Angels who had egregiously violated the rules, including three who had stabbed someone, and seven for public drunkenness. Five had refused to follow orders, even after multiple chances. Most of the rest were in for stealing. Somehow Angels had resorted to taking whatever they wanted from others. It caused more than a few fights, and sometimes depending on severity, they were jailed for that too.

The knock came again, this time louder. "Commander Marcellus."

"Coming," said Marcellus, as he threw off his blanket, swung his feet off the bed, and slipped on his sandals. He stood and put on his tunic, then walked over and opened the door. It was one of his headquarter guards.

"What is it?" asked Marcellus.

"There has been trouble. Your Host Commander Jonathan has been badly injured."

"Injured? How?"

"His lover, Sansa, impaled him with a sword."

"What?" Marcellus grimaced. He was growing tired of all the trouble in this realm, but this was a most egregious act. He had not dealt with its like before. "Where is she now?"

"She has fled, Marcellus."

"Assemble the guards and capture her. This cannot go unpunished. Notify the other realms, too, in case she tries to go to any of them. Also, have Jonathan taken to the Healing Springs."

"At once, sir," the guard said, smiling at some of the others. No one liked Marcellus as their leader. There was nothing particularly wrong with him, per se. It was rather that they loved Luminé and all looked forward to the day he would return.

Marcellus closed the door and laid back down for a few minutes. He needed to think. Things were escalating. Was it because Luminé was returning? Was all of this planned to unseat him? Trouble was brewing in a big way, and it was coming right at him.

The Hunt

At the crack of dawn, the new day's sun was just shedding its long rays across the surface of the sea and onto the shoreline of the 2nd Realm. Sansa crouched down under a large pine tree in the dense forest not far from the coast, trying to decide what to do. The night's rest on the soft pine needles had enabled her to gain a sense of feeling under control again. She was still in disbelief that Jonathan had betrayed her like this, but she had given him exactly what he deserved, and now the feelings of rage that drove her practically mad, were all but dissipated.

She was one of the more petite Angels, slim with short auburn hair and deep green eyes. Jonathan was the only Angel she had ever loved, and now, with time to reflect, her memories of happier times with him came rushing back to her. They had met in the 2nd Realm, only three days after the Angel Games had finished, both of them having been assigned to Luminé's realm. You might say it was love at first sight. Sansa had been at the headquarters, and Jonathan, a new Host Commander for Luminé, had ridden in on a beautiful brown horse. Sansa would never forget how prominent he looked atop that horse. She simply stared at him, wondering who he was. Jonathan had seen her too, and he stared right back at her. Sansa remembered every moment of his actions, how he had dismounted without turning his gaze from her, and how he walked over, introduced himself, and kissed her hand. From that moment, they had been practically inseparable, until of late that is.

Now, everything was confusing, and her mind kept lamenting his actions, trying to reason it out. *Why Jonathan! Why was I not good enough for you! We could have... could have... parted, as friends, and entered into a Season of Reflection. Why did you cheat on me!!!*

After a long while, the sun grew stronger, and she began to calm down. The soothing rays of the morning sun were bringing her back to reality, to the reality of what she had done and what she may have to face. She wondered what her options were. She could go to Oxana's house on the other side of the realm and plea for her protection. Oxana had no real say in the governance of the realm right now, not during Luminé's absence, but everyone knew she was his right hand, and Luminé would be coming back soon. What Oxana wanted to be done mattered, though Marcellus nor the Lords would ever acknowledge it.

Sansa crept down to the shore and scooped some water to drink. She looked across the horizon; it was empty. Throughout the night, she had seen patrols of Angels scouring the skies and land from above. She was sure they were looking for her. Perhaps she needed to make a break for it and go to another realm to hide. Perhaps even she should escape to the uninhabited Olympus Islands to cool off and think. There had to be a way for her to get out of this. If Luminé was reinstated, and he well might be, her friendship with Oxana would take care of everything else. She only needed to hide out until then.

Suddenly she heard the rustle of branches moving behind her. She whipped her head around and saw them: several Angels with swords drawn, spread out, creeping through the woods. Sansa bolted up, caring no longer about concealing herself; there was no time for that. She flew through and around the trees, looking back at the Angels who now had her in their sights and were closing in. She flew straight up out of the trees, turned at an odd angle, then dove back down into the forest, skillfully zigzagging her way through the dense forest.

She looked back; she had lost them. Bam! Her head slammed into the shield of an Angel who had been hiding behind a tree in her path, just as the Angels chasing her had intended by purposefully driving her in his direction. As a great net fell on top of her and one, then two, she fell to the ground, then four Angels quickly arrived. They grabbed the edges of the net and raced into the sky, closing it around her. "Let me go," she screamed as her body painfully jack-knifed inside the net. They ignored her and whisked her back towards the headquarters.

The News

Oxana sat alone in her house on the northern shore of the 2nd Realm. It was a one-story abode made of stone and pinewood with a thatched roof. It had several windows, including a large one in the center that looked out to sea. Inside, the furnishing was sparse, with a few comfortable chairs, neatly carved from forest wood, and one couch adorned with maroon material. Though there were fewer things inside than other Angels had, it was enough for her. She had ordered the building of it to be kept simple, knowing she would rarely be there. The simplicity gave it breathing room to allow her and anyone visiting to comfortably sit and look out the large window facing the sea. Over the last year, in Luminé's absence, it had become her temporary home, and her refuge, and her place to think. She'd had plenty of time for that lately. Seeds of doubt were haunting her for weeks now, throughout almost every night, stealing her ability to get any sleep.

She sipped her morning coffee, still in her sheer nightshirt, looking out over the horizon, glimpsing the beginnings of the sunrise toward the east. Her great champion and lover Luminé would be coming home soon, coming to sweep her back up into his arms and again put her at his side as the defacto co-ruler of the 2nd Realm. She took another sip of her coffee as a feeling of doubt suddenly swept up her spine. She gasped, choking on her coffee, coughing incessantly. She stumbled to her cooking area and quickly poured some water, drinking it, continuing to cough up the coffee that had gone down the wrong pipe. Finally, it subsided, and she leaned on her counter, breathing heavily, trying to normalize her breathing. What if Luminé had changed? What if he did not love her, or even need her anymore? What if this wretchedly simple abode was to become her permanent home, and she was to return to being nothing more than a lowly Angel, doing meaningless work? Worry began to overwhelm her, and she went back to her living area and sat down.

A knock at the door jolted her out of her worry. She looked over and wondered who could be there so early. She opened. It was Antonio, one of Luminé's trusted top commanders. Antonio was the picture of masculine strength. He was tall with broad, well defined tan chest. His waist was slim but packed with strength. He had an air about him too, a no-nonsense attitude that struck fear into others. It was one of the reasons Luminé had chosen him.

Oxana asked, "Antonio? What are you doing here so early?"

He glanced down at her body, then quickly back up at her eyes. "It's Sansa. She has been arrested."

"Sansa? For what?"

"For stabbing, her lover Jonathan."

"What is Marcellus going to do with her?"

"He has set her trial for tomorrow," replied Antonio.

"Hmmm… tomorrow, you say." Oxana paused, suddenly feeling a degree of hope. Her sudden spiral into worry seemed to be finding a solution. Of course, it did, she thought to herself. All the Angels had learned that worry was useless and nothing more than failure to trust. But she needed things through, and she might need help. "Antonio, go now. I will speak to you and the other key commanders later. I need to work some things out."

Calla and Sadie

The morning sun fell warmly onto the top of Holy Mountain, bringing the new day's life to the trees, birds, and small animals who made their home around the land that surrounded the Throne Room. Commander Sadie arrived on the portico landing and hustled up the seven steps to the vast marble floor located just outside the Throne Room. On the other side of the vast floor, the large wooden doors that led into the Throne Room stood closed, bathed in sunlight. There were other Angels there, but Sadie took no notice. Her visit was urgent. She walked hastily across the floor to the guard waiting by the doors on the other side. "Commander Sadie here to see Lord Calla."

"Do you have an appointment?" asked the male guard standing stiffly at attention.

"No, I do not. But this is a matter of utmost importance."

The guard did not look at Sadie but said, "And what makes your 'utmost importance' any different from all of theirs?" He glanced at a long line of Angels waiting against the opposite wall. Sadie glanced over, taking notice of them for the first time. She looked back at him with a determined look on her face, "Because it has to do with Eve."

The guard darted his eyes to Sadie, then back, and nodded, "Wait here." He pushed open one of the large wooden doors just enough to get through and went in, pulling the door closed behind him. A few minutes later, the door pushed open again, and he stepped through, waving for her to come. "Come. Come. Lord Calla will see you now."

Sadie brushed past him and walked onto the floor of the magnificent Throne Room. The morning sun bathed it in marvelous light. The sound of trickling water and the lush green plants that were now maturing gave a most peaceful ambiance.

Sadie saw Calla on the other side, waiting with her hand folded. Sadie smiled and walked over. She knew Calla would know what to do, and she was glad she had decided to come.

As she neared, Calla said, "Good morning, Sadie."

Sadie bowed, "Good morning, Lord Calla." Sadie felt the warm feeling she always felt around Calla, and it made her realize how lucky she was to be doing the things she was doing right now. She was in charge of guarding Adam and Eve and the Garden of Eden, which was now under complete lockdown, and she got to work closely with Calla. The freedom she felt was enormous, and she was suddenly glad Rana had cheated her out of becoming an Archangel.

Calla's long blue gown fluttered gently in the mountain top breeze as she smiled and slowly walked over to greet Sadie, taking her by the hand, leading her, "Come with me, Sadie. We can sit and talk by the overlook." Calla's hair was long, brown, and silky smooth, and it obvious she had just washed it. She looked happy, peaceful, far more than she had looked during the trial.

They walked across the Throne Room and sat on one of the seven soft cushioned royal blue benches arrayed in a semi-circle looking over the mountain's eastern side. The view was spectacular from here, stretching for miles and miles across the Heavenly green valley and winding blue rivers below.

Calla asked, "What can I do for you?"

"My Lord, it is Eve. I am afraid she is sick, and I am worried about her."

"How long has she been sick?" Calla asked, her face showing slight concern.

"For over four days now. I don't know what happened, but I suspect some kind of insect bit her."

Calla nodded. She was worried about Eve. It had been over a year now, and still, Eve was not expecting a baby. She could not understand why, as nothing in her design of the males and females had suggested this delay could happen. "I will come with you. Let us go now."

~ ~ ~ ~

Calla and Sadie flew to the Earth and circled over a clearing several miles west of the now closed-up Garden of Eden. It was a large clearing of sandy-brown dirt surrounded by miles and miles of dense foilage and was located about 100 yards from a small river. In the center of the clearing was a hut made of palm tree leaves and branches. They landed, and Calla walked up to the hut, but it was empty. "Where are they?" she asked.

"Up there," Sadie said, pointing up to a large tree located at the far end of the clearing. There was a ladder leading up the trunk of the massive tree, and twenty feet up was a primitive-looking treehouse, also made of palm tree leaves and branches.

Calla stared at it. She found it primitive, sparse, no place for creatures of her creation. She furrowed her brows and looked at Sadie. "What are they doing up there?"

"My Lord, they were being attacked by the lions. We defended them, but the truth is, we cannot be here every minute. I had my Angels build that house in the tree so they could sleep peacefully."

"Lions? Did they get hurt?" Calla was suddenly tense. She looked around her quickly, flicking her eyes all around the clearing as if in search of predators. This went against her design—animals and humans were meant to live in harmony. That there were problems among them troubled her greatly.

"No, but one of my Angels did. It was over there." Sadie pointed to a spot in the clearing where blood stained the ground. "She is home healing, but after that, we decided to move Adam and Eve up there right away."

"When did this happen?" she asked.

Sadie grimly replied, "last week." She kept her eyes down. Sadie, too, knew this was serious.

Calla sighed, thinking. The past year had brought more and more bad news about how difficult life was for Adam and Eve, news that Calla tried to ignore. She had no good reason, except perhaps she was in denial that their entire plan had collapsed. She had been unwilling to get involved, relying on Sadie to handle things. But here she was, and there could be no brushing such a serious matter aside.

"When did this happen?" she asked.

Sadie grimly replied, "last week."

Calla tightened her lip and marched across the clearing, followed by Sadie. When she reached the ladder at the base of the tree, she looked up, wishing for a moment she had changed out of her long blue gown. "Should we fly up?" Sadie asked.

"No, I want to experience it just as Eve does." She hopped up onto the first rung and began climbing, arm over arm, up the side of the massive tree.

Sadie followed, and when they reached the entry point, Calla knocked on the makeshift door. There was no answer. She knocked again, listened carefully, and again heard nothing. She glanced at Sadie, then went inside. Eve was lying on the bed, sound asleep, with her body covered in sweat. Calla went over and gently woke her, asking, "Eve, are you all right?"

Eve squirmed, wincing, unable to speak. Her hair was disheveled, and her cheeks were pale and slightly gaunt. Beads of sweat were on her face. Calla placed her hand on her forehead. "She is very warm." Calla suddenly regretted her inaction over the past year. She had unconsciously kept her distance from Adam and Eve, relying on the help of Sadie and the few Angels working under her. She was upset with Adam and Eve for disobeying the only law in the Garden. Though they were tricked, their actions had caused everything to fall apart. But now, she looked on with pity at the misery on Eve's face and thought, *Perhaps I expected too much from them.*

Calla frowned, and a tear welled up in her eyes. Nothing was going as it should. Their beautiful plans for the Angels and the Humans were all in shambles. Eve was supposed to have born children by now, though only the Lords knew. Had Legion's dark successes somehow thwarted this? Then it hit her. She had a strong inkling as to why Eve was not expecting a baby yet. It was something she had never considered. Stress must be a factor in Eve's ability to conceive. She looked up at Sadie, with an almost jubilant look on her face, "I'm afraid I have been negligent by not giving them the help they need."

Sadie thought it strange that Calla's words did not match the look of hope on her face. She watched as Calla turned and placed her hand on Eve's forehead, holding it there, whispering a sacred blessing. "Child of Earth and Heaven be made whole."

Within moments Eve slowly opened her eyes and looked up at them, "Lord Calla? Sadie? What are you doing here?"

"We are here to help you," Calla said.

Eve shuddered, and she bravely replied, "I have been very ill, but... I... I feel better now."

Calla said, "I'm sorry I have not visited you more often, Eve. Are you happy?"

Eve's eyes grew moist with sadness, "No... we are not happy. Everything is hard... and I'm worried about Adam. Some of these animals are very frightening. It's dangerous to leave our home, let alone find food or retrieve water from the river." She looked up at Sadie, "I don't know what we would have done without Sadie and her Angels helping us."

Calla looked to Sadie, her eyes moistening, "Sadie, I did not realize how much you were helping, but thank you."

Feeling the emotions in the room, Sadie nodded and wiped a tear from her own eye and said, "Look at all of us, tearing up."

Calla smiled. She loved Sadie's passion, as well as her wit. She resolutely turned back to Eve, "Eve, we are going to help you even more.

I don't want you to have to worry anymore." She looked up at Sadie, "Sadie, see that even more protection is given and that more food and drink is supplied. We have to get you healthy again, Eve. Please go find Adam and get him back to the compound." Calla stood up and looked out the window. She knew Adon would disagree because of his hard stance on free will, but she didn't care. She turned, "Sadie, one more thing. I want a stockade fence built all around this place so they can be at peace."

Sadie smiled, "My Angels and I will see to all, at once, my Lord."

Calla bent down and kissed Eve on the forehead, saying, "Be at peace, woman. All will turn out."

Conspiracy

Oxana went to her bedroom, completely disrobed, and stepped into her shower. She washed her body slowly, feeling a rising sense of hope as the confidence in her budding idea grew. It was time to make her move. She had been biding her time, unsure of herself, but now she realized that she had lulled her hope to sleep, and now it was awakening and rising and lifting her spirit like she had not felt in ages. The time was now. Luminé's return was imminent. *Yes, this is the moment I have been waiting for.* She dressed methodically, putting on her dark brown tunic, maroon belt, silver necklace, and brown sandal-type shoes laced up and around her calves to just below her knees. She adorned her head with a silver braid and fastened her sword on one side and her dagger in the leather sheath on the other. She wanted to look like she felt today, strong and in control of her destiny.

She headed to the earth, to the coastal cave where Legion had strategically set up his lair to avoid any notice of the Lords. She alone knew the location, and she had come here frequently during the last year, not only for advice but to satisfy her increasingly dark sexual urges.

As she flew near, she saw Legion sitting on the nearby cliff-side plateau, overlooking one of the Earth's vast oceans. He was wearing a brown tunic and cooking two pieces of fish on two sticks propped up over the fire. She landed behind him and walked up to him, "Greetings, Lord Legion."

Legion turned abruptly, his hand grasping for his sword, then he saw it was Oxana, and he relaxed. "Oxana, what brings you here today?"

"There is to be a trial tomorrow for one of my friends. With Luminé's return imminent, I believe it would be a perfect time to further humiliate Marcellus."

Legion was quiet as he turned the fish over. He leaned his head back, letting his long blonde hair hang down onto his chest. He closed his eyes, thinking, "No, Oxana, not now."

"But why?" She asked, her brows sunken in anger.

He snapped his head back up and glared at her. "You dare to question me?"

Oxana stood her ground, "Yes, I dare. I need to know why." Her tone was deliberate and authoritative.

Legion seethed. He hated her defiance, and yet strangely, he allowed for it. No one else had ever been granted this privilege. But Oxana was no ordinary Angel. She had not only captivated Luminé, but she had done so to him too. He held his anger and replied, "The reason, Oxana, is that it is not time yet. We need to wait for Luminé to be reinstated as the Archangel in charge of the 2nd Realm, and we want nothing to get in the way of that."

Oxana listened, nodding, then bowed, but she was not in agreement. She was going to make sure Luminé was put in place and that Marcellus was humiliated. She was going to wait for Legion or buy into his plan. She had come for help, and now that he said no, she would go forward without him.

She was turning to leave when Legion gripped her wrist more tightly than was comfortable. "Where are you going?" He arched an eyebrow at her and drew her in closer.

Oxana knew what he wanted, and she wanted no part of it right now. She was determined to go through with her plan—no matter what, she'd take down Marcellus. But she couldn't let Legion know that, so she pacified him with a tender kiss. "Another time," she said. Then she flew off just as quickly as she'd flown in.

Legion watched her, pleased with her strength and confidence, and yet he was beginning to worry that someday she would not be able to be contained. He needed to maintain his power over her, or he would have to replace her and put someone else at Luminé's side.

~ ~ ~ ~

Oxana flew to the designated meeting place. She had wanted Legion's help, but his hesitancy would not be her hesitancy. She would no longer place her destiny in anyone's hands except her own and Luminé's, of course.

As she drew near the grassy area in the small valley situated at the high elevation where two small mountains blended together in the 2nd Realm, she saw they were all there waiting, sitting around in a circle on the fallen logs they had placed there earlier in the year when it had become their regular meeting place. Present were Antonio, Lisala, Lito, Enzola, Diana, Siotte, and Thaddus.

While the seven of them only directly commanded 7,000 of Luminé's 100,000 Angels, they were well known by all to be Luminé's favored commanders. Their opinions mattered not only to other Host Commanders but to thousands upon thousands of rank and file Angels who spoke of Luminé and his henchmen often around countless evening fires.

It wasn't just the Angels in Luminé's realm who felt this way. Angels all over the Heavens felt he had been unjustly punished. They felt that it was Adam and Eve who were the ones to blame for the fall of Creation, not Luminé. A great underlying division simmered beneath the surface of all of Heaven's Seven Realms.

Oxana landed at the edge of the valley and slowly paraded toward them then through the circle of logs, around the ash-filled fire pit, eyeing each of them, walking beyond them out of the circle, until she stopped and turned to face them with a sinister smile on her face.

Though she held no rank or title, she was their leader. They all knew this, and they all respected her. She represented Luminé, the great one, who would be returning. She was part of him, and no one dared question her. Her actions now telegraphed that she had something important to tell them.

She began, "It is time to destabilize Marcellus. Luminé will be returning soon, and we must demonstrate Marcellus's inability to govern this realm. Why? So we may assure everyone that only Luminé is capable of leading us. Tomorrow's trial presents the perfect opportunity."

Antonio alone began to snicker, nodding his head, drawing the attention of the others. He loved the chaos in the Heavens, and he had been noticed early on by Luminé as someone like-minded. Since Luminé's absence, Antonio had stayed loyal to Luminé by being loyal to Oxana.

Oxana saw him snickering and asked, "Is there something you want to share with us, Antonio?"

"Yea, there is. I have only one question. How bad do you want it to be?"

Oxana smiled widely, glancing around at the others, signaling to them how pleased she was with Antonio's willingness to go to any extent she wished. She looked back at him, "Let's just say, as bad as we can make it. Lots of turmoil, fights, maybe even a riot. Am I making myself clear?"

Antonio's face broke out in a wide smile, "Then bad it shall be." He started laughing, as did the others. Oxana allowed it for a few moments, then raised her hands, signaling for them to stop. "Our great leader returns soon. We must do everything we can to make sure he is reinstated as the Archangel of the 2nd Heavenly Realm. You will all be rewarded. I will make sure of it. Now go, and do your duty."

Sadie

Sadie went back to headquarters and called her Headquarters Guard unit together. She asked for volunteers to help build the stockade fence and other volunteers to help with patrols and gathering food for Adam and Eve, but strangely, only 11 Angels stepped forward. Sadie ground her teeth and worked her jaw. She had heard the under-current of Angels blaming Adam and Eve but had not imagined it affecting her unit.

She squared her shoulders as she addressed her brigade. "All right," she said. "The 11 of you step to the side. As for the rest of you, I'm disappointed in you. I expected better from the angels of our realm — we are a proud realm, determined to help others, are we not? Why such reluctance now?"

Nobody answered her, either because they couldn't find the words or because her words had made them feel ashamed. It was clear she would need to take matters into her own hands.

"Very well then," she said, folding her hands behind her back. "I will select you myself." She then walked up and down the line of Angels, all trying not to be noticed, and handpicked 13 more to complete the 24 Angels she had in mind for the team.

"All right. Now, Calla wants us to clear and build a stockade fence. She wants it done quickly because Adam and Eve are in danger from wild animals. So we will work in two shifts, each 7 hours long. I want you to break into two groups of 12 Angels and choose a leader. The perimeter of the clearing and fence should be an area approximately three stone throws. Are there any questions?"

One Angel raised his hand, sheepishly looking at the others. "How big of an area is three stone throws?"

Sadie walked up to him, "Are you trying to be smart?"

"No," he said. "I've never heard that."

Sadie stared at him, trying not to look embarrassed. She realized she had only shared her novel way of measuring with the guards at the

Garden of Eden, and not to her wider command. But she couldn't show her shame—she knew it was important that she maintain her air of authority at all costs. "Fine, I am very surprised you have not heard of it, but I will demonstrate. Pay attention, everyone." Sadie looked around, picked up a stone, faced the headquarters' front gate, and threw the stone as far as she could.

All eyes followed it as it sailed through the cloudless blue sky. It tumbled through the tall grass and landed near the open gate, bouncing through a short distance, settling onto the road in front of the headquarters. Everyone held their gaze on the stone for a moment, then almost in unison, turned back to Sadie.

Sadie smiled, "That's one stone throw. Two more of those makes three, and that is how wide I want the open space within the perimeter of the fence to be.

"But I can throw farther than that!" said a tall Angel named Sylvia.

"Look, it's an approximation," Sadie said, sorry she had brought up stone-throwing at all. "One of you does the stone-throwing, and one of you mark the perimeter, then start building the fence. We need this fence built quickly."

"I thought we were just Headquarter's Gate Guards. Shouldn't we get other Angels to build the stockade fence?"

"No!" Sadie said in a stern voice. "And do you know why?"

The air in the courtyard was flat. Sadie could tell by their postures that they were bored with her, that they weren't taking her seriously and probably never would. Sylvia was biting her nails, and Steven was making eyes at a young angel Sadie couldn't remember ever meeting before. Nobody was looking at her. She clenched her fists and raised her voice. "Because we are the best Headquarter's Gate Guard unit in the Heavens. We do our own handy work. Everyone clear on that?"

Slowly, casual nods and forced smiles came. Everyone seemed to be mumbling.

"We start tomorrow morning," Sadie said, "Dismissed."

She'd never seen a group of Angels scatter so fast. They truly couldn't wait to get away from her.

~ ~ ~ ~

Sadie went home and made herself something to eat. She cooked some beans and greens with herbs in hopes it would become a delicious soup. After getting it cooking, she sat on a chair near the window, thinking of ways she might earn the respect she deserved. She had tried everything. She'd ruled with fear as Luminé had. She'd ruled with wisdom, like Calla. She'd been trying to maintain a delicate balance of fearful and wise, walking the tightrope of generous understanding and total control.

It was clear she could walk that line no longer. Something would need to change, and soon.

Suddenly, a messenger bird arrived. She untied the message from its leg and unfurled it.

Dear Sadie,

There is trouble brewing here. I need to discuss it with you tonight.

Marcellus

She finished cooking and ate her soup. Then, she freshened up and left. As she approached the coastline, she saw a crowd of Angels in the courtyard, angrily chanting. It was clear they were together, but they were arguing and fighting amongst each other as if to just add to the chaos of the scene. She landed in the dust at the center of the compound and walked over to them, recognizing many of them. They were some of the rank-and-file Angels under Antonio's command. Most of the Angels she had understood to be troublemakers or classic under-achievers. They fit well in Luminé's realm.

"What's the meaning of this?" Sadie demanded.

One of them shouted, "We want Sansa released!" Her face was gruff, and her teeth were gritted. Others ran up beside her, shouting, raising their fists, "Release Sansa!"

Sadie looked behind them. Near the eastern wall of the headquarters ' compound was Oxana's friend, Sansa, seated in a large iron cage. Sadie knew Sansa only in that she was one of Oxana's close friends. It told her enough. Her blood began to boil. Of course, Oxana was at the heart of it all, and now through the devious works of her friends.

She turned and walked into the headquarters, up the stairs and down the wide hall to Luminé's old office, that was now occupied by Marcellus. The door was open, and Marcellus was sitting at the large oak desk. Sadie walked right up to the front of the desk and pointed out the window, "What is going on with Sansa?"

Marcellus looked up at her with a grim look on his face. "This is the trouble I spoke of in my letter." His forehead was furrowed with worry, and he looked tired. Sadie had never seen him looking so defeated.

Sadie snapped back, "I gathered that. What did she do?"

"She ran her sword through the back of her lover, Jonathan."

"What! Why?"

"She said he was cheating on her with another Angel. Apparently, she caught them in the act."

Sadie exhaled loudly and lamented, "Marcellus, everything is falling apart."

Neither said a word.

Marcellus walked to the window, looking out at the protesters. One of them was throwing rocks at some of the others across the courtyard.

Sadie asked, "What are you going to do?"

"She is being put on trial in the morning. She is guilty. I am sure of that. The only question is what is should her punishment be. She hurt Jonathan very seriously."

Sadie said nothing for a moment, thinking, "Marcellus, I fear this could be a setup." She didn't know how she knew, other than all the right actors were in play. This could have happened by accident.

"And if it is? What can I do about it? I don't think things can get any worse." He hung his head dejectedly. It was clear that ruling the realm had taken its toll on him. The bags under his eyes were round and protruding. His shoulders slumped under the weight of the entire realm. His nails were bitten down to nothing, his cuticles torn and ragged.

Sadie raised her eyes, "I think they want things to get much worse. Luminé is being released soon. They will try to take advantage of that." Her voice trailed off into silence. She wanted to push back. She wanted to charge out there and shut down the protests. But it was too complicated, and there were too many hidden enemies.

Marcellus looked out the window again. He leaned his hands against the sill, his shoulders sulking and dropped his head.

Sadie walked up beside him, "Marcellus, those Angels outside need to be sent home."

He looked up at her, "I'm allowing it for now. It's not worth the trouble of more arrests."

Sadie pounded her fist against the wall in frustration, "This is outright insubordination! You cannot let this stand!"

Marcellus wheeled around and snapped at her, "I don't think you understand. There is a dark spirit over this whole place. Rebellion is in the air. Many of my commanders have attested to this subtle defiance from the rank and file. Those we can trust are an increasingly small number."

Sadie noticed the sad, worn-out look on his face, and she realized she was pushing too hard. She tightened her lip, "When is the trial?"

"Tomorrow afternoon."

"I will be back," she said. She was worried about not only what this had already done to him, but more so, for what was coming, and something was coming. She could feel it.

Luminé and Rana

The early morning sun lifted itself above the horizon as Luminé stood naked, looking out of the small thatched window of his hut on the remote island he had been sent to for his year of repentance. It was a beautiful tropical island with a white sand beach on all sides. Inland was a freshwater spring Luminé used for drinking water, and which fed a small clear-water pool he could use for refreshment when he did not feel like going into the sea. His hut was modest, built by a few Angels with his help when they brought him in chains. But Luminé outfitted it with comfortable chairs and a bed made from the wood of palm trees, grass, and dried palm leaves. There were window openings cut into the side walls looking in almost every direction to allow maximum light. The floor was strewn with sand that Luminé had brought from the beaches. He preferred this to a grass or dirt floor. While it did not possess the elegance of his headquarters in the 2nd Realm, its simplicity inspired him.

Being out of the limelight for so long had also inspired him, or rather, changed him. He felt more thoughtful and more introspective than he had ever been. In many ways, he regretted what had transpired. He understood that he had let his jealousy for the Humans get the best of him, but in another sense, he did not blame himself for what had occurred, after all, he was not the one who had set the creature Serpe loose in the Garden of Eden, nor was he the one who had told Eve to eat the forbidden fruit. Yes, he deserved to be reprimanded, but being sent away, with the possible stripping of his title, was a gross miscarriage of justice. He sighed; it didn't matter now; the year-long exile was almost over.

He quietly glanced over his shoulder, his eyes gazing at Rana's exquisite long blond hair, wildly wrapped around her sumptuously curved body, only half covered by the sheet. Rana was his first lover, and no matter how he felt about Splendora or Oxana, Rana was the most sensuous.

Rana stirred and stretched her long slim body like a panther. She opened her eyes and noticed him gazing at her, "Luminé, what are you doing up so early?"

He smiled and turned back toward the window, "Just thinking."

Rana swung her long legs off the bed and stood, dropping the sheet to the floor and pranced over to him. She stood behind him, wrapping her arms around his chest, resting her head against the back of his broad shoulder. "You are so strong and handsome, Luminé. I love you."

Luminé clasped her hands, holding her close, feeling her warm body against his back. He turned to face her, placing his hands around her waist, pulling her in closer, feeling himself readying again. "We only have a little more time," he said, "Let's not waste a moment."

An hour later, Luminé opened his eyes and saw Rana now standing across the room, fully dressed, fixing her hair. He watched her quietly until she noticed him. He smiled and said, "I'll miss you."

"Oh, I will be back. Give me a week or so." She winked.

"I don't know what I would have done without you, Rana," said Luminé, "You were the only one daring enough to come here, and I won't forget it during this last year."

Rana turned, "It's our little secret, Luminé. It will always be our little secret."

Mutiny

Marcellus grimaced as he peered out the headquarters' window at the nearly ten thousand Angels gathered in the courtyard. They had begun gathering just after lunch, and they were loud and raucous, shouting and shoving and laughing and arguing.

It was now mid-afternoon, and standing before him in his office was a group of his most trusted commanders. He turned to face them, "We're going to have trouble today. I can feel it."

"Don't worry, Marcellus," said Myrnia, "We can handle it."

Myrnia was his favorite. She had been appointed as his right-hand commander from day one. She was loyal and smart and a real fighter with the sword. Luminé had never acknowledged her skills, but Marcellus promoted her to Host Commander in charge of his old command.

Marcellus nodded and looked back outside. "I hope you are right, Myrnia." He peered along the back of the gathering. Some of his other commanders, the ones loyal to Oxana, were conspicuously mixed in with the crowd. He could see Rodrigo, a swarthy scoundrel who had always remained loyal to Oxana. His hairy fist was raised in the air, and he was yelling so loud his face was turning red, trying to whip the crowd up into a frenzy.

From what he could see, Oxana was not there. This worried him. She was behind all of it, and the fact she was not there could only mean she was making sure no blame would be associated with her. Something big was about to happen.

In the distance, he spotted Sadie flying in with several Angels from her command. He watched them land and take up a spot near the back of the crowd.

He turned to his commanders, "It's time. Let's go."

Marcellus walked down the long wide hallway toward the stairs leading down to the first-floor courtyard. He again lamented the predicament he was in. It was true that the Archangels in the other six Heavenly realms were having problems, but none like in his realm. There was a concerted effort to thwart his authority, and his not being an 'official Archangel' only added fuel to the fire.

He followed his commanders down into the courtyard and over to the large wooden table sitting on the ground where the trial would be held. He felt nervous today, not ready for anything major, and yet, everything told him that was coming. But despite his apprehension, he needed to gather himself now. He was the leader, and this was his duty.

He stood behind the table next to his commanders, paused, and raised his hand high, signaling for quiet. In a booming, commanding voice, he shouted, "Bring Sansa forward."

Several Angel guards went to the cage, unlocked it, placed chains around her hands, then marched her across the courtyard. She looked worn out, and her clothing was still dirty from her capture. She had not bathed in days, he was sure. The look on her face was one of deviousness, with her eyes sparkling and a half-smile pinned to it.

The crowd began shouting and clamoring loudly as they reluctantly parted to let Sansa and the guards through. Finally, Sansa and the guards reached the table and stood in front of it.

Marcellus raised his hand, calling for quiet, then pulled out a scroll and looked up, making eye contact with Sadie. He could see the worry on her face. He proceeded in a strong voice the Lords would expect him to use. "Sansa, you are charged with using your sword to cause great injury to the Angel Jonathan. How do you plead?"

"I am guilty," she said defiantly.

Marcellus had not expected her to reply so. Witnesses were standing by to corroborate her act. It was clear to him now that whatever was about to happen was surely orchestrated to be efficient.

He gathered himself and stood resolutely, knowing what was now expected, and knowing it would ignite the crowd. "Do you have anything else to say before I pronounce your sentence?"

Sansa held up her chained hands, "He cheated on me. He deserved what he got." Her face looked distressed, but Marcellus could tell it was contrived. He listened without flinching. Now, all eyes turned to him. The words he would speak would set their plan into motion, undoubtedly causing chaos. He could still take the easy road of letting her off, and this course of action and what it would mean briefly swept through his mind, but only for a moment. He delivered his verdict, "I understand you believe you had reason to assault him. However, it is my judgment that this does not absolve you from your violent behavior. I hereby sentence you to one year in a cage."

Immediately the crowd began growing boisterous and louder. Shouts of "Not fair! Free Sansa!" began to ring and grow louder in the crowd.

Sansa fell to her knees and theatrically screamed, "But he cheated!"

Her words seemed to set a match to the crowd.

Suddenly, bedlam ensued. The crowd rushed forward, sweeping up Sansa, knocking over the table. Marcellus and his commanders fell back, calling for reinforcements. He watched as Rodrigo, Antonio, and other commanders loyal to Oxana charged forward with their swords held high, egging on their willing followers.

Sadie looked up and saw Antonio shouting, "Mutiny! Mutiny!"

The compound's rear gate was knocked over, and thousands of Angels poured into the courtyard, racing into the fray. Fires were set along the wall as smoke began to billow upwards.

Sadie flew up into the air to assess the unfolding scene. She scanned the courtyard and saw that Marcellus and his loyal guards had formed a large circle and were fending off the attackers. Rodrigo charged forward, breaking through, and began battling with Myrnia. He pushed her back, back, and up onto the courtyard platform. Myrnia leaped up, narrowly missing his swinging sword. She came down hard, slicing his hand away. Rodrigo screamed and fell, then ran back, writhing in agony, as Myrnia jumped back down into the circle with Marcellus and the others.

Sadie scanned the courtyard. Everywhere, thousands of Angels were engaged in the fight. Marcellus needed help badly. She shouted to her companions, "Go and help Marcellus. I am going for help!" She rushed off through the billowing smoke into the distant blue sky.

~ ~ ~ ~

Splendora stood at attention in the Throne Room alongside Arcano and Fernando, her two most trusted commanders. They were waiting to give their weekly report of events in her realm.

There was a hushed, peaceful silence hanging over the vast room. Sunlight from the descending afternoon bathed the floor in a warm, welcoming glow. There was a peaceful aura, light and easy, full of hope that nature brought.

The golden doors at the back of the Throne Room that led to the Lords' quarters opened, and Calla and Adon walked out together, smiling. Moments later, Yeshua followed, and they all took to their respective thrones and sat down.

Splendora and her companions bowed. "Greetings, my Lords."

Calla smiled, happy to see her favorite Archangel, "Greetings to you Splendora, and to you, Arcano and Fernando. How are things going in your realm?"

Arcano resolutely stepped forward, "My Lords, with the exception of some unexpected incidents, all is going well in the 1st Heavenly Realm."

Yeshua asked, "What unexpected incidents are you referring to?"

Arcano's lips tightened as he momentarily glanced at Splendora. He had agreed with Splendora that he would not offer details unless asked. Now, he had been asked. He said, "They are minor in nature, nothing worth mentioning."

"Such as?" asked Yeshua, not willing to let this pass.

Arcano sighed, pulled out a scroll from his belt, and unfurled it. "My Lords, there have been incidents involving the following: fighting, not reporting for duty, not following orders, and violations of Heaven's Law of Love." Arcano stopped abruptly, rolled up the scroll, and stepped back. He was sleek and strong but never confident when dealing directly with the Lords as they intimated him.

Calla grimaced, "I told you, Adon. Not only the Earth, but the entire Heavens have fallen into the grip of this darkness. The knowledge from the Tree of the Knowledge of Good and Evil has been unleashed upon the world too soon."

Yeshua nodded, "It seems this knowledge of evil is becoming a temptation."

Calla replied, "Yes, the desire was to do good, is becoming, for many, the desire to do evil."

Adon nodded, "This is what free will looks like."

Calla looked over at him, shaking her head, "Yes, but Legion's escape so soon is ruining everything."

Adon nodded, she was right, but he would not say any more.

Suddenly the Throne Room doors opened, and the guard walked in. "My Lords, I am sorry to bother you, but…" Behind him, through the doors, walking at a hurried pace, came Sadie. The guard turned, trying to signal for her to wait, but Sadie marched right past him. "My Lords, there is a battle raging in the 2nd Realm." Her face was hurried and showed alarm.

Splendora turned, "A battle?"

Sadie said, "Yes, there was a trial. As soon as the judgment was pronounced, the Angels watching the trial began fighting with all of Marcellus's guards. There are thousands of them fighting in the courtyard. It is like a mutiny."

Calla stood, exclaiming, "Mutiny?"

Calla said, "Splendora, summon your Angels and go at once. Arcano, you go to the 3rd Heavenly Realm and summon Michael and his Angels. Fernando, Sadie, go to the 4th and 5th Realms and summon Raphael and Gabriel."

Everyone dispersed. Calla turned to the other Lords. "We need to go and see what is happening."

Adon replied, "Calla, we vowed to stay out of the affairs of Angels and Humans as much as possible. I fear if we get involved, it will destroy the very foundation of the concept of free will. They need to resolve this themselves."

Calla dropped her head back, "Free will! I am sick of hearing about it. It is destroying everything."

Adon shot back, "No, Calla. The knowledge of evil is destroying everything."

Yeshua said, "Calla, Adon is right. We should not intervene directly. However, I want to understand what is happening. I will disguise myself and go see."

~ ~ ~ ~

Splendora flew near the shores of the 2nd Realm, followed by hundreds of her Angels. They were all set upon their goal and determined, like their leader, to quell this rebellion. All had their swords drawn, ready to engage as soon as they arrived.

As they neared the headquarters, they could see thousands of Angels packed into the courtyard fighting each other, and thousands more were on the roads surrounding the compound. Most were using their fists, but a fair number were using swords. Splendora pulled up in the air and looked at the roads leading in. It seemed that everywhere, Angels were rushing to the scene. With 100,000 Angels living in the realm, she knew she was greatly outnumbered.

She and her Angels flew down into the center to join Marcellus and his small band of Angels. They formed a circle and began pushing outward, widening it, pushing the rebels farther and farther into the unruly crowd.

Nearly a half-mile away, Yeshua landed on the shoreline. He pulled the hood from his tunic over his head and began a brisk-paced walk up off the beach and onto the road that led toward Luminé's headquarters. All around him, Angels were rushing past him toward the fighting, anxious to find out what was happening. Up ahead in the distance, he could now hear the shouts, and screams, and clanging of swords.

It did not take much longer before he came across the edge of the growing crowd. Angels everywhere were indiscriminately engaged in fighting. Yeshua observed them, wondering how things had gotten so bad, so fast. The anger and rage coming from many of the Angels astonished him. Yes, this was mutiny, but it was much more. It was the influence of Legion's dark reign spreading.

He walked into the midst of the chaos when suddenly a female Angel, with sword drawn and gritted teeth charged toward him. Yeshua gently raised his hand, signaling for her to stop. The Angel did, and Yeshua engaged her eyes, with a calm look on his face, and said, "Put down your sword."

The Angel looked at the sword in her hands as if she had been unaware it was there. She dropped it and looked up at him.

Yeshua said, "Go home."

She nodded, turned slowly, and began walking away with a somber look on her face.

Yeshua kept walking into the midst of the fighting. He turned, looking at Angels, saying the words, "Return to your homes."

One by one, they began dropping their swords. But there were tens of thousands on the roads, and thousands more in the courtyard, too many for Yeshua to reach. In the sky, he saw the thousands of Angels from Michael and Raphael's realms approaching. He knew he was no longer needed. He quietly turned and walked back toward the shore, burdened now more than he had ever been before.

~ ~ ~ ~

Moments later, Gabriel and Sadie, accompanied by 10,000 more Angels, arrived in the skies. Sadie shouted, "We need to arrest the leaders!"

Gabriel turned and gave the command, "Find the leaders and arrest them. Arrest anyone else who tries to resist." He turned to Sadie, "Tell us who the leaders are."

Sadie shouted each name, "Antonio, Lisala, Lito, Marco, and Thaddus." She paused and turned to Gabriel, "And Oxana, but I will go and find her."

Gabriel gave the signal, and he and the small army of Angels charged downward into the fray, while Sadie took off alone toward Oxana's home.

Gabriel's forces engaged others with their fists and swords when needed, driving a wedge into the center. Initially, the fighting intensified, with the addition of hundreds more into the mix. The noise grew louder, the fires burned higher, and the smoke intensified. At one point, the north wall was knocked over. But then, the tide began to turn, and little by little, the mutineers were subdued and tied up. Soon, their leaders and other their followers were located, arrested, and the fighting came to a stop.

By the end, over two thousand Angels had been arrested and were seated in the courtyard in chains.

Oxana, who had not participated in the fighting, was brought in last by Sadie. Her wrists were chained, and she was marched to the stockade where those under arrest were corralled. As she neared them, thousands of the Angels began chanting, "Luminé, Luminé, Luminé."

Visitations

Luminé lay in his hammock, tied between two palm trees, thinking about Rana's visit two nights earlier. Her beauty enthralled him, and he longed for the next meeting with her. Suddenly he heard a voice in the distance. "Luminé!" He sat up, listening. The voice grew louder, and he recognized it. It was Adon.

He jumped up and quickly looked around to make sure there was no trace of Rana having been there. Had she been discovered, it would not go well for him. When he was sure there was no trace, he shouted, "Over here, Lord Adon."

Moments later, Adon and Calla walked out of the jungle into the small neat clearing Luminé had made for himself in front of his light brown grass hut. Luminé was startled to see Calla and suddenly wondered where Yeshua was.

"Good morning, Luminé," said Adon,

"Good morning, my Lords." Luminé was happy to see Adon coming to visit him. He looked warm and fatherly, not like the regal, stoic Lord he had last at the trial. Calla looked very different. She was dressed as the strong warrior and Lord she was, wearing a light blue tunic with a gold belt and golden laced up sandals. Her long brown hair was braided back, and a golden headband adorned her head along with golden metal bands on her wrists. She looked unflinching and ready for battle.

Adon asked, "How are you doing?"

Luminé bowed, "I am doing fine. As you know, my time here is coming to an end, and I am anxious to return." Even as he said it, he knew he would miss his secret liaisons with Rana. But it was fine. He would have other days with her. They had an understanding.

Showing little emotion, Calla said, "That is what we are here to discuss, Luminé. We want to know what you have learned here during the last year."

Luminé studied Adon's warm smile. It seemed kind, even forgiving. He had the sense Adon held no animosity toward him, but he could not tell with Calla. Her face gave nothing away. He said, "My Lords, in my year of reflection, I have come to regret my actions. Being here has stripped me of all pride and contempt, and I want nothing more than a chance to humbly serve you and the Humans. I was wrong to have not trusted you and to have disrespected you." Luminé was lying about some of what he said, though he wanted to mean all of it. But he could not let go of his disdain nor suspicion of the humans entirely.

Knowing that Luminé's reply sounded rehearsed and worried it was not enough to sway Calla, Adon asked, "Luminé, have you changed your ways?"

Luminé nodded with a sorrowful look on his face, "I have, my Lord."

Calla said, "Your actions have caused utter chaos in all of Heaven. Perhaps being sorry isn't enough." She breathed deeply and narrowed her eyes, watching his reaction carefully.

An uncomfortable silence fell upon all. Calla broke it. "We will determine your fate upon your return." She looked over to Adon and waved her hand, signaling they should leave.

As Luminé watched them walk away, Calla's words simmered. He still blamed Adam and Eve. They were the ones who ate from the tree, and they were the ones, in his mind, who truly deserved to be punished.

~ ~ ~ ~

Calla and Adon returned to Holy Mountain and walked across the Throne Room floor toward their quarters in the back with neither saying a word. They knew they were not in agreement, but neither felt it was time to hash it out. Adon stopped, "Calla let me say one more thing. It was Legion's persuasive power that was at the root of all this."

Calla nodded, "Yes, Adon, that is true, but by his careless actions, Luminé made himself an easy target. Can we afford for one of our Archangels to be so reckless?"

Adon nodded, not showing agreement but acknowledging her point.

Yeshua walked in. "I am afraid we have trouble in the 2nd Realm."

Adon asked, "How bad is it?"

"There are over 5,000 wounded."

"What!" Calla exclaimed.

"Yes, it was a mess. Thousands upon thousands of the Angels were embroiled in a massive fight, with no clear distinction as to who they were fighting or who they were fighting for. They were all just fighting each other as if each was enemy to the other."

Adon clenched his teeth in disappointment. Things were indeed spiraling out of control.

Yeshua asked, "Where were you?"

"We went to see Luminé," replied Adon.

Yeshua said, "Luminé needs to be put back in charge. It is the only way to bring order without getting directly involved. The chaos is... well... as I said, it is out of control."

Calla replied, "Luminé is not repentant in the least. He told us what we wanted to hear, but I don't think he believed any of it."

Yeshua sighed. There was no easy answer. "Well, it still may be our best option."

Calla snapped, "How can we simply reward him by putting him back in charge? It is an affront to us, and to everything good."

"Well, you both make good points."

"And what do you say?" Calla asked in a heated tone.

Adon replied, "I am still undecided."

~ ~ ~ ~

Sparkis waited until the moon was nearly set before setting out toward the Southern Realm. As he was ready to leave, it started to drizzle. He grimaced and set out, flying low across the unsettled waters of the Great Heavenly Sea. His red curly hair and brown tunic he wore to help avoid detection became drenched quickly. When he reached the Olympus Islands, he waited to make sure he had not been followed. Finally, he flew across the narrow strait and landed in the pre-dawn darkness on the shore of Luminé 's island.

He knew exactly where he was to go. He shook the water off his short legs and walked up the sandy beach into the dark jungle, and made his way down the lush, winding, jungle path, pushing large leaves and branches out of his face, until he reached the darkened clearing. There he stopped and called out Luminé's name. "Luminé?"

No answer.

He called out again, louder this time, "Luminé?"

An angry voice came from the darkness, "I heard you the first time, Sparkis."

Sparkis said, "It is me, Luminé."

"I know it's you, Sparkis. Wait there."

Sparkis felt proud to be one of those Luminé trusted to periodically visit him. But he also felt demeaned as Luminé looked down on him. Still, Sparkis accepted this. After all, Luminé was the greatest of Archangels. He waited for a while until finally, he saw Luminé light a lamp inside. He waited longer, listening to movement, and humming, and more movement, and more humming. Eventually, Luminé came out. "What news do you have for me, Sparkis?"

"Great Luminé, there is major trouble." Sparkis puffed his chest out, honored to have been chosen to bring such important news.

"What do you mean, major trouble?"

"Mutiny. The entire realm mutinied yesterday. Thousands have been arrested, including Oxana."

"What! Why?"

"Sansa ran her sword through the back of Commander Jonathan. Marcellus found her guilty and tried to imprison her. There was a mutiny."

Luminé was quiet. Suddenly he realized why the Lords had visited him. They must have been considering putting him back in charge to restore order.

"What is to happen to them, Sparkis?"

"Splendora said their judgment would be decided after your return when the new leader of the realm is established." Sparkis was moving from one foot to another with nervous energy, his head bobbing slightly.

"The new leader of the realm, hah! She knows it will be me." His face grew cross, "What was she doing there?"

"All the Archangels came to put down the rebellion. Tens of thousands of Angels were all fighting and destroying the headquarters compound."

Luminé thought for a moment, "Why weren't you arrested, Sparkis?" Luminé had the feeling Sparkis stayed out of harm's way.

"Me... well... I managed to stay out of the limelight. Only the leaders and those bold enough to resist were arrested."

"But where are your scars, Sparkis?"

Sparkis put up his dukes, smiling, bobbing back and forth, "I gave out a number of them, Luminé. But I received none."

Luminé raised his eyes, amused at his old friend's cavalier demeanor. "Come with me. I want to go see the sunrise. I need to think."

They went down the jungle path to the shore just in time to see the sun cresting over the horizon. Luminé was beginning to feel his destiny return. An excitement he had not felt in a very long time began inching its way back into his mind.

"Sparkis, go back to my hut and retrieve a parchment and quill for me."

"What for?"

Luminé looked at him, annoyed, "So I can write a letter, Sparkis!"

"Oh, sure. I'll be right back."

As he left, Luminé smiled. Sparkis had indeed been a dose of comic relief since the first day he had met him. Annoying, yes, but also funny, and at times, like this, useful.

Moments later, Sparkis came back and handed Luminé the parchment. Luminé turned away from him and began to write in earnest. He finished and sealed the parchment shut. "Get this to Oxana."

"But she is in the stockade with the thousands of others."

"I don't care how you do it, Sparkis, but this letter must get to her. Do not read it either, do you understand?"

Luminé handed him the letter, "Go now. Make sure she gets this today. Is that clear?"

"Yes, it is clear, great Luminé." Sparkis already knew there was no way he could get the letter to Oxana today. He had things to do, important things, but there was no point in trying to tell Luminé any of that. He took the letter and left.

The Return

Three days later, Oxana sat alone in the corner of the stockade staring into the distance with her chest forward and her jaw set firmly. A self-satisfied grin crept across her face. She had done what Luminé asked, secretly alerting his vast followers throughout all seven realms of his return. The response, according to her network of informants, had been more than she ever hoped for. Now, she needed to wait to see if his plan would work.

Antonio and Thaddus walked over and sat down next to her. Although their every move was being watched by the guards above, they were allowed to move around the stockade. Thaddus said, "I am worried, Oxana. What if Luminé is not put back in charge?"

Oxana glanced over at him with a stern look, "Do not doubt Luminé, Thaddus. We owe him our loyalty."

"Yes, yes, I know, but what if…"

"Stop!" Oxana said in a harsh whisper.

Antonio glared at him too, "Yea, stop Thaddus, and quit being so weak. They are not going to put 2,000 of us in cages." Antonio was getting tired of the lack of zeal and confidence in the co-conspirators he had to deal with.

"Well, they put 2,000 of us in a stockade."

"Enough!" Oxana said. She turned to Antonio, "What did the guard say?"

"He said he knows nothing yet, only that there are hundreds of thousands waiting for the signal." A sly smile crept over Antonio's face. He was amazed that Oxana had orchestrated this so quickly.

The news of so many being ready caused Oxana's worried brow to lighten. She nodded subtly, thinking if there was anything else, then asked, "Who is giving the signal?"

"Sparkis," said Antonio, and his sly smile started to fade.

Oxana frowned. She liked Sparkis. Everyone did. But he had a way of fouling things up. "Isn't there anyone else who could give the signal?"

Thaddus echoed her lament, "Yea, Isn't there anyone else?"

Antonio's eyes narrowed, and he glanced up and down the stockade, "We are all here in this stockade. Sparkis was the only one left."

Oxana exhaled loudly, then recollected herself. "It doesn't matter. The plan is in motion."

~ ~ ~ ~

Calla took in a deep penetrating breath of the sea air coming into her bedroom. She was at her villa, finally alone with time to think. She had been spending too much time at the Throne Room and her living quarters there. It was fine, and it was necessary, but it was not home. She drew in another breath and closed her eyes, exhaling slowly. She felt peaceful again, rested, and she was going to need it.

Today was the day Luminé was to return, and it would be decided whether he was to be reinstated or not. Luminé did not deserve the command, but Yeshua thought otherwise. It was clear that Adon would determine the outcome. This worried her. Adon knew more about everything than he was letting on. She never imagined her ancient lover and best friend would be working against her, but it seemed as though he was.

As she gazed out at the distant horizon, she saw something that at first looked like just a tiny spec. But then there were more and more. She stood and peered out, focusing her vision. They were Angels, groups, and groups of them, flying toward the shoreline near Holy Mountain.

She quickly dressed and rode her horse Willow across the plains toward Holy Mountain. As she neared, she thought of their journey on the first day of Creation when the Angels were given life. It was along the same path, through the sleeping Angels, where they had felt such great joy and hope, a stark difference to the dread she felt today.

She stopped Willow and reflected on how much had changed. The day they created the Angels, she was happy and full of hope for a bright future. She was about to embark on another Season of Love with Adon. Now, she was tired, and she faced a myriad of problems, and her mind held too many worries, and she was far from loving anyone. How did it all happen?

She pulled on the reigns and moved Willow forward again, picking up speed now, galloping with the wind at her back. Finally, she reached the base of the mountain and rode up the path leading to the top. When she entered the Throne Room, Adon and Yeshua were seated on their thrones waiting for her. Neither of them looked particularly happy, for today's decision was difficult, and no matter which way it went, it felt like they were losing something.

Calla stopped in the middle of the Throne Room and pointed to the hundreds of thousands of Angels gathered in the distance at the shore where Luminé was to land. "I thought this was supposed to be a private affair."

Adon shook his head disapprovingly, "It seems as though they have somehow found out about Luminé's release date. There is nothing we can do."

"Where is Luminé now?" she asked as she walked over to the southern edge of the Throne Room to get a closer look. It made her nervous that the Angels were somehow driving destiny. It reminded her of the trial a year earlier and their boisterous and rebellious tone.

Yeshua replied, "He is on his way... in a boat."

"A boat!" she exclaimed, turning abruptly, with her eyebrows touching in the middle.

"Yes," Yeshua said, "apparently, he wanted to ride in a boat instead of flying here."

Calla let out a loud sigh. In a frustrated tone, she said, "Luminé was supposed to quietly return, and we were supposed to decide his fate. Now, he, or someone, has orchestrated a grand entrance. Instead of a hearing, this has turned this into a parade."

Adon sighed and shook his head. Calla was right. It seemed as though events were once again unfolding with the help of an unseen hand. "We will handle this properly, Calla."

"Well, I am not going to allow the Angels who support Luminé to push us into reinstating him. I am perfectly happy with Marcellus being promoted to Archangel."

Yeshua nodded, "It is your right to want this, Calla. We will decide after the hearing."

~ ~ ~ ~

Splendora and her old friend Sparkis waited on opposite ends of the dock where Luminé was to arrive. They had been tasked with meeting him at the shore and bringing him to meet the Lords. Splendora was frustrated. Someone had found out and spilled the beans about Luminé's return. She could tell simply by looking behind her at the hundreds of thousands of Angels who had come to greet him. No one was supposed to have known about his return, and the endless possibilities as to how the word got out went through her mind.

She doubted Sparkis could have orchestrated such a thing, but the only other person who knew the exact date he was coming was Luminé himself. The Lords had assured her of this. And he was in a solitary exile. This was not a good sign of his "having changed," and it was not a good sign either, for her secret desire to perhaps someday love him again. Was he up to his old tricks again, with Oxana, with Rana? Had he not learned his lesson?

There was a shout, and someone pointed in the distance, and the crowd began to clamor. The boat was in sight, and as it drew nearer, she could see Luminé standing at the bow. As it got closer and glided toward the grassy dock, he raised his arms, and an immense cheer went up. Splendora looked around, watching the faces of so many of the Angels. They were excited, full of hope, exuberant. She knew it was wrong for her to smile, but she could not help it. She had not seen so much happiness in Heaven in a very long time. That was Luminé's way. It was his style; making everyone around him feel excited. Now, he was back, and everyone was glad about it.

Luminé's pulled alongside the dock and stepped off. Splendora was waiting and reached out her hand to greet him. "Welcome back, Luminé. The Lords are waiting to meet with you." She watched him taking a moment to look at her, taking her in. His eyes spoke of the eternal fire they both carried for each other. But they were not alone, and there was no time for anything to be said other than what was expected.

"Splendora, thank you for being here. It is… good to see you."

"It is good to see you, too."

Sparkis stepped into their midst, "Great Luminé; welcome back."

Luminé nodded, "Thanks, Sparkis," he said more curtly.

Splendora turned and began making her way from the dock through the immense crowd. She had never seen so many Angels not gathered in the skies. All were crowded on the land behind the dock, cheering, shouting, smiles, and happiness on their faces.

As Splendora brushed past Sparkis, she noticed Sparkis was acting strange, almost nervous with Luminé in tow. She walked a few more steps, then looked back. He had jumped onto a rock near the edge of the road and raised his fist, shouting something, but he fell off the rock into the crowd. She paused, and the crowds quickly overwhelmed him. She shook her head, wondering what he was up to, and continued walking. But then she heard Sparkis' voice shouting faintly, and she turned again. He was back up on the rock, shouting, "Luminé, Luminé, Luminé."

"What is he doing?" she said to Luminé, who merely shrugged his shoulders. But then the crowd started catching on, and within moments, the chant of Luminé's name began to grow and spread, until, within mere moments, the entire crowd of hundreds of thousands of Angels were shouting in unison, "Luminé, Luminé, Luminé."

Luminé raised his hands, acknowledging the crowd, and the chants grew louder. Splendora grabbed him by the sleeve, pulling him forward down the road, utterly annoyed. Their chants alluded to worship, which was only to be given to the Lords. Frustrated at the spectacle, she snapped, "Let's go, Luminé." She flew up into the air with him, and the crowd followed. As they arrived, the thousands of Angels quickly raced to the open spaces in the sky to get the best view of the coming proceedings, while Luminé and Splendora flew down to the Throne Room entrance. The air above was filled with electricity, and it seemed obvious what the Angels wanted. They wanted Luminé to be restored.

~ ~ ~ ~

Legion stepped from behind a grove of trees not far from Holy Mountain. He was wearing a plain tunic and sandals, the way many of the Angels dressed in an attempt to blend in. He placed his arm on a tree branch and watched the crowd of Angels taking their places above the sky. Everything was going according to his plan. He had chosen wisely when he zeroed in on Luminé. He had also acted wisely on the first day of creation when he conjured up and spread his seeds over as many of the sleeping Angels as he could. Those seeds were bearing fruit. They were feeding into the spirit of rebellion. He was casting over those who were susceptible. Now, he needed Luminé to be put back in charge.

~ ~ ~ ~

Luminé and Splendora walked through the Throne Room doors and saw the Lords waiting on the other side and the skies above filled with Angels. All eyes were upon them. Splendora looked at Luminé, and he at her. It seemed for a moment to her, that this was how it was always supposed to be, Luminé at her side, both of them the most splendid Archangels, joined in their allegiance to the Lords.

All grew quiet as they crossed the floor together. The Lords were waiting, dressed in regal robes, all wearing laurels on their heads.

Suddenly the chants began, slowly at first, but quickly gaining steam, "Luminé! Luminé! Luminé!"

While this was fine at the dock and part of the plan, Luminé now realized it was not playing well in front of the Lords. He turned to the crowd and crossed his hands above his head, signaling them to stop. He then turned to face the Lords and bowed, "Greetings, my Lords. I am sorry for this outburst."

Adon stood up, "Greetings, Luminé." A long silence ensued as the crowd settled in. Adon continued, speaking in a loud and regal tone, "Are you prepared to answer our final questions before we render our verdict?"

"I am, my Lords," he replied in a calm and resigned tone.

Adon nodded and sat, and Yeshua turned to him, "Luminé, what have you learned during your year of solitude and seclusion?"

Luminé paused for effect and turned to look at the hundreds of thousands surrounding him in the sky, "My Lords, I wish to say to you, and to all of these Angels present, that I was wrong. I formed a distrustful attitude against the Humans that ultimately led to acts against your very wills. I repent for what I did and take full responsibility for it. I have come to realize that I am nothing more than a humble servant created in your image. I want nothing more than to do your will. Give me a second chance to show you I have changed."

Adon nodded, and Luminé could tell his answer had pleased him. He had always loved Adon, like a father. Ever since the first day of Creation, Adon noticed his natural leadership qualities when he helped serve the other Angels fruit.

He asked, "And how do you feel about the Humans now, Luminé?"

Again Luminé paused, dropping his glance momentarily before nodding slowly. He raised his head, "My Lords, Adam and Eve are beautiful specimens created in your image, worthy of love and acceptance by us all."

Calla then asked, "Luminé, what evidence do you have that you have changed?"

Luminé had expected this question, and he was ready, "My Lords, stripping me to nothing has allowed me to find within me roots of humility as I have reflected on my core my purpose, which is to honor and obey you and all you create. And, to prove this, I am perfectly willing to be stripped of my title of Archangel to serve and protect the Humans."

Calla looked out at the crowd murmuring amongst themselves. She overheard a voice gasp, 'No! It can't be!' and another boomed, "Save us, Luminé!"

Adon then stood with a solemn look on his face, "We will now vote."

Luminé bowed and waited for the verdict. The crowd grew silent.

Adon stepped forward, "I believe you have learned your lesson. I vote to reinstate you." He sat down as the crowd grew jubilant.

Calla stood, "Luminé, although you have apologized profusely, what has occurred has been too grave and can never be reversed. Therefore, I cannot reinstate you. My vote is no."

A disappointed murmuring shot through the skies and all eyes turned to Yeshua.

Yeshua sat for a long moment. He had always trusted Calla's intuition, and the words she had just spoken resonated loudly within him. He slowly stood, "Luminé, I have heard all that has been said. It is difficult for me to render this verdict for reasons you may never understand. I understand that you were sincere in your apology, and… because of this, I restore you to the rank of Archangel and to command the 2nd Realm. Now you may…"

Yeshua was cut off by the sudden, deafening, outburst of cheering from the crowd. Luminé turned, smiling up at them all. He turned back to face Yeshua, knowing he was not finished.

Yeshua raised his hand high, and the crowd died down, "Luminé, your first order of business will be to pronounce judgment on those who mutinied in your realm and restore order and peace. They await your judgment; remember our example as you rule."

Luminé bowed, "Yes, my Lords."

He's Back

Thaddus and Antonio ran through the seated prisoners inside the stockade to the corner where Oxana was seated.

"He's back!" Antonio shouted.

"Has he been reinstated?" she asked, her eyes pregnant with hope.

"Yes!" Thaddus declared, just I thought he would be.

Oxana glared at Thaddus, who how doubted everything for a moment, then jumped up and hugged Antonio. "I knew he would return to us. I knew it." Oxana could barely contain herself.

One of the guards walked over, "Did you say Luminé is free?"

"Yes, he is," snapped Thaddus. "And if you're smart, you'll open that stockade before he gets back."

The guard's face grew pale.

Oxana shouted, "No, Thaddus, we will stay here and wait for Luminé." She turned to the guard, "You have nothing to fear. Go and make sure you and the others do your jobs until Luminé returns."

The guard nodded and walked away.

~ ~ ~ ~

Luminé flew triumphantly away from Holy Mountain toward his realm. Behind him were not only the Angels who called his realm home but thousands upon thousands of others who wanted to see his return complete. When the realm came into view, Luminé's heart leaped within him. He had feared never being able to return, but now his fears were a distant dream. Now he had been given a second chance.

He landed in the middle of the courtyard to the cheers of thousands upon thousands of Angels. He looked around and saw the devastation and chaos caused by the mutiny. For a moment, it unnerved him that his kingdom was in disarray, but then he realized they could rebuild, and it had all been necessary. He turned to the crowd, raised his hand high, took in their accolades, then resolutely turned and walked into the headquarters.

Behind him walked a long line of Angels desperate to see what would happen when he took back command from Marcellus. Luminé stopped and turned, "All of you wait here until I receive my report."

He went inside alone. The place was desolate as he walked stoically down the long hall. While this was a moment of triumph, it also reminded him of the emptiness of his life. He was going to miss the solitude of the beautiful island.

He continued down the hall, opened his office door, and walked in. Marcellus was standing behind his desk, waiting. "Greetings, Luminé."

"Hello, Marcellus. I heard we had some trouble." Luminé knew Marcellus was not ambitious enough to have tried to unseat him truly, so he felt no animosity toward him.

"Yes, we did, lots of it…"

Luminé interrupted, "Are you ready with my report?"

"I am," said Marcellus, as he handed Luminé a scroll. Marcellus watched him quickly peruse the report, then said, "Luminé, as you know, there was a mutiny here following the trial of Sansa. The details of all those charged are contained in…"

Luminé cut him off and held up the scroll, "I have what I need, Marcellus."

"Very well," Marcellus said as he saluted, then stepped from behind the desk. Luminé made his way behind his old desk. He put on a fake smile and said, "Marcellus, it is best if you take some time off, away from all this. Get some rest and report back to me in a few weeks."

"Very well, sir."

Luminé smiled, then turned and walked back down the hall and out into the compound. Over a hundred thousand Angels were outside, waiting to see what he would do with those imprisoned in the stockade. Luminé resolutely walked across the compound, and the crowd grew silent. He walked past the gate and along the fence until he reached the place where Oxana was sitting with her hands still bound. He paused and looked at her as she slowly raised her eyes to meet his. He missed those eyes, those smart, cunning eyes. He'd forgotten how mesmerizing they were. He took out his sword, raised it high, and mightily slashed the fence in two.

He stepped inside, helped Oxana to stand, and removed the chains from her wrists. He then took her by the hand and stepped out of the stockade. The crowd went wild as Luminé kissed her hand and had her stand next to him. He raised his hand high, signaling for all to be quiet, then turned to face the nervous guards as silence fell upon all. "Guards, I hereby order the release of all prisoners. Just as the Lords forgave me, all of my beloved Angels are also forgiven."

The crowd ran to the stockade and tore it down, welcoming those who had been imprisoned. On Luminé's order, fires were lit, wine barrels were opened, and a celebration of music, dance, with roasting boars and venison commenced.

~ ~ ~ ~

The following evening, when the celebration was over, and all had gone back to their homes in the 2nd Heavenly Realm, Oxana looked into the living room of their quarters. Luminé was sitting on the couch with his head leaning against his hand, immersed in thought. It worried her. She had not been able to get close to him since his return, and her thoughts began to fear many things. Has he lost interest in me? Was someone else there on the island? Has he decided to get rid of me and is just waiting for the right time?

She poured two glasses of wine and brought one into him. "Here, Luminé, enjoy this wine. It will help you to relax."

He raised his eyes to meet hers, and they held a look she had never seen. It caused her to pause. He then said, "I have to take you somewhere, first."

"Where?" she asked.

"Just come with me. It will not take long."

Oxana did not like the tone, but she went along. To her surprise, they flew into the evening sky and headed toward the Earth.

"Where are we going, Luminé?"

"To the Garden of Eden. I have to show you something."

"But why are we going there?" she nervously asked.

"Just come with me."

They landed at the gate of the garden, and suddenly a guard stopped them. "I am sorry. No one is allowed in the garden."

Luminé half-smiled, trying to use his charm to disarm the guard, "I only need a couple of minutes."

"I am sorry, Luminé, but I have strict orders from Commander Sadie. No one is allowed in."

Luminé leaned into the guard with his eyes narrowed, and said, "In case you haven't heard, I am back, and I am an Archangel again, and I am best friends with Commander Sadie's boss, Gabriel. We can keep this simple, or I can get Gabriel and trouble him to come down here. Now, I only need a few minutes."

The guard swallowed hard, glanced at Oxana, then back to Luminé and said, "All right, but you have to make it fast."

Luminé smiled, and the guard opened the gate.

He and Oxana walked for a while, then flew up into the sky, above the trees, and headed to the abandoned hut, where Adam and Eve once lived. It was already overgrown and beginning to become covered with weeds and vines. There was a stark emptiness and a dark stillness to the place that gave Oxana the creeps. "Luminé, why are we here."

"Just wait and stay with me."

They peered inside the open door of the abandoned hut. There were turned over chairs, a broken table, cups and plates on the floor, also broken. Oxana watched Luminé scan the scene. His face looked sad, even reflective, something she had rarely seen in him. It struck her too at that moment, and she realized for the first time how this little scene represented the collapse of so much more.

"Let's go," Luminé said, and he headed toward the middle of the garden. They landed on the path they had walked long ago, when he, Oxana, and Marcellus had first visited Adam and Eve. Oxana began to fret as she saw in the distance the Tree of the Knowledge of Good and Evil. It was not the shining tree from long ago. Instead, it looked sickly, with over half of its leaves withered, though its trunk still appeared healthy. Black vines were growing all around it, hanging from the lower branches. Luminé stopped and pointed.

"Why are you stopping?"

He looked at her with his jaw set and his lips tight, "It was there."

"What was there?" she asked, knowing full well what he was talking about.

"The wooden crate, Oxana. It was there you saw the crate that scared you."

Oxana felt her heart sink. Had he discovered something about her alliance with Legion? If he did, he would never believe that everything she ever did was for him. He would surely abandon her.

He stepped closer to her, putting his face near hers, saying very slowly, "I need to ask you now, Oxana. Did you have anything to do with this?"

Oxana ground her teeth, and her eyebrows grew cross. She could not believe he was questioning her in this matter. She blurted out through gritted teeth, "I already told you everything!"

"I don't think you did!" he growled.

"Don't you know what I've done for you!" she yelled, as the year of waiting for him and worrying and plotting suddenly felt like it was going to be brushed aside in a sweeping dismissal of her from his life.

He pointed at her, shouting, "Did you have anything to do with this!"

"Nooo!" she cried.

She cringed as he grabbed hold of her shoulders, scanning her eyes, searching them for an answer. "Stop!" she said.

He said again, louder this time, "I need to know if you are with me or against me."

"I'm with you!" she cried, as she knocked his arms away, and turned around, holding her face in her hands, weeping. "I am with you," she said, her voice trailing off into quiet sobbing.

Luminé's mouth dropped open as he watched her cry. Confusion swirled through his mind. He had been sure she had been involved, and yet, he also knew she was not.

Oxana perceived his silence and confusion. She turned abruptly with anger on her reddened face and eyes and said, "Luminé, you need to decide, one way or the other. I cannot go on if you don't believe me."

He stepped forward, lost in his doubts, and took her by the shoulders, again, "I... I am sorry. I believe you."

Oxana snapped her head away, angry, but he pulled her close, hugging her tightly, "I am sorry, Oxana. I'm sorry."

Woman

Sadie opened the latch on the wooden gate that led into the compound surrounding Adam and Eve's home, shaking it a few times to test its sturdiness. She and the Angels under her command had built it along with the fence several weeks earlier to keep wild animals out, and so far, except for a few instances that were resolved quickly within the compound, it had worked. She crossed the 100 feet or so of the compound they had cleared and looked up at the large hut in the tree. Eve insisted they keep their home off the ground for now. She would not trust that they were safe from the animals just because of the fence.

Sadie called up from the base of the ladder, "Adam, Eve?"

Eve poked her head out the window. "Oh, Sadie."

Sadie smiled. She really enjoyed being around Eve, especially since she knew her and her team's work was making a difference. Eve's countenance was improving, she was smiling more, and her formerly gaunt face was now full of color and vigor. Sadie and her Angels had indeed removed all her worries.

Sadie climbed up the ladder and looked around, the spacious hut made of branches tied tightly together and rugs covering the floor. "Where is Adam?"

"He went with one of your guards to get some water from the river," she said with a light-hearted lilt in her voice.

"That's great. So, are you feeling better?"

"I was, but lately, I've been feeling a little sick again, only when I wake up, though."

"I'll let Calla know. Do you or Adam need anything?"

Eve reached her hand across the table, resting it on top of Sadie's. "Sadie, you and the others have been so kind to us. I don't know what we could possibly ask for, except... well."

"What is it?"

"Sadie, what is going to happen to us?"

Sadie had been so busy she had not herself considered where this was all going. But she could see Eve was concerned. "I don't know, Eve... but I am sure the Lords have a plan."

Eve tried to smile, but she had so many concerns. "Have a good day, Sadie. Thank you."

Sadie went down the ladder, crossing the compound immersed in thought. Where was this all going?

~ ~ ~ ~

Luminé and Oxana landed near the mouth of the Tigris River and flew toward the compound where Adam and Eve lived. Luminé wanted to see them again, but privately. As they were walking through the forest, Oxana suddenly said, "Get down."

"What's going on?" asked Luminé.

"It's Sadie."

"What?" Luminé said as he peered at the hut in the distance, "Why is she here?

"She's been helping them," Oxana said, frowning. Oxana never disliked Adam and Eve, but the fact that Sadie was now their ally and helper cast a shadow on it all. She hated Sadie and knew full well Sadie hated her. Oxana stepped a little closer, peering around a tree, watching Sadie walk through the compound toward the gate. She felt Luminé lean into her, looking beyond her shoulder. "There she goes," Oxana said as Sadie flew away.

Moments later, Eve climbed down and walked over to a basket and gathered several pieces of fruit, placing them in a small pouch, then went back up the ladder. Luminé remarked, "So there is the woman who disobeyed the Lords and ate of the forbidden fruit."

Oxana turned to look up at him, smirking, then turned back to watch Eve. She was surprised, though. Luminé's had told everyone in the Heaven's that he had no grudge against the Humans. His words now conveyed otherwise.

Luminé said, "Look, there is Adam." Adam and another Angel came from the woods to the compound gate and went inside.

Luminé asked, "Why do they have that fence anyway?"

"To protect them from the animals," said Oxana.

"Oh, yes," Luminé said, frowning, realizing the Humans were in many ways at a disadvantage against them.

They watched for another few moments until Luminé remarked, in an annoyed tone, "I still don't know why there are only two of these Humans."

Oxana shrugged, "I imagine the Lords planned to create more, but now... who knows."

Luminé chuckled.

Eve came down the ladder and greeted Adam. He kissed her warmly."

"I've seen enough," said Luminé. He turned to leave, but Oxana stayed for a moment. Something about Eve intrigued her, but she didn't know what it was. Adam intrigued her as well, but not like Eve. There was an aura around her, a warmth to her attachment to Adam, that she could not comprehend.

Chase

Yeshua walked at a brisk pace along one of the dirt roads in the 2nd Realm that led from the sea to Luminé's headquarters. He had seen clearly into Luminé's heart and soul during the hearing. Luminé was divided, still. Yeshua did not blame him for this, but he did not like the fact he was not honest about it. Even so, the fact he was divided was something Yeshua could work with.

It was a warm morning in the Heavens, and he could not help but remember a month earlier, the last time he had traveled the very same road. It was the day of the rebellion that occurred during Sansa's trial. This morning there were no fires and smoke billows and bloodied Angels punching and wounding each other with swords. No, instead, there were birds chirping and animals running around and Angels milling about in the course of their typical day.

Ahead of him, he saw a group of three Angels all dressed in the official uniforms of the realm, flying hastily toward him. As they drew near, Yeshua could tell it was Antonio and Thaddus, and Thomas, obviously on guard duty. They landed on the road in front of him.

Antonio bowed, "Good morning, Lord Yeshua. We did not expect you here today."

Yeshua paused, looking at each one of them over. He was smiling as he truly enjoyed seeing those he had created. But when he looked at Antonio, he had to hold his smile and not allow the concern he felt to cross his face. Antonio's spirit was distraught, and it saddened him. "Good morning to you, Antonio, and to you, Thaddus and Thomas."

The Angels smiled, and Thaddus remarked, "You remember our names?"

"Yes, I remember everyone's name. It's part of my job."

They all chuckled together. Thaddus asked warmly, "What can we do for you, my Lord?"

"I am here to visit Luminé."

Antonio replied a bit more curtly, "Very well, Lord Yeshua, follow us."

Yeshua raised his hand and gently waved them off, "It's okay, Antonio. I won't need an escort. Go ahead and tell Luminé I am coming."

Antonio knew full well Luminé would not like one of the Lords, nor anyone, just popping in on him, especially now when it seemed to them all that the Lords were against their realm. Antonio feigned to smile and asked, "Shall I tell him what it is about?"

"Just tell him I have something to ask him."

Antonio nodded, and they took off.

As Yeshua walked, he wondered about this attitude he perceived from his Angels. Some were interiorly hostile, others only going along, but why? What was brewing inside? It was Legion, but how? He finally reached the headquarters compound and walked through the gate. Luminé was seated on the porch, dressed in his full uniform. Next to him was Oxana, also dressed in the uniform of the realm. They both were still with only half-smiles on their faces. To Yeshua, they seemed nervous, and he'd wished he had been able to come unannounced.

He walked up to them and greeted them, warmly, "Good morning, Luminé. Good morning, Oxana."

Oxana smiled now, "Good morning, Lord Yeshua." Luminé stood, "Good morning, Lord Yeshua. What can I do for you?"

"I am inviting you to dinner tomorrow at Adon's mansion."

"Oh… yes… I will come." He glanced in Oxana's direction and asked, "Can I bring anyone?"

"Well, the thing is," he paused, half-smiled, and turned to Oxana, "I must apologize, Oxana; it's a small gathering with just a few of the guys."

Oxana nervously smiled, "That is fine, Lord Yeshua."

Luminé asked, "Who is coming, my Lord?"

Yeshua smiled broadly, "Adon, Gabriel, Michael, Raphael, and me. It is set for early evening, a few hours before sunset."

"I will be there," said Luminé.

Yeshua nodded, and started to turn, then stopped, "Oh, I almost forgot. Bring your horse."

Luminé smiled, "I will."

Yeshua walked back out of the compound, waving at a number of Angels who acknowledged him and headed back to the road that led to the sea.

~ ~ ~ ~

As soon as he left, Oxana got up and nudged Luminé, "Come inside."

Luminé followed her in, "What's wrong?"

"Luminé, this may be a trap. They may be trying to trip you up or something. You have to be careful."

"Why do you think that?"

Oxana hesitated. The reason she did was her own deep insecurity that somehow, she was going to lose Luminé, and worse, lose her status and have to return to being a nothing in the Heavens. "It just seems to be coming from nowhere. I think you need to be aware of my concerns."

She watched him weigh her words, and his eyes gave away that he did not trust her intuition like he used to. He nodded, but only out of courtesy and said, "I will be careful."

Oxana wanted him to understand she had reasons to warn him and that it was her role to be his confidant, and counselor. Her eyes widened, "What are you going to say to the others? Have you forgotten that Michael and Raphael both voted against you?"

"I can handle them."

She sighed, not satisfied, but knew the conversation was over.

~ ~ ~ ~

The following morning Oxana was awakened by a messenger bird at her window. She rarely received messages, and it surprised her. She reached over and took the small rolled-up message tied to the bird's leg.

Dear Oxana

I am hoping you will respond this time. I see how well you are doing, and I hear how fun things are in Luminé's realm. Can you please find a way for me to transfer there? I miss our days together, swimming, laughing. I know you are busy with more important things, but just being part of the realm that you are helping to lead would be wonderful.

Please get back to me.

Your friend,
Mylia

Oxana stared at the letter for several long moments. It the third letter she had received from her during the last several months. Before, she had been too busy to be bothered. But now, she had time, but now, the stakes were very high. She worried about Mylia being around her. She was too good and too innocent to drag her into the complex dynamics now at work in Luminé's realm. She got up, grabbed a quill and parchment from her top drawer, and then sat back in bed to write her response.

Dear Mylia

It was so good to hear from you. I will keep you in mind for any openings that come up. Right now, though, it is not a great time because of all that happened here. However, things could change someday.

Please take care of yourself.

Your friend,
Oxana

~ ~ ~ ~

The next evening, Luminé raced on his horse across the plains that led from the sea toward Adon's mansion in the Great Forest. He had trepidation for seeing everyone again, alone like this. Oxana was right. Most of them were set against him, or at least were in a position to judge him. He loathed that they had this authority over him. But he also knew now that this was the way the Heaven's worked. His fellow Archangels and indeed, the Lords, would hold him accountable for his actions.

He reached the forest edge, then began winding up the pathway that led to the top. As he exited the forest, he could see the others were already there, sitting on their horses in front of Adon's magnificent forest-side mansion. The sun was shining on the two-story log structure, gleaming against the windows. Not far from the porch was a fire burning with some type of meat roasting.

Michael was the first to notice him, "Oh, look who decided to show up." He smiled, then glared, "Don't worry, Luminé. We have not been sitting here waiting that long." Michael was still not happy Luminé had been reinstated, and now here he was, once again being late.

"Oh, you were waiting for me, great Michael," Luminé said, smirking, happy he had unsettled is rival.

Before Michael could respond, Adon walked out of his front door carrying six long mallets and a wooden ball. His face looked solemn, and he walked very upright as if he was about to deliver some very important news. He paused, allowing everyone to fix their attention on him, then said, "Welcome, everyone. Before we begin our festivities, over there," he glanced over at the meat cooking on the fire, "we are going to have a little test of our strength and skill, over there." He pointed in the other direction, to a distant field, where there were two nets set up at either end.

Yeshua looked out, "Adon, I thought we were having a feast. What is all this about?"

Adon gave him a bewildered look, "Why, it's a game of skill and strategy."

"What game?" Yeshua asked, playing along.

"A game I made up," said Adon.

Yeshua looked to Michael, Gabriel, Raphael, and Luminé, and said, "I say we take a vote, and maybe we skip right to the feast."

They all glanced out at the field, then over to the venison, "I'll second that motion," said Michael.

"No, no, no, we have to play," Luminé said as he trotted his horse over next to Adon. "It will be fun. I will race you there."

Luminé slowly pulled his horse around, glanced at the others, giving them a moment to get ready, then yelled, "Yaah!" He took off, storming across the terrain toward the distant field. Everyone immediately took off too, and soon the race was on. Luminé maintained the lead until Yeshua finally caught up. It was neck and neck as they bore down, both reaching the field at the same time. They jumped off their horses, laughing as the others came up, and they all dismounted.

Adon arrived last, jumped off his horse, and set down the mallets near the net at one end of the field. "Alright, everyone gather around. I have to explain the rules."

Gabriel replied heartily, trying to give formality to his request, "We are ready, Lord Adon. Tell us the rules."

"The only rule is this..." he said, pausing as he slowly looked each of them in the eye before saying, "There are no rules."

Everyone laughed. Michael asked, "Well, hold on. So, no rules, fine. But what is the goal?"

Adon chuckled to himself. The goal was for him and his key male Angels, along with Yeshua, to form a closer bond. That was the goal. The silly game he had dreamed up the night before. But no one seemed to be embracing it. He replied, "Michael. the goal is to hit this wooden ball, with your mallet, into one of the nets."

Michael walked over to the three-foot-wide net and examined it. He looked down at the other net at the far end of the field and said, "That does not seem too hard."

"Well, it is," said Adon, "if you are on a horse… and someone is trying to stop you."

Michael sat up tall on his large horse and laughed, glancing at Luminé with steeled eyes, then boasted, "I don't imagine anyone here will be able to stop me."

Yeshua chimed in, "Do you think you might be a little overconfident today, Michael?"

"Not without good reason."

Luminé chimed in, "Well, don't forget, Michael. I am pretty good at games. Do you remember… what did we call them… oh yes, the Angel games."

Raphael laughed, "How could we ever forget them, Luminé? You remind us every time we see you."

Adon said, "All right, everyone, mount up."

They all got on their horses, and Adon handed each one of them a mallet. He then took the ball and led them out to the middle of the vast field. Adon turned his horse to face them all and said, "There is one more thing we need to consider."

Yeshua shook his head, saying, "I should have known. I can't wait to hear this one."

Adon chuckled and said, "We will divide into teams. Team one is Yeshua, Michael, and… and…."

"And who?" asked Yeshua.

"And Luminé. Team two is me, Gabriel, and Raphael."

"Well, that seems unfair," said Yeshua. "We have the three best players on the same team."

Adon laughed as he swung his horse around next to Gabriel, "That's funny. I was worried about the same thing."

Adon raised the wooden ball in the air and yelled, "Go." He dropped it, and they all collided in the opening moments, trying to reach the ball with their horses and mallets. Finally, someone knocked it away, and they were off. It took a while for them all to get the hang of hitting the ball, let alone passing it to each other. All were laughing and thrusting their mallets, knocking the ball back and forth, with no one making any headway. Finally, Luminé broke away, knocking the ball ahead of everyone. He was galloping to it when Adon jumped off his horse onto Luminé's back. Luminé shouted, "Hey!"

Adon laughed loudly, "There are no rules, Luminé!"

Michael shouted, "Over here, Luminé."

Luminé broke his arm free from Adon's grip and knocked the ball to Michael. He tried to hit it toward the net but missed it. Gabriel then followed Adon's lead and jumped onto Michael, knocking them both to the ground. Yeshua raced past them with Raphael right with him. Yeshua knocked the ball forward, then swung the mallet, knocking it into the net.

Luminé shouted and jumped off his horse, running with his arms upraised. Michael ran up and jumped on him, tackling him, yelling, "We did it! We did it!" Within moments, Adon piled on, then Raphael, then the others as they all laughed, tangled together, all crushing Luminé.

One by one, they got up, all wide-eyed, all happy, all one again for the first time in ages, ready to feast for the night.

Turnings

Over a week later, Luminé stood by some trees at the top of Holy Mountain, a short distance from the portico at the Throne Room entrance, waiting for Splendora to come out from delivering her weekly report. Having been put back in charge and now enjoying a night of camaraderie with the Lords and some of the Archangels, he was beginning to rethink his goals. Perhaps he needed to lay down all his misgivings about the Humans.

Splendora walked out and down the steps. She looked happy, as usual, diligently taking care of her duties. He marveled at her beauty, knowing too the strength and flare behind it all. He called out, "Splendora?"

"Luminé, what are you doing here?"

"I was looking for you."

"Oh, really," she said, surprised. She was delighted to see him, and more importantly, to see him without Oxana hovering over him.

He smiled and asked, "Are you busy?"

"I have things to take care of in my realm later, but… I don't have any plans."

Luminé smiled, "Well, if I can borrow you for a while. I wanted to talk with you."

"Sure," she said, "Where?"

"It's a surprise," he said, "Follow me." He took off, and they flew toward the south, passing over the great Heavenly Sea, to a small island that Splendora immediately recognized. She turned to Luminé, smiling, "I love this place."

"Me too," Luminé said as he swooped down and flew low over the trees until they reached the lagoon with the waterfall, the one Splendora had hit her head on so long ago, the one where she first fell in love with Luminé. They landed and sat down on the smooth stone ledge overlooking the lagoon. Luminé stretched out his legs and rested his elbow on the ground. "Do you remember that day?"

"Yes, I do. Even my head remembers that day."

"I heard you are in the middle of a Season of Love with someone named Anthony."

She looked into the distance, "Yes, I am…and look. I have to go. I have a meeting.

~ ~ ~ ~

Calla pushed herself, running faster along the jungle path next to the spring-fed river near her villa. She felt good today, better than she had felt in a very long time, and it had put a spring in her step. Finally, there was news about Eve, news she had been expecting to hear for a long while now, and while it was late in coming, it was here.

She reached the river source and waded in to begin her two-mile swim back down the river to her sea-side villa. This was her morning ritual that kept her strong and fit, mentally and physically. When she reached the end, the point where she had started, she got out and laid naked in the warm morning sun, drying her body naturally as she did on most days. She was not in any hurry today and wanted this day to be a memorable one for her, so she took her time.

After a while, she dressed and flew to the Earth, where she had instructed Sadie to meet her outside the compound gate. Sadie was waiting for her. Calla said in a warm, hopeful tone, "Good morning, Commander Sadie. How are you today?"

"I am doing fine, Lord Calla. You look very refreshed this morning."

Calla smiled, "Yes, I am refreshed. Now, we have some important business to attend to. Come with me." They opened the gate and walked across the compound of Adam and Eve's home. Calla stopped before reaching the ladder to the treehouse and said, "Sadie, what you are about to hear, must be kept absolutely secret. Do you understand?"

"Yes," Sadie replied, feeling honored to be told something confidential from Calla.

Sadie followed Calla up the ladder. Calla stepped onto the rugged floor of the treehouse and walked a few steps in. "Greetings, Adam, and Eve. Eve, Sadie told me you have not been feeling well."

"No, I have not," Eve said, adding, "But only on some mornings. I feel fine now. I just got finished straightening everything up."

Sadie looked around at the sparse furnishings and small baskets and bowls containing fruits and herbs. She marveled at the simplicity of their life.

Calla nodded reassuringly and said, "I have something to tell you both." A slow smile crept over her lips. "Eve is going to have a baby."

"A baby?" asked Eve, with uncertainty in her voice.

"Yes," said Calla, hardly able to contain her excitement. "When we created you, we gave you the power to generate life. That is how the Human Race is going to grow. Eve is going to give birth to a small male or female human."

Adam looked over at Eve, his face showing some confusion.

Calla continued, "During the sexual dance, an egg inside the woman can be fertilized. This has happened. Now, a tiny child is growing inside Eve's womb. When nine months have passed, then it will exit her body and come into the world. It will either be male or female and will grow into an adult. Although you may not understand everything, I am telling you now, with time, you will."

Eve's eyes lit up, and her mouth opened in awe. She looked at Calla, then Sadie, not knowing what to say, then instinctively turned to Adam and hugged him tightly.

Sadie watched the moment of joy between Adam and Eve that words could never capture. Their hug, the emotion they were showing, the love, was something she had never seen. She wondered again, what that might feel like, and wondered why the Lords had not allowed the Angels to have babies.

Legion

Legion waited until well into the dead of night before leaving the make-shift home he had built in one of the Earth's unoccupied forests. He flew toward the Heavens to the murky lands surrounding the Dark Mountain, his old habitat. He landed on the shore, retrieved the canoe he had kept hidden in the woods, and paddled across the Dark Sea. As dark and dank as his old home was, it reminded him of an important part of his life, the time when he learned his true destiny. But tonight, he had no time for nostalgia. He needed to see the abyss again. It was in the Prophecy, and he hoped, being near it, he might understand what it meant. He had timed his visit so the dawn light would rise *after* he had made it safely there.

In his pocket was the Prophecy he had written down long ago. Adon had alluded to the fact that the Prophecy foretold Legion's demise, but Legion thought otherwise. Of late, one line of it was haunting him — the line about the Golden Sword. If the Prophecy held the key to the future and to ultimate power, then surely the Golden Sword was key to it all. What was this Golden Sword? Did it possess power only the Lords would understand and be able to use? Would the Golden Sword give Legion a distinct advantage over the Lords? Perhaps even allow him to kill them?

He labored up the dark, familiar path of the isolated, cold, Dark Forest. He was glad to be free from there, but part of him missed it. It was the place where he had been forged, where he had gained his strength, where he had matched wits with Adon, and tricked him into freeing him.

When he reached the top and stepped onto the plateau's cold, rocky ground, he immediately noticed the fire amidst the waters of the abyss was extinguished. This alarmed him, as it had always burned brightly. Something inside him told him it meant that it was not time. The end, seemingly foretold by the Prophecy, was not now. The fire would have to be lit for that time of the end to be upon them all.

He walked over to it and peered in. It was still too dark to see into the calm waters, so he built a fire nearby and sat down to wait for the sunrise.

In the light of the fire, he pulled out his parchment and unfurled the Prophecy, studying it again, hoping for some revelation. He read each verse, slowly, trying to process the cryptic words, wondering what he could learn.

In the tree, the secret lies
The ancient seed, bearing life
Whose fruits reveal both dark and light
And opens eyes to the age of strife.

When sea doeth yield the Golden Sword,
Forged and burnished from the fire.
The virgin warrior again will rise.
Bringing hope to listless band.

When armies face eternal doom
And the holy one is lost for good
The feared day has now arrived
Darkness reigns, yet even still...

The fiery column signals time
Seven days, no more may pass
But yea, cannot beyond delay
For sunset yields eternal night

If the fire consumes the host
Unto the end, the dark must go
And Sacrifice will save the day,
And Sacrifice will save the day.

"Arrgh!" he yelled as he threw the parchment down in frustration. Despite having read it over a hundred times in the past, he still could gain the insight he had hoped to. He needed to understand. He sensed the time was nearing. He picked it back up and began to read again.

The sea will yield the Golden Sword,
Forged and burnished from the fire.

He stopped and looked over at the ten-foot-wide circular abyss, carved into the surface of the plateau rock. It was filled with dark water. Legion's eyes widened, and his mind began to piece together a puzzle. *The Sea? The water in the abyss is the same waters as the Dark Sea. It must feed it. The sea will yield the Golden Sword?* He glanced up at the horizon.

It would only be another half hour before the sun rose. He would be able to see more clearly then. So, he waited.

Eventually, the sun burst over the horizon, and the entire plateau lit up. Legion smiled, extinguished his fire, and walked over to the edge of the watery abyss. He knelt next to it and peered down into the dark water. *Forged and burnished from the fire.*

He put his face closer to the water, straining to see down. Then he saw it, a momentary glimmer from 20 or 30 feet down. His eyes widened, and he put his face closer still. His nose touched the water, and he screamed, jumping back, holding his face in agony. Had the water burned him? He hesitantly touched the tip of his finger to the water and yanked it back in pain. The water *was* burning him. But he had seen something. The key to power, the key to the ancient text, had to be the Golden Sword.

A noise from the forest startled him as he whipped around. It was a boar rummaging through the forest nearby. He smiled. He had an idea. Perhaps it burned him because he was a Lord. He got up, walked over, standing perfectly still, then leaped forward and snatched the squealing beast by the back of its neck. Legion pulled his dagger from his side and ran it across the boar's neck, severely wounded it, but he was careful not to kill it.

He took it over to the abyss and, holding it by the hind legs, dipped half its body, face first, into the water. The animal at first only began to writhe, trying to free itself. Legion wondered why it had not recoiled in agony instantly, as he had. He kept it partially submerged, waiting. After nearly 45 seconds, the surface of the abyss waters was now covered with the animal's blood. Suddenly, the nearly dead boar began to squeal wildly. Something was causing it to revive from the edge of death, and it was not renewed strength but rather extreme pain.

Legion held it fast for another few seconds until he saw its skin smoking and starting to dissolve. The final moments of squealing from under the water were so loud it unnerved Legion, but he held the beast steady. When he pulled it out, half of its face was melted away. He threw it down on the rocky plateau and watched as it writhed in its final death throes. Then, before his eyes, the half that had been submerged slowly dissolved into dust. Legion laughed and picked up the now still hindquarters and threw them off the side of the plateau, into the brush. He now knew something. The waters seemed to only affect the Lords. Now he needed help in order to be sure, and he needed it soon.

Time was running out.

Currents

Luminé jogged along the beach of the 2nd Realm. He was well into his fifth mile, and he showed no signs of stopping. He was strong today, he had hope, and he knew why. It was because he had seen Splendora, and though she rebuffed him, seeing her caused those age-old feelings, he would always have for her to resurface.

He sped up, moving at a faster pace for the final mile, his bare feet barely touching the sand, then stopped. He caught his breath for several minutes, then threw off his tunic and high-stepped into the incoming surf, finishing with a dive into the shallow water, rinsing his body, refreshing his mind.

He popped up, standing naked in the knee-high surf, and thrust his arms into the air, closing his eyes and taking in the warm morning sun. He did not ever remember feeling so strong or so happy.

In the distance, he saw a horse and rider coming down the beach. He walked out and put on his tunic, looking down the beach to see who it was. The rider waved, and Luminé knew. It was Oxana. He waited, thinking, while she closed the distance. He still loved her, there was no doubt, but a year away had cooled everything about their relationship, including his reliance on her for advice.

"Luminé!" she shouted as she neared.

Luminé smiled, waving, but he noticed the irritation bubbling up within himself. She had interrupted his thoughts of Splendora.

Oxana pulled on her horse's reins, pulling it to a stop in the sand, then jumped off, her long black hair twisting in the wind. She felt fresh and alive today, playful, and she smiled as best she could so he might know. "Luminé, I've been looking all over for you."

She stepped closer and put her arms long tan arms around his neck, "I was hoping to spend some time with you."

Luminé shook his head, "Oh, you're kidding. I have to go to my office. I have too many reports to go over."

Luminé stared into her eyes; they still mesmerized him, but things were changing. He was not moving away from the Lords anymore; he needed to move toward them. Did that mean toward Splendora too? He let her reach forward and give him a long amorous kiss, then pulled back gently, smiling, and whispered, "I will see you tonight at dinner." Even as he said it, the old thrill of saying such a thing to Oxana was not there.

Oxana stepped back with a manufactured smile, "Tonight, yes... I will see you at dinner." She turned, trying not to show her disappointment, then hopped up on her horse, kicked the sides, and rode away fast, leaving him alone on the beach.

~ ~ ~ ~

Rana was in the middle of an affair with one of the guards under the command of Sadie. His name was Samuel. A few weeks earlier, she left her friend and fellow Archangel Gabriel's office after having stopped in to say hello. Samuel was a guard under the command of Sadie. As soon as she saw him, their eyes locked on each other. Rana was unable to look away. He was tall, with broad shoulders and black wavy hair, and he one of the most handsome Angels she had ever seen. She had crossed the courtyard and spoken to him about his duties there. When she left, she winked at him and whispered, "Write to me some time. I would like to get to know you more."

He had sent her a message that night, and the following night she met him on a secluded beach where they made love for hours.

Rana had sworn him to secrecy for the simple reason that neither she nor he, thought of this as the beginning of some Season of Love. There was no penalty or punishment for doing so, but it was generally understood that Seasons of Love were important, and it was a law to be followed as a way of life for the good of all Angels.

Besides that, Rana would never be involved, publicly, with one of the Angels under Sadie's command. Her disdain for Sadie would not permit it. Samuel was remarkable, though, and he was a voracious lover who displayed a ravenous hunger for her beauty. He adored her body, and this was all she needed to make sure it kept going.

Today, she left her home just after dusk and flew to the 5th Heavenly Realm, where he lived a few miles from the shoreline. She landed on the earthen road and walked the rest of the way, careful to stay along the edge to avoid being seen. She reached his house, a modest one-story ranch style home in a large clearing at the bottom of a range of hills. She walked to his back door, opened, and walked in. He was waiting on his couch, wearing only shorts. The room was darkened, lit only by several candles he had stationed around. Samuel stood up and said nothing. He took her by the hand and led her into his bedroom, where they undressed and within minutes were rolling on the bed together. After they had finished loving each other, they lay still for some time, not speaking, thinking about the myriad of things males and females think about after such intimate encounters.

After a long while, Rana asked, "So, how is it going with Adam and Eve?"

"I think it is going fine. We built a fence for them, which is helping a lot. I don't know how much longer this is going to go on. It's getting boring, to be honest with you."

Rana turned over onto her elbow, running her hand slowly up and down his broad chest. "Boring! How can babysitting Humans be boring?"

"You'd be surprised," he said as he marveled at her long slender body lying on its side facing him.

Nothing was said, and Rana rested her head on his chest, listening to his breathing. She loved how warm and sensuous he always felt after they made love.

Samuel looked at her long beautiful blonde hair spewed across his chest, and he smiled. "There is one thing that is odd," he said.

"What is that?" she asked, listening intently.

"Eve has been sick. And... she is gaining weight. She has quite a little stomach on her."

Rana lifted herself off him and rolled off him, asking, "A little stomach? I've never heard of such a thing. What do you mean?"

"Neither have I. I wonder if something is wrong. These Humans... it is a lot of time from a good number of us doing not much more than standing around. I wonder if they are going to be a big flop."

Rana realized that while the Lords had not anticipated the Humans eating from the Tree, but even still, they were not going to let this turn out to be a big flop. Something else must be going on. She looked up into his eyes with a sly smile, "Keep a close eye on things. Find out what you can for me. I am interested in knowing more."

Mylia

Mylia, walked down the secluded path in the morning sunlight toward the lake she and Oxana used to swim in. She felt bothered today. Her duties under her Host Commander were taxing, and like Oxana so long ago, they felt meaningless to her. She had been thinking about contacting the now powerful Oxana and gaining a transfer to Luminé's realm.

She and Oxana were old friends, having worked together in Gabriel's realm before Oxana wisely transferred out. They used to go swimming together at the inland lake. Mylia was disappointed that Oxana was not helping her. She wanted out of Gabriel's realm. She wanted to be with Oxana and enjoy the benefits of her friend's rise to power, but Oxana was not cooperating.

She reached the top of the path where the final stretch to the cliff's plateau was. She looked around, making sure she was alone, disrobed, stretched her arms up into the air, then started out, running down the short stretch, then dove off the edge. It was the same ritual she and Oxana used to do, the same one she did every day by herself now. It was a stress reliever and a moment of exhilaration she looked forward to during her work every day.

But she was not alone today. Hiding nearby was Legion. He was in the midst of his third day by the inland lake. He found Oxana here long ago, and something told him he would find another worthy Angel there. He recognized Mylia from long ago and knew it would be easy to tell his lie.

He watched her swim for a while. She was the other Angel who had been with Oxana long ago. She was quite beautiful and could serve his needs in more than one way. He waited for a while, enjoying the sight of her naked body moving through the water. Then, he made his move. He took off his shirt, keeping on only his black pants. He brushed his long hair back and walked out onto the plateau, waiting for her to notice him.

Mylia rolled over in the water then dove down, pulling herself through the clear water. When she surfaced, she saw something out of place. An Angel was standing on the plateau, looking down at her. He waved to her.

She stopped swimming and treaded water, embarrassed at being caught without any clothes. She shouted up, "Who are you?" The Angel looked handsome and pleasant, with long blonde hair and a broad smile on his face.

He shouted down, "I am a friend of Oxana's. Come out, so I can talk with you."

"Can you wait over there?" she pointed, "So I can get dressed?"

He laughed, then nodded, and walked a good ways away.

Mylia swam to the shore and climbed up some rocks, peered through the trees to make sure he was where he was supposed to be, then jogged over to her clothing and put her tan tunic and sandals on. She then said, "I am over here."

She watched the tall, muscular Angel walk over to her. He was gorgeous, and his smile was warm and inviting. She was surprised Oxana had never mentioned him before.

Legion said, "You are one of Oxana's friends. I remember, she told me you both used to come here to swim."

Mylia nodded, "Yes, I am. Who are you?"

"I was... once very close to her," he said, with a warm, inviting smile, suggesting he knew Oxana very well, even perhaps intimately.

"Oh, what is your name?" she asked.

He stepped closer, looking deeply into her eyes, and extended his hand. She took it and felt his gentle touch drawing her, warming her. He said, "My name is Legion."

She pulled her hand back, just a little, but something about his grasp invited her to hold on, "But I thought, that you... "

"You believe everything you have been told to be true? Oxana knew better, and I helped her to become who she is today. You see, Mylia, I am a Lord."

Mylia finally withdrew her hand. Something was disarming about him, and his chest, his eyes, they mesmerized her.

"Would you like my special favor, too, Mylia?"

She nodded, "I... I would."

"Then meet me here this evening when the sun sets. I will have something special to show you."

Mylia's body quivered, and she knew why. He was incredibly sexy. She said, "All right, I will be here."

She went home full of excitement about what might be coming.

~ ~ ~ ~

Sadie entered the compound of Adam and Eve's home and walked over to the ladder that led to their home in the tree. She heard a voice, "Sadie?"

Sadie turned; it was Eve walking from the fruit trees situated near the back of the compound, holding a small basket filled with fruit. Her stomach looked larger than ever before; the baby inside her was growing fast. She looked tired, but in a good way, as it was not the haggard, sick-looking tired she had before. Now there was a glow about her, undoubtedly connected to the new life growing inside of her.

"Good morning, Eve," Sadie said, as she walked over, "Here, let me take those for you."

Eve gladly gave up the basket of fruit, and put her hand on her stomach. "I sure feel tired lately. I can't believe I am having a baby. Oops, there it is again."

"What is it?"

Eve took the basket back from Sadie and set it down. "Here, give me your hand."

Sadie extended her hand, and Eve placed it on her stomach. "Now, wait just a moment."

Sadie held her hand there, wondering what they were waiting for, then suddenly gasped and drew her hand back, "Oh my gosh. What was that?"

"It's the baby. I think it is kicking or something."

Sadie's mouth dropped open, and she put her hand back on Eve's stomach, waiting. "Ooh!" she said, "It did it again!"

Suddenly, out of the corner of her eye, Sadie saw movement outside the compound. She signaled for Eve to wait and quietly walked over and peered through the fence. It was one of her guards, Samuel, with his ear to the fence, listening to them. *What is he doing back there?*

Just then, Adam came down, and Sadie whispered, "Adam, keep talking to Eve for a moment." She eyed the fence and nodded, signaling someone was listening in. Adam nodded and began talking with Eve.

Sadie quietly hustled across the compound and went out the gate. She circled along the outside of the fence to the back section. There was Samuel with his back to her, still leaning with his ear against the fence, listening to Adam and Eve talk. Sadie crept up behind him until she was within a few yards, then snapped, "Samuel!"

Samuel leaped up, almost falling back, then turned quickly and stood at attention, with his eyes pegged to the sky above her head. "Yes?"

"What are you doing back here?"

"I was… was just…"

Sadie stepped up, her eyebrows slanted together, and her lips tightly pursed, and cut him off, "You're supposed to be at the front gate!"

"Yes, um… I was just taking a little break."

"Well, the break's over. Now get back to your post!" Sadie waited while he looked at her to be sure she was done, then hustled back to his post at the front gate.

Sadie watched him run off and wondered. Something did not sit right with her. He had been close enough to overhear their conversation. She only wondered how much he had heard. It would be more and more challenging to keep this baby a secret, but she would not let her guards be the ones to break the news.

~ ~ ~ ~

Mylia walked along the path toward the secluded forest lake. It was still evening, though it would be drawing to a close within the hour. She had her misgivings, unsure about meeting Legion. They had been taught to fear him, but he did not seem dangerous, and he had clearly helped Oxana to reach great heights. He was also incredibly handsome, with long blonde hair she had not seen on many of the male Angels. His body, too was strong, and tan, but it was more than his physical features. There was an air about him, a confidence that could not help but feel enticing to her.

As she neared the place where they were to meet, she heard him call out her name in a warm, calm voice, "Mylia?"

"I'm over here."

In a moment, Legion stepped from a grove of trees, walked over, and took her by the hand. "Let us walk together."

Mylia took his hand; it felt warm, secure, and the fear she felt left her.

Legion asked, "What is it you want me to do for you, Mylia?"

"Do?" she asked, hesitant to reveal what she wanted.

"Yes, what is it that you want most?"

"I want to transfer to Luminé's realm as Oxana did. I want to be near her and be part of all that she is doing."

Legion nodded slowly as a smile began to creep across his face. He said, "I can do this for you, but what will you do for me?" he asked.

She looked into his mesmerizing eyes and drew closer to him, saying, "Whatever you want."

"I will lay with you, Mylia, and tomorrow morning, when the sun comes up, I have a task for you. Then, I will grant your request. Now, come with me."

His bold request did not phase her. Mylia could not believe she was holding the hand of a Lord, much less about to do even more with him. He turned, leading her, and began walking.

"Where are we going?" she asked.

"To the Dark Forest, where the deed will be done."

What should typically frighten her sent a warm sensation through her body. Legion flew up into the air, bringing her along, and they flew over the sea and across the Land of the Lords until they finally neared the edge of the Dark Sea. They landed on the opposite bank, and Legion retrieved the canoe he had hidden in the brush. He loathed that he had to cross in a boat, but for some reason, the laws of the universe would not permit anyone to cross over any other way.

Mylia stepped into the canoe, with Legion in the front, and went across with him. The air was warm, and the waters perfectly still. She watched his broad shoulders in front of her, paddling from side to side. He was so strong and Lordly, and her body was beginning to moisten, anticipating what was to come.

They reached the shore and stepped out. Legion again took her by the hand and led her up along a darkening pathway under a thick canopy of trees. The fading twilight was barely visible. When they reached the immense stone plateau at the top, the canopy of trees yielded to a darkening sky in the final moments of dusk. Stars began to dot the night sky. Mylia looked around, amazed at the place. On the other side of the vast, barren, stone plateau, a fire was already burning, and a lamp was lit inside a hut. Her body quivered, knowing now where they would lay together. Legion took her hand and walked over to the hut with her. She stepped ahead of him and peered in. There was a comfortable looking thatched bedding and two glasses of wine waiting. Her body grew intensely excited, knowing the time was coming when she would lay with a Lord.

Legion handed her a glass, and they toasted. They wasted no time, neither interested in the wine, but only in each other. They both let their clothing drop to the floor and stood naked, kissing, exploring each other. Legion led her backward and gently laid her on the bed.

Mylia moaned loudly as his body entered her. Within a short time, a magnificent dark pleasure swirled through her mind and body as all went black.

The Humans

Luminé sat in his office, late in the evening, as he unfurled the small parchment he had just received. It was from Rana.

Luminé,

Meet me at my home after dark. I have something important to share with you regarding the Humans. I also must tell you, Luminé, I miss our days on the island when we had no one to disturb us. You have loved me like no one else ever has, and I always cherish you for that.

Rana

Luminé stared at the letter. *What is Rana up to? Is she trying to seduce me?* He chuckled but then stopped.   The *'regarding the Humans'* part was most curious. The Humans had nearly been his undoing, and he had survived it.   He penned a response, sent it off, then crumpled up her letter. He dropped his head back, thinking not about the Humans but Rana and her magnificent body. She was the most fantastic lover he had ever been with, but he had no time for her now. Still, whatever she needed to tell him must be important. He would leave after dark.

~ ~ ~ ~

Two hours later, Oxana walked out of the living quarters, down the steps, and across the compound, and over to Luminé's office. It was late, and no one was working at the headquarters. She expected Luminé would still be there, at his desk, working.

Only a few guards were on regular guard duty within the compound. Oxana smiled at the guard to the headquarters entrance and went up the stairs. She walked down the quiet hall, but his office was not lit. She went inside and lit the lamp, wondering where he was. She sat in his chair, glad he was back, glad she had so skillfully maneuvered Marcellus out of the role. She looked over and noticed a crumpled parchment on the floor next to the wastebasket. She picked it up, uncrumpled it, and began to read. It was from Rana. She fumed as she read each line twice, making sure she was clear about what it said, then slumped down, feeling like someone had just punched her in the stomach and knocked the wind out of her completely. She quickly turned off the lamp and sat in the dark, rocking back and forth in his chair, periodically wiping a falling tear from her eye.

She was losing him. She could feel it. She had feared Splendora more than anyone because of how deeply Luminé loved her, but there was no ignoring Rana and her beauty. Luminé had always been enthralled with her, but that was the old days. It was supposed to have been long ago. Now, since his return, her plans were all falling apart, and the walls were closing in.

She got up to leave then stopped. *What did she mean, something important regarding the Humans? I need to tell Legion. Maybe I can use this to keep Luminé for myself.*

The Watery Abyss

Mylia opened her eyes. She had not stirred since she had passed out after her romp with Legion. Her body felt warm and thoroughly satisfied. She had been with several other Angels in her life, but none like this. She laid her head back, closing her eyes, trying to remember the night before, but it was all a blur for some reason. She glanced out of the window and around the hut. It was the break of day, and Legion was not there. She got up, still feeling the excitement of the previous night, and glanced out the door. Legion was sitting out by a small fire. Mylia stretched up on her tiptoes, grabbed her tunic and shoes, put them on, and then walked out of the hut. Legion was sitting on a large log by a small fire. He was dressed in his black robe, with a golden chain around his strong tan neck. His hair was perfectly combed back, and his eyes looked dark and piercing.

He smiled at her, looking her body up and down once, then stood up and extended his hand, saying, "Come with me, Mylia. I have something you must do for me." He took her by the hand and led her over to the ten-foot-wide circular abyss filled with churning seawater and pointed. "The water is about 30 feet deep. Look down at the bottom. There is something shiny. I believe it is a sword. I simply need you to go in and retrieve it."

She looked up at him quizzically.

"Go on, take a look. You will have to adjust your eyes, but you can see a small glimmer from here."

Mylia half-smiled, wondering, then knelt and peered in for several long moments. "Oh, I see it now."

Mylia looked up at him again, "Why don't you just go in?"

He glared at her, then smiled, and said in a subtle yet angry tone, "Mylia, are you forgetting? I am a Lord. It is not for you to question me. Touch the water; you will see there is nothing to fear."

Mylia swallowed, then hesitantly reached out and touched the water with her finger. The water was warm and pleasant. She did not see any danger in entering the ten-foot-wide water hole. "All right. I will do it." She turned and sat on the edge, lowering her legs in first, then slipped in. She used her hands and the walls to push herself down. Finally, after what seemed like an eternity, her feet touched the bottom. It was pitch black. She looked up and could see the light; this momentarily comforted her. She began to feel around with her hands on the floor. Then she felt it; a piece of steel; it was a sword. She lifted it up and kicked herself up to the surface.

Legion watched with delight as he saw the Golden Sword nearing the top. It's shining metal burst through the surface, followed by Mylia. Legion smiled, took the sword, brandishing it in the air, as Mylia climbed out. She watched him for a moment, wondering what the sword was, but then she began to feel her skin tingling, subtly at first, then more intensely. She said, "I... I don't feel right."

Legion looked over momentarily, then back at the sword, brandishing it, marveling at it. It was a long, thick sword, one of the largest he had ever seen. It was shiny gold-colored and heavier than any normal sword, yet light to maneuver, and sharp as a razor.

Mylia looked down at her hands and arms, her skin was starting to smoke and peeling, and she began to feel a burning pain all over her body. A piece of flesh fell off of her cheek. She reached her hand up, feeling her exposed tissue, and screamed, with panicked eyes, "Legion! Please! Help me!"

Legion again looked over at her, then back at his sword, holding it aloft, eyeing all angles of it, and said. "I cannot help you."

Mylia winced, and fell to her knees, then forced herself up, "I... I... have to get... out of here!"

Legion stepped closer to her. He smiled, and for a moment, she imagined he would help her, that he was going to stop whatever was happening. But his eyes narrowed, and his smile turned to a look of determination. He rammed the sword into her gut. Mylia's eyes widened in horror. She let out a feeble scream, the pain too profound for her to do anything else.

Legion withdrew the sword, watching her grow weak. He then pushed her into the pool of burning water and watched her frantically struggle to get to the surface. He placed the sword on her head, holding her down, watching her life ebb away, and her body dissolve.

Moments later, a small tuft of hair floated on the surface, followed by her bloody tunic. Legion laughed and scooped up the tunic first. He walked over into the brush on the side of the plateau and placed it inside an old log. Then he returned to take hold of the tuft of hair with the tip of the Golden Sword, then cast it across the stone plateau. The wind would take it away. He peered into the waters. There was nothing. Mylia had completely dissolved. He turned to leave but then heard something rise to the surface. He turned and walked back. It was something white and round, floating. He reached out the sword and rolled it. It was Mylia's skull. He laughed, thinking of the pain she must have endured, then put the tip of the sword into her teeth, lifted it out, and flung it deep into the woods.

Discovery

Calla swam through the spring-fed river toward her sea-side villa two miles away. The sun warmed her face each time she surfaced, as she dove down with broad strokes to see the wonders of the smooth river bottom then surfaced to feel the sun again. She had just finished her morning jog up to the source that kept her healthy and fit, mentally and physically. She felt strong today and hopeful. With the news of Adon and Yeshua having had such a good time with the male Archangels at the event Adon hosted, she had a feeling that perhaps things could come back together.

She swam a little further when a strong jolt reverberated in her mind. It was a thought, but one with power behind it, powerful enough to startle her profoundly. She kicked upwards, frightened, breaking through the surface, choking up the water she had swallowed. She quickly swam to the bank and climbed out, laying on the sandy trail, breathing hard, scared at what she had just experienced, wondering what it could mean.

The plateau at the Dark Forest had flashed into her mind, and something else, something gold, something long, and sharp. *The Golden Sword?* She shuddered again, never before feeling so frightened. She ran to get her clothes and quickly raced back to the villa.

She immediately penned a letter to Yeshua

Yeshua,

Meet me to the north of Holy Mountain, on the road to the Dark Forest. Something has happened.

Calla

She went to her bookshelf and pulled down the book, where she kept a copy of the Prophecy. She was sure she had seen something gold, and she knew instinctively, the only thing it could be was the Golden Sword. *But why did I see the plateau? The fire has been extinguished for a long time. Nothing can be forged in it.* She already knew the Prophecy by heart, but she reread it.

In the tree, the secret lies
The ancient seed, bearing life
Whose fruits reveal both dark and light
And opens eyes to the age of strife.

When sea doeth yield the Golden Sword,
Forged and burnished from the fire.

The virgin warrior again will rise.
Bringing hope to listless band.

When armies face eternal doom
And the holy one is lost for good
The feared day has now arrived
Darkness reigns, yet even still...

The fiery column signals time
Seven days, no more may pass
But yea, cannot beyond delay
For sunset yields eternal night

If the fire consumes the host
Unto the end, the dark must go
And Sacrifice will save the day,
And Sacrifice will save the day.

~ ~ ~ ~

Calla and Yeshua stood on the bank of the Dark Sea, waiting to go in. "We will have to swim," Calla said.

"That is fine," Yeshua said. "You saw the Golden Sword."

"I am almost certain, Yeshua."

The news did not sit well with him. How possibly could the events of the Prophecy be coming true? It was far too early in the game. He started to step into the water when Calla said, "Look!"

He turned. There was a canoe hidden in the brush.

"How long has this been here?" She asked.

Yeshua stepped back up onto the bank, went into the brush, and pulled it out. He bent down and examined the bottom of it and said, "Someone used this very recently. There is water still inside."

"I knew it," she said. "Something has happened."

They pulled the canoe out and paddled across the Dark Sea. A mist hung above the waters, giving an eerie feeling to them. Neither said a word as they both knew Legion might very well be on the other side waiting for them. Yeshua paddled while Calla sat in the back, carefully scanning the shore.

They got out on the Dark Forest bank, drew their swords, and started up the dark foreboding forest trail towards the plateau of the Dark Mountain. As they neared, the canopy of dense trees opened, letting light in. They smelled the fire, then stepped onto the plateau, seeing the smoldering fire by Legion's now abandoned hut.

Calla started forward, but Yeshua grabbed her arm, signaling to wait. He stepped in front of her and waved for her to go around the other way. They approached the hut from two sides. Yeshua went in, first, as Calla peered in behind him, keeping her eyes on the surrounding plateau.

Yeshua looked at the bedding and could see it was freshly slept in by more than one person. He glanced over to Calla, "Someone was here last night."

Calla scanned over to the watery abyss that once held fire. She was trying to understand what she had seen in her vision. She began walking over, wondering what, wondering why. Yeshua caught up to her, and they walked to the edge of the water together. Yeshua bent down and touched his finger to the water, then pulled it back quickly, startled. He cried out in pain.

"What's wrong?" said Calla, concerned.

"It burned me!"

Calla looked at him strangely, then bent down and barely touched her finger to the water. She, too, yanked her hand back, feeling the same burning pain. She looked at him wide-eyed, "I... I saw the Golden Sword in my vision." She labored to see into her mind's eye and added hesitantly, "I...I am almost sure, but how could it be?" She looked down and began talking to herself, "The Prophecy said the sword is forged amidst the eternal flame... How could it have been forged here? The flame has been out for years now. Surely we would have found it long ago."

"Perhaps Legion forged it before the flame went out before he left."

"No, he could not have. He would have used it on me when he attacked me in the forest."

Yeshua nodded, thinking. He walked around to the other side and bent down, peering into the water. He heard a cry, not a real cry, but a cry in his mind. Something in his mind, a voice, was screaming, calling, desperate more than he had ever heard before, and then the voice was gone. He stared down. "Perhaps the sword was here all the time. Perhaps..." he looked up, "Perhaps it... it has been found."

Calla stared down, concerned, trying to understand. If the sword had been found, it could only mean that Legion had it. This would surely sway the balance of power in the Heavens. Legion would be empowered as he had never been before. Exactly how, she did not know, but to possess the sword of the Prophecy had to have immense implications. Then, she noticed something. She pointed, "Yeshua! What is that?"

Yeshua looked to where she was pointing. There was a small tuft of hair on the stone surface just behind him, and it looked like blonde female hair. Yeshua looked closer. He picked it up and quickly dropped it. "It too burns, as if..." He looked up, mystified, unwilling to finish his own sentence.

Calla looked to the water, then back at him.

"Get leaves and wrap it up. We need to take it with us."

They headed back down the path, worried, wondering whose hair it was. It was female. They were almost sure of it. But whose?

Calla turned momentarily, "From now on, this entire forest must be guarded. No one can come in, and no one can go out."

The Guard

The Seven Archangels stood at attention in full uniform at the Throne Room. It was mid-afternoon, and the entire floor was lit up by the clear blue skies and a bright sunny day. The air was warm, and a light breeze carried the fragrance of the cherry blossom trees behind the Throne Room across the entire area.

Calla opened the meeting by saying, "We have come to the conclusion that the Dark Mountain, especially the watery abyss at the top, has to be guarded. Gabriel, do you think the guards of your realm can do this?"

Gabriel stood at attention with his black hair waving in the gentle breeze. His face wore a half-smile and his blue eyes shined in the sun. He did not answer immediately but was thinking, then he nodded and stepped forward, saying, "My Lords, we can. However, I would defer to someone else because our guards are already spread thin guarding the Garden of Eden, as well as assisting Adam and Eve."

Calla nodded, then asked, "Who would like to take responsibility for this?"

Rana glanced over at him as a confident look crossed her face. She pushed her long hair back and stepped forward. Her stature looked particularly magnificent on this perfect day, with her white uniform perfectly complementing her sleek strong body and golden-tanned skin. She announced, "The Angels of the 6th Heavenly Realm will be able to provide the guards, my Lords."

Michael, with his brown hair, perfectly combed back, and his deep brown eyes narrowed, stepped forward also, in a hurried gesture, announcing in his booming voice, "The Angels of the 3rd Heavenly Realm would also be happy to provide the guards, my Lords." He bowed slightly and stood tall, his large jaw set with determination.

"Very well," said Calla. "It seems we have an abundance of volunteers." She turned to Rana and said, "Rana, you will be in charge and will use Michael and his Angels also to assist you. No one is to go in, and no one is to go out. Put plenty of guards there and make sure they are visible. We want to deter Legion from ever going there again."

"Yes, my Lord," Rana said, as she glanced at Michael, wondering if perhaps this would be a time when they could finally learn to like each other. She did not really know why she didn't like him. Maybe it was because he and Luminé were always at odds with each other, and she, of course, always sided with Luminé.

As the Archangels were dismissed, Rana raised her hand high, asking to be recognized.

Adon called upon her. "Yes, Rana?"

"My Lords, I have heard from some of the Angels that the Human, Eve, has been very ill. It is reported that she does not look well, even that she looks very different." Rana hoped that she had managed to make her voice sound concerned.

Adon turned to Calla, "Calla, I have not heard anything about Eve not feeling well. Have you?" Adon was hoping his face did not give away his worry. They were not ready to tell the Angels about Eve yet.

"No, Adon, I have not," said Calla. She turned to Rana, "Rana, Adam and Eve are living out their existence in the world. Life has demands there that can render them, well, stressed at times. I am sure that is all you have heard about."

Luminé listened intently. He could tell that the Lords were not forthright. Something was wrong. He stepped forward, "My Lords, if there is anything we can do to help them, please let us know."

Splendora glanced over at him. She sensed that Luminé, too, was not being forthright, and she had the sneaking suspicion that he and Rana were in this inquiry together.

Calla responded, "Thank you, Luminé. The Angel Sadie is helping me to make sure Eve and Adam have everything they need."

Luminé nodded, "Very well, my Lord."

The meeting was adjourned, and the Archangels silently made their way out while the Lords sat still. The air in the room was heavy, heavy with the inquiry that had not been answered.

~ ~ ~ ~

Adon, Yeshua, and Calla went into their quarters behind the Throne Room. As soon as they were alone, Calla said, "Rana and Luminé know something about Eve."

Yeshua nodded, "I sense it too."

Adon said, "Perhaps it is a mistake not to tell them."

Calla grimly nodded, "It is ironic that this is our crowning achievement, and yet I have dreaded the day when we must tell the Angels. I fear they will be jealous."

Adon lowered his glance, "Yes, we knew this might happen. There is nothing we can do except to tell them."

Calla reluctantly said, "We will call a meeting next week."

~ ~ ~ ~

Calla rode Willow through the Cherry Blossom trees down the dew-filled fields that made up the mile-long incline to the back of the Throne Room. The sun rose in the East, causing the entire landscape before her to glitter with its reflection off the dew drops. When they reached the bottom, she headed out across the fields, riding as hard as she could. After an hour of hard riding, they reached the shoreline and bolted her and Willow into the sky, flying over the Heavenly Sea toward Gabriel's realm. She landed on the beach and rode up the coastline until she reached the home of Sadie.

She dismounted and took in the sea air. It had been a brisk ride here, one which she needed. She wiped the sweat from her brow and went up the stairs. She did not like coming unannounced, but she knew Sadie might very well be asleep, so there was no sense in sending a messenger bird, even earlier.

She knocked on the door. There was no answer.

She knocked again. There was no answer.

She knocked a third time, and suddenly the door opened. Sadie was in her nightgown and wearing a tan robe. Her hair was all over the place, and her eyes were narrowed, only partially opened.

Sadie squinted, then said, "Lord, Calla?"

"Good morning, Sadie. I need to talk with you. I hope I did not wake you."

"Oh... no... I... I had to get up to answer the door anyway. Come in, please.

Calla walked past her and sat down at the kitchen table. She looked around at the simple furnishings and décor, and it warmed her. Sadie was one of the Angels she had come to trust more than any other, and she understood why. She was honest and loyal and not interested in any show or flare. Calla appreciated this quality in her. She waited for Sadie to sit down and said, "Sadie, I am afraid we have a problem. Yesterday, at the Throne Room, Rana asked a question that unsettled me. She seemed to imply that she knew something was going on with Eve. Is that possible?"

Sadie glanced out the window, grimacing, and lamented, "Samuel must have overheard us."

"Who is he?"

"He is one of my guards. He was listening in by the fence the other day when Eve was talking to me about the baby. I don't know what he heard." Sadie slammed her fist on the table, "Rana! It figures."

"Is he connected with Rana?"

"I don't know for sure," said Sadie, "but I have heard rumors they are seeing each other."

"Well, that all makes sense now." Calla was disheartened to hear of one of her Archangels involved with what certainly did not seem like a proper Season of Love, but she was getting used to news like this. She said, "I am sorry to barge in like this, but I needed to find out. You won't have to keep the secret for much longer. We will tell the Archangels next week." Calla stood up and smiled, "Have a nice day, Sadie."

Oxana and Legion

Oxana rose early and flew to the Earth. Legion had set up his new lair there, away from the Heavens and the Lords. It took her a very long time to get near the place, and she began to understand how vast the Earth was, and she could not understand why the Lords had created something so immense just for Adam and Eve. She was not as bothered about the Humans as Luminé was but seeing this vast world caused her to wonder if perhaps Luminé was on to something, something that she had not yet come to realize.

She was looking for the high mountain, next to the smaller pointed mountain and rocky stream that Legion said would mark the entrance to the forest. Finally, she found it and landed at the entrance, and began walking into the dense pine forest down what appeared to be a narrow pathway.

She walked a ways further, then called out, "Legion?"

There was no answer. She looked around, wondering if she should venture in further. The forest was dark, with an eerie presence to it, and it reminded her of the Dark Forest. There was very little sunlight coming through the canopy of trees. There was minimal sound, too, only the occasional calling of distant crows. She wondered how it could be so eerie and so like the Dark Forest and realized that perhaps Legion's presence was the driving force. Perhaps his dark, mysterious powers shaped the places where he stayed. Her need to talk to him could not wait, so she continued down the narrow forest path.

Then she saw him, ahead some 100 feet down the path. Legion was standing in his black robe, perfectly still, his long blonde hair pushed behind his shoulders, and with his hand on the handle of his sword. He was watching her as if he'd been watching her since she entered the forest. Something about the way he stood though, caused her to realize perhaps he was not as powerful as he once was.

She put her eyes down and kept walking, feeling the uneasy feelings that always stirred within her when Legion was around her. Part of her needed him, part of her desired him, and part of her loathed him. When she was within hearing distance, he called out in a deep, commanding, and foreboding tone, "Oxana, I see you found me."

"Yes," she said, as she watched him turn and continue down the path. She followed until they reached a small clearing where there were a hut and a fire burning. Legion sat down on a large stone and beckoned for Oxana to do the same on one across from him. He asked, "What is happening in the wretched Heavens?"

"Everything is happening. There is chaos in every realm. My friend, Mylia, is nowhere to be found. It has been over a week since anyone has seen her." Oxana knew as soon as she said it, she was wasting her time. Legion did not care about her concerns. She gathered herself and was about to get down to the reason for her visit when she noticed a small smirk pass Legion's lips and then disappear as quickly as it had appeared. He said, "Mylia, you say? She was of no importance to anyone."

"You knew her? Have... have you seen her?"

"That is none of your concern," he said sharply.

Oxana cringed, suddenly concerned that he knew something, but knowing she dare not question him. There was a subtle evil force about him that Oxana knew he had not shown her, but something within her feared he was capable of great violence. Had he done something to Mylia?

"What else do you have to report?" Legion said sternly, shaking her out of her thoughts.

Oxana looked up, trying not to show her growing horror that perhaps Mylia had been harmed by him. She swallowed, trying to collect herself, to put her fears about Mylia aside. She needed his help right now.

"What do you have to report, Oxana?" he said in a coarse, demeaning tone, his eyes narrowed and bordering on anger.

She hated it when he talked to her this way, and she would not stand for it from anyone, except he was a Lord who she had not figured out how to deal with yet. But she would. She replied, "I have news about the Humans, my Lord."

"What news?"

"I cannot know for sure, but Rana wrote to Luminé, telling him there was something urgent she needed to see him about, regarding the Humans. I think it might be something the Lords are hiding from us."

"Find out what it is, Oxana," he said, his voice sharp and full of venom.

"Yes, my Lord." The words surprised her. They were not her own. She recalled following his dictates blindly in the past. In the past, she would turn now and leave, doing his will, but not now. Being away from him for so long had loosened his power over her. She would do what suited her.

"And what of Luminé?" he asked.

"I am losing him."

A concerned look came over Legion's face. Luminé was the key to everything. He asked, "Why do you say this?"

"Because he is involved with Rana… and I know he has always been in love with Splendora. I fear he may be growing tired of me. I do not have the hold over him I once did."

Oxana observed his reaction. He did not flinch, and yet, she could see a hint of worry in his eyes. He obviously still had plans for Luminé, and the worry told her he needed her to be in the driver's seat alongside Luminé. He needed them both, and this gave Oxana a great deal of comfort. He would help her.

Legion stood up, "I will need time to think about this. Come with me, Oxana."

"No," she said, standing and turning back down the path. "I have to leave. I will wait to hear from you."

She could feel his eyes on her back as she left. She had never disobeyed him, and she knew there could be consequences. But first, she had a score to settle.

Legion watched her go with curiosity. This was not the first time she had defied him. He needed to remedy this, and he would do so at the time of his choosing.

Sadie

Sadie flew at a hurried pace through the skies toward the Earth. She needed to check on Adam and Eve and find out how they were doing, and more importantly, how Eve was doing with her pregnancy. She also wanted to assess the safety of the compound as well as the supply of food. These were matters of routine for her, but today she had little time.

She zeroed in on the compound, only a few miles from where the abandoned Garden of Eden still stood and landed inside Adam and Eve's compound. As she was climbing the ladder to their house in the tree, she saw movement outside the rear compound wall. *Samuel!* She thought, gritting her teeth. She had already caught him spying once. This time his punishment would be severe. She would see to it that Gabriel would formally reprimand him at the very least.

She quietly went back down the ladder and out the gate. She walked around the compound fence and through the trees and tall grass that surrounded it. As she neared the place where she suspected Samuel was standing, she slowed her pace, determined to catch him red-handed. Up ahead, she saw part of his tall figure, partially concealed behind a tree. At least the little she could see, his clothing seemed different from the tunic he normally wore. She thought, *Perhaps he is not on duty.* She stepped quietly for the remaining 20 or so steps, then stepped up next to the tree he was right behind, and shouted, "Samuel!"

Legion turned, glaring with dark grey steely eyes, and roared as he bared his teeth and drew his dagger. Sadie's heart leaped out of her chest in fright. He swiped at her, barely missing her neck. She stumbled backward several yards, almost falling as she grabbed for her sword. A wave of fear, threatening to paralyze her, shot through her veins. She swallowed and stood up, holding her sword aloft, ready to engage him.

Legion glared at her, "You dare to challenge me!"

His words shook her soul, but she remembered her lesson from long ago when she stood up to him. Summoning all the courage she could quickly muster, she shouted in a trembling voice, "I'm not afraid of you, Legion." She leaped forward, swinging her sword violently, slashing his arm. Legion kicked her backward. She stumbled back several yards, then got ready to charge again.

In the next moment, Legion forcefully threw his dagger at her. It whistled through the air and buried itself deep into her chest.

"Ahhh," Sadie screamed, wincing in pain, her breath taken away from the force of the dagger blow.

She raised her sword, trying to move forward, but fell to her knees. Everything went hazy, and she fell onto her side. Her chest burned like fire, and she could feel the blood pouring out down her stomach. She looked up, trying to see where he was, fearing he would now come and wound her even worse. Slowly, her vision blurred, and she began to lose consciousness.

"Sadie!!", a voice cried. It was Eve, crying out in a frightened voice from the window in the treehouse above.

Then the gate guards came running around the back, finding Sadie motionless on the ground covered in blood, with a dagger in her chest. "What happened?" exclaimed the guard.

Sadie opened her eyes slightly and whispered, "Legion."

"Legion!" he said, looking around for Samantha, the rear guard who had been guarding the back of the compound.

"Look!" said the other guard, pointing. Samantha was lying on the ground fifty yards away, face down, her back covered in blood. The guard shouted in a commanding voice, "Take them both to Gabriel's headquarters, at once."

~ ~ ~ ~

Gabriel was the last to walk into the meeting of the Archangels at the Throne Room. He had just returned from his headquarters, where Angels were attending to Sadie and Samantha's wounds. He joined the others and stood at attention. He was flustered and agitated. Sadie was one of his favorites, and her wound was severe. He did not know Samantha as well, only from a distance, but her injuries angered him. He was not known as a fighter, like Michael, or Luminé, or Raphael, but he was raring to go.

Adon said, "Gabriel, please update us on the situation and on the condition of the guards."

"My Lords, there are 20 Angels now guarding the perimeter of Adam and Eve's home. The Angel Samantha was badly injured. Her recovery will take time. Sadie, too, received a severe dagger wound, only inches from her heart. Her recovery, too, will take time."

Gabriel watched as Calla cringed at the news. He remembered she too had been wounded by Legion, and her reaction further angered him, realizing the fear Sadie and Samantha must have endured at Legion's hands.

Adon asked, "Was Legion wounded?"

"We don't know."

Calla thrust her head back in frustration, "What was he doing there? How did he know!"

"Know what, my Lord?" asked Michael in a loud, somber voice.

Calla knew she had said too much, but it did not matter. Right now, her concern was for Eve. She stood up, "I have to go see how Adam and Eve are doing. We will meet back here in the morning at first light. You are dismissed."

Gabriel interrupted them all, "My Lords, there is one more thing I think must be said right now, as it may be connected to this series of strange events."

Calla asked, "What is it?"

"One of my Angels, named Mylia, is missing. Her commander has not seen her in over a week."

"Missing?" said Yeshua. "What do you mean?"

"We have searched every inch of my realm. She is nowhere to be found. There is no sign of her, and no sign at her home that she was going anywhere."

Calla asked, "What does she look like?"

Gabriel replied, "She is skinny, of medium height. She has long, stringy bleach blonde hair."

A shudder ran through Calla as she glanced over to Yeshua, then back to the Angels. The hair they found at the watery abyss at the top of Dark Mountain matched that description.

Calla said, "All of you, have your realms searched, and report back here in the morning. We have an important announcement."

Questions

Luminé sat at the long oak dining room table, turning over his salad greens and other vegetables with his fork. His mind was on Splendora. Seeing her today at the Throne Room had only reminded him of the one central truth of his life. She was his destiny. Oxana sat at the other end of the table, also uninterested in eating. She knew full well where Luminé had been, and she knew full well when his mind was somewhere else.

Oxana broke the silence, "So, you seem preoccupied. Was everything at the Throne Room okay?"

For the first time, Luminé wondered what good it would be to talk to Oxana about anything. "Yes, everything was fine. Just the usual."

Oxana heard his reply, and the detachment of it, loud and clear. She looked down at her food, then pushed the plate slightly away.

"Oh, there was one thing," said Luminé. "Your friend Mylia is apparently missing."

Oxana's eyes grew concerned, "I know that, but... how did you know?"

"Because Gabriel told the Lords. It was odd, though. They asked him what color hair she had."

"Why would they..." She stopped and put her hand on her forehead, shaking her head. Something must be wrong. Legion's smirk came to mind, and now the Lords were asking about her. They must know something.

There was a long uncomfortable silence. Oxana waited, then decided to ask, "So, was Splendora there today?"

Luminé shot back, "She is none of your concern."

"Well, it is my concern when you have been so distant from me."

Luminé sat for a moment, thinking. Perhaps it was time. Splendora was his destiny. He had been thinking about it for days now. Loving her was what the Lords expected, and it was what Splendora wanted. He was sure of this. Maybe now was the time. He flippantly said, "Oxana, sometimes I feel that our relationship is no longer of use to me."

"Use to you!" She shouted as she stood up and slammed her hand on the table. "I have done nothing but serve you! And you think you can just cast me aside! You would be nothing without me!"

Luminé, too, stood angered at her boldness, "You do not make me who I am, Oxana. I am more than you will ever be. It is I who made you, Oxana."

"Oh, really. Is that all you think of me!"

"You know what, why don't you just leave."

"Leave!" she exclaimed, her voice trying not to show the terror she felt at what his words meant for her destiny.

"Yes, leave! I don't want you around anymore," he snapped as he coldly looked away from her.

She swallowed hard, suddenly adrift, and alone for the first time in as long as she could remember. Her world had just collapsed in a moment of heated aggression. She said, "Mark my words carefully, Luminé. You will regret the day you sent me away." She picked up her glass of wine, shattering it into the fire, then stormed out.

~ ~ ~ ~

The next morning, at first light, the Archangels gathered again at the Throne Room. There was a lightheartedness in the air, and they were all smiling, and relaxed News was forthcoming, and after yesterday's difficult meeting, they all imagined today's news would be more joyful.

The living quarters' rear wooden doors opened and Calla, Adon, and Yeshua all walked out, wearing regal robes, their faces all bearing smiles. Calla especially looked radiant in her royal blue robe with white trim. The three walked up the three steps and sat in their respective Thrones.

Yeshua began, "Archangels, there is something you need to know about Adam and Eve." He paused, "The reason Eve has looked different and has seemed ill is that she is expecting a Human child."

Gabriel glanced over at Splendora. He could see she was still trying to grasp the meaning. He looked at Luminé, and it caused him to pause, as Luminé's eyes were already furrowed with concern.

Yeshua continued, "When we created the Humans, we gave them a special power; the power to procreate."

Gabriel spoke first, "Procreate? What does that mean?"

Calla replied, "When man and woman experience the sexual dance, there is a chance they will produce a tiny child. The woman will hold the tiny child in her own body until it grows to a viable size, and when it is time, the child will leave her body as either a male or female Human. It will take years for the child will grow into a man or woman, capable of procreating, and so the cycle will go on forever."

Luminé did not hold back, "You are saying the Humans will share in the divine power to create life."

"Yes, Luminé," said Calla. She figured she might as well get it all out, so she added, "The animals of the Earth will also have babies as a way to ensure the survival of all species we have given life to. That will not start until the first Human child is born.

Luminé was aghast. "My Lords! Why were the Angels not given this power?"

Michael, too, in a rare joining of concerns with Luminé, chimed in, "Yes, I too am wondering why?"

Adon said, "Look, we want you to understand, as our Angels, you are closest to us. You have been given special powers, and you have been given life eternally. The Humans are different, and they need this because… their lives are very fragile."

Rana raised her chin, her eyes trying to hide the suspicion she also felt, asked, "What do you mean by fragile?"

"They will die!" Adon replied, "And it will be very remorseful for them. It is their children that will give them comfort that will help them to let go of their life on the Earth."

Calla said, "You may all go now."

~ ~ ~ ~

Luminé walked out with the others but quickly flew away. He went to the place where he had first met Splendora, to the place where he had carved his name and his vow to himself on the rock. He sat on the edge of the stream bank, saying nothing, staring down at the gently flowing waters with a look of dismay on his face. *Share in the divine power. The cycle goes on forever. We cannot create anything! Why should the Humans be the chosen ones?*

He remembered too the first day of creation when he felt so discontented, so uneasy at all that was happening. He felt it all again today, and it reminded him that despite several years of trying to come to terms with his life, nothing had changed.

~ ~ ~ ~

Later that afternoon, Marcellus landed in the courtyard of Gabriel's Realm and asked to see Sadie. He was taken to a room where she was recovering from her wounds. He peered in. She was asleep. He quietly stepped in and walked over to look at her. Her face looked pale, and her chest was bandaged, with blood seeping through in the center. She must have suffered a great deal and, indeed, was probably still in a lot of pain. He bent down closer, admiring her beautiful face, looking so peaceful while she slept, and decided not to disturb her. He turned to leave, then heard a faint voice say, "Aren't you going to kiss me?"

He smiled widely and turned back. Her eyes were open, and though they looked tired, they were a welcome sight. He walked over and sat on the bed, brushing her thick black hair back out of her face, and leaned his face close to hers and said, "Well, of course, I am."

He gently kissed her and whispered, "I'm proud of you. You are so brave."

Her body shuddered, remembering the fearful encounter. "I had to be, Marcellus. There was nothing else I could have done. I had to fight him, or... or I don't know."

Marcellus pulled up a chair and sat close to her, grasping her hand, rubbing it. Sadie closed her eyes, stealing a moment of needed rest. She opened her eyes again, gazing at him, grateful for his love. There was silence for a while, as they both relished in the love they shared, love, that at times like this, seemed all the more essential in their lives. After a little while, Marcellus said, "I have some news."

"What news?" she asked.

"It's Oxana. She has left Luminé."

"What? That doesn't make any sense. She has been with him since the beginning."

"Well, maybe Luminé is changing. Maybe all of this trouble is finally coming to an end."

Sadie shook her head, "I don't know, Marcellus, I feel trouble is just getting started."

Splendora

Splendora closed her eyes and laid her head back, slowing her breathing. "Oh, Anthony, that was wonderful."

She looked over at the ruddy Angel lying in her bed, his eyes too, closed, he too, slowing his breathing. He smiled without looking over, "You are beautiful, Splendora."

Anthony had been her lover for several months now. She had met him while visiting Raphael's realm. He was one of his commanders, and he was a great guy. He made her laugh, and it surprised her as she had never considered humor that important. He was of average height with blondish brown hair and piercing brown eyes. His hands were strong, and whenever he took her into his arms, she felt instantly captivated. She had not planned on entering a Season of Love, but she needed to begin one with someone. What troubled her, though, was she did not know if she was truly in love.

"What are you doing tomorrow?" he asked.

"Oh, I am just taking care of my duties."

"I was hoping we could get away for a few days, perhaps go down to the beaches in the Southern Realm."

Splendora smiled, but her mind was racing. She did not want to spend a few days away. She had things to do, nothing that important, really, but... she replied, "I really can't. I have some pretty important meetings with my commanders. I should not miss them." It surprised her that she had lied to him.

"All right," he said as he sat up to get dressed. She watched him, admiring his strong backside. After he dressed, he walked over to her side of the bed, kissed her warmly one more time, and then left.

~ ~ ~ ~

The following morning, Splendora rode her horse toward the rising sun. The plains of the 1st Heavenly Realm seemed to go on forever. They were vast in the middle of the realm with endless rolling hills of grass and beautiful winding streams running toward all the coasts of the vast island. Today was exceptionally beautiful, with a light sprinkle of dew slowly drying with the sun's strengthening rays.

She felt grateful for the long ride. She needed to think. Luminé's reaction yesterday at the Throne Room greatly disturbed her. The same discontent she had seen long ago had reappeared, and it scared her. It could only mean trouble, and this time, she was not going to let it get out of control. No one imagined that the Heavens and Earth's chaos could get any worse, but Splendora knew they could. She did not know how, but just as the Lords' plans for good seemed to have endless new designs, she imagined Legion also had unlimited designs to ruin them.

She reached the far eastern edge of her realm, jumped off her horse, and walked down to the beach. She glanced around to make sure she was alone, took off her clothes, and ran naked into the surf, high stepping as far as she could, then fell forward into the warm waters, letting them wash away her worries. She surfaced, then dove down again, sweeping her way along the smooth sandy sea bottom, pulling herself farther and farther out to sea.

The water felt magical today, and being naked gave her a sense of exhilaration she desperately needed. Luminé again came to her mind. She knew he had goodness within. *Did I fail him by not loving him?*

~ ~ ~ ~

An hour later, she landed in Luminé's Realm's courtyard and walked up to his headquarters' office. His secretary said, "Good morning, Splendora. To what do we owe this honor?"

"I am here to see Luminé."

"Oh," she said, glancing out the window to his living quarters. "He has not come in yet. Would you like me to go get him?"

Splendora smiled, "No, it's okay. I'll get him myself." She walked across the courtyard. There was a large group of Angels gathered around a pole reading a proclamation. Splendora walked over to see what it was. She stood at the back of the crowd reading. It was from the Lords.

To all Angels in the Seven Heavenly Realms

When we created the Humans, we gave them special power, the power to procreate. During the sexual dance of the male and female, there is a chance they will produce a tiny child. If a child is conceived, the woman will hold the tiny child in her own body until it grows to a viable size, and when it is time, the child will leave her body and be born into the world as either male or female Human.

The child will be separate from its parents and have his or her own identity and personality. Throughout many years, the child will eventually grow into a man or woman capable of procreating, and so the cycle will go on forever.

Adam and Eve are now expecting their first child. There will be more, many more, and over time, this is how the Human Race will expand and grow.

Once the baby is born, the animals of the Earth will begin to have offspring as well.

This is the next step in the unfolding history of the Lords, the Angels, and the Humans.

We will hold an event to celebrate at the Haldansa in five days.

The Lords

Splendora carefully watched the reaction of the Angels. These were the very Angels who rebelled less than a year ago, and the spirit of rebellion was rising again. "Why are they so special?" asked one.

Another female said, "We should have been given this power, too."

Another said, "The Humans are weak. This will fail miserably."

Only one turned to face the others, saying, "We have to trust the Lords," but her words were met with a few noticeable scoffs.

Splendora went up to Luminé's quarters and knocked. Luminé answered, looking disheveled. "Splendora, what are you doing here?"

"I came to talk with you."

He smiled, pausing, contemplating her motives, and said, "Come in."

She walked in, looking around, "I did not see Oxana at your office."

"That's because I sent her away."

"Why?"

"Because I am tired of her. That's why."

Splendora was surprised, and this gave her hope. She sat down, "Luminé, you looked pretty upset yesterday."

"I am upset!" he said. "Why are these Humans so special?"

"Luminé, don't go there. Don't you remember what just happened? You were almost put into a cage as a prisoner. Have you forgotten?"

"No," he grimaced, "I have *not* forgotten."

"Your Angels seem to have forgotten. They are out there, complaining about the proclamation."

Luminé walked to the window to see the clamoring crowd gathered around a pole, reading. He turned to Splendora with an angry look on his face, "Can I help it if they are angry? They have a right to be!"

Splendora snapped, "Why don't you try being a leader for once, Luminé!"

"I am a leader, Splendora. And in case you didn't notice, I have a lot of followers!"

"Just make sure you lead them to the Lords, Luminé, and not away from them." She turned to leave, "I'm sorry, Luminé. I obviously made a mistake coming here."

She opened the door and left before he could reply.

Servants

Thaddus, Antonio, and Sansa marched down the road toward the house where Oxana was staying. All along the way, they had discussed or rather lamented the fact that the Humans were being given special powers. Antonio had rallied the others to go and find out what Oxana thought about the matter. She alone would know how Luminé would feel about things, and besides, they all wanted Oxana to come back. She was their connection to power.

They reached her home and walked into the back to find her sitting in a chair, looking out at a rough sea. The winds were strong today and the Heavens' relatively new phenomenom since the chaos brought on by what happened in the Garden of Eden over a year earlier.

Oxana heard them coming and turned, trying to keep her smile from showing. She was glad they were there. In truth, she was powerless right now, subject only to Luminé's will. Perhaps her friends coming would give her the courage she needed to find a way back.

She didn't get up but only looked up and asked in a serious tone, "What are you all doing here?"

Antonio asked, "Where have you been?"

She glared momentarily, saying, "That is none of your concern, Antonio."

Antonio had heard the rumors that Luminé had told her to leave, but he dared not press her.

Thaddus jumped in, "Oxana, we came here to see if you heard about the proclamation?"

"No, I did not. What proclamation?" she asked, annoyed that he knew something she did not.

"The Humans are able to have babies, little Humans that will grow up and have more Humans."

"I don't understand," Oxana said.

They all took part in explaining the entire proclamation as Oxana listened intently. She was not sure how to feel. She remembered Eve and how special she had seemed to her, and now she knew why. Eve, even then, had the power within her to create life. That is what Oxana had sensed. She was happy for Eve. She held no ill will toward her.

Sansa asked, "So what do you say, Oxana? What should we do?"

"I don't really care. That's what I say. The Lords can do what they want." As soon as she said it, she knew she had finally parted ways with Luminé.

"You know what I think?" said Thaddus, "I think we are going to end up being servants to the Humans."

"That's ridiculous," said Oxana in a scoffing tone, as she stood up and walked toward the sea before stopping to listen more.

"Oh, really," said Antonio. "It was not very long ago Luminé felt this very way."

"It makes sense," Thaddus said. "Why? Because we are meant to serve them. Look at a... what's her name? Sadie, yea. She is serving them with almost thirty Angels, and there is only Adam and Eve. Imagine if there were more of them."

"Enough, Thaddus!" Oxana said. It bothered her that her underlings seemed to have more opinions and knowledge than she should and usually did possess. Being a leader who was not in the lead was irritating.

Just then, a voice came from the top of the hill, "Hey everyone!" They all turned. It was Sparkis, with his red hair cast in every direction by the wind and a broad smile on her stubby face. He came running down the hill with his short legs taking extra short steps. They all watched each of them, concerned he was about to topple over, though none said it. He made it to the bottom, and sped up, then came to an abrupt stop, completely out of breath. "I just… saw… the proclamation. Did you guys… hear about it yet?"

"Yes, we did," said Sansa, rolling her eyes.

"Well, Luminé and Splendora are talking about it right now. I heard them arguing."

Oxana's face grew cross as she looked back out to sea. "Where were they arguing?" she asked.

"Inside Luminé's Quarters."

"Are you sure?" asked Thaddus.

"Yes, I was listening in," he paused as everyone looked at him with an annoyed look. Then Sparkis added, "Splendora was warning him about something."

Sansa shook her head at the news, then looked at Oxana for her reaction, fully aware of her jealousy toward Splendora. Oxana would not react; she just turned away and stared out at sea, thinking. Why would Splendora be warning him, unless, of course, this news had put Luminé back into a state of deep discontent? She could use this, but should she? Would she be better to leave it all alone and go away, as Luminé had asked? She turned back, with her chin lifted in proud defiance of this news and said, "I must ask you all to leave. I will let you know what I decide to do."

~ ~ ~ ~

Oxana waited till she was sure they were gone, then she began to cry. All she had worked for, all her hopes and dreams of being beside Luminé, were about to become a distant memory. What was going to happen to her? How could she stay in Luminé's realm, knowing he didn't love her anymore? She let out some more tears, trying to get it out. Then she grew quiet and sat up. *Luminé does love me. Luminé does need me. He is not going to have Splendora. If he did, he would have taken her long ago.* She stood up confidently, facing the sea, and said aloud, "This is my destiny, and I need to go take it back."

She turned and walked into her home, put on a sexy outfit, and took off for the Legion's hidden lair on Earth. She would gain Legion's help this day, just like she had long ago.

An hour later, she walked down the now familiar forest path. When she felt she was far enough in, she called for Legion. He appeared within moments on the path, surprising her, as if he had been expecting her. "Oxana."

She watched his eyes look her up and down, undressing her in his mind. "I have come with important news, my Lord."

"Come with me. I have a fire built."

She followed him to the clearing that held a lavish-looking hut with curtains and rugs at the entrance. Outside was a small fire pit surrounded by sitting logs and a table that held pitchers of water. Legion motioned for her to sit in front of the fire as he sat across from her. He did not have his black robe on this evening, only his brown tunic and brown sandals adorning his tan, muscular legs.

He waited until she sat and asked, "What news?" He asked in a strong and capable voice, one which reminded her of when she had been with him in the very beginning.

She sat tall and replied confidently, "The Humans have been given special powers. They have been granted the ability to have children, little Humans, and the Human Race is set to grow."

Legion did not react, his face showing no emotion, as he began thinking, trying to understand. He said aloud, "Of course; that is why there were only two of them."

"There is more, my Lord," said Oxana. "Luminé has cast me out. He is moving toward Splendora. I fear you will lose him as someone you wanted to influence, as well."

"Cast you out?" Legion said, his eyes narrowed, and his voice angry.

"Yes, he told me to leave."

Legion looked at her for a long moment, measuring if she had suddenly lost the ability to help him. If she had, he would need to be rid of her for good. He had one question, though. He asked, "How does he feel about the news of the Humans?"

"He is angry, I am sure, though we have not been able to discuss it."

Legion stood up and stepped into his hut for a moment, then returned, leaving the door open. Inside, Oxana could see his bed covered with a maroon quilt. It distracted her momentarily. He went over to the table outside the hut, took two flasks, and poured two wine glasses. "Here, Oxana. Let us have wine."

She slowly raised her eyes to his and accepted the flask. She had just taken one step forward. Legion sat again, across from her, sipping his wine, thinking. He said, "How could he not be angry? Do the math, Oxana. If the Humans are going to procreate, they will outnumber the Angels in a matter of 10 generations. They will expand exponentially. Eventually, the Angels will be a mere blip on the radar of history and exist only to serve the Humans. It is the Humans who are the focus, Oxana. The Angels will be nothing. Luminé will hate this."

Oxana said nothing, thinking to herself, *Luminé was right. Thaddus was right too. We are to serve the Humans.*

"But what can I do?" she asked.

"You must show him this. You must tell him this."

"But what will it accomplish."

Legion had already planned what he was about to say a long time ago. It was the first step in establishing his rule on the Earth and in the Heavens. He needed someone to take this crucial step. He needed Luminé. "Luminé must have his own kingdom."

"His own kingdom?"

He stood up and walked over to her and held out his hand. She took it and slowly stood. He whispered into her ear, "Yes, Oxana, with you as his queen. Luminé needs to rule his own kind, all those Angels who think as he does. He will never be happy serving the Humans. It is all that is left."

Oxana's face grew worried, but then she started to smile. "Yes, it is all that is left."

"Would you like to be his queen, Oxana?"

Oxana knew what this question meant. He wanted her, and it was his way of confirming her loyalty. She wanted him too, and the dark rush he alone gave her. She stepped forward, putting her arms around his neck, pressing her excited body against his, "Very much so, my Lord."

Findings

Calla galloped across the plains in the hot mid-afternoon sun, passing Holy Mountain, heading to the north. She wanted to be sure that the Dark Forest and Dark Mountain were being properly guarded. Part of her knew it was already too late. Something had happened at the watery abyss, what, she was unsure. Did Legion have the Golden Sword? Something told her, yes, and at the same time, there was a murkiness to her vision.

As she neared, she did not see any guards, and this alarmed her. She began to grow anxious. She carefully stepped into a canoe then paddled across the dark, cold swirling waters. After a short while, she stepped up onto the embankment, and immediately two Angels came out from the woods. "Halt, who are you?"

"It is I, Calla," she said, relieved that the guards were alert.

"We are sorry, Lord Calla. We did not expect you."

"Carry on," she said as she started up the path. She passed two female Angels part way up. They were talking and suddenly stood at attention when they saw her. "Good day, Lord Calla."

"Good day to you," Calla said as she smiled warmly and passed them. She was not far away when she heard one mutter to the other, "So, we are not good enough."

The other scoffed too, thinking Calla was out of earshot.

Calla paused for a moment and thought of turning and confronting them, but she kept on walking. She was stopped at various points and was greeted with smiles and just as many emotionless faces, which told a story all to themselves. Discontent was growing. At the top, she saw Rana standing on top of the plateau, wearing her finest uniform. Calla was impressed at how stunning, and intense Rana looked, and she was glad she had chosen her for this task. She called out, "Rana."

Rana turned, with a look of warm surprise on her face, "Lord Calla, I did not expect you."

"I just wanted to see how things are going. Any trouble?" Calla, too looked stunning today. She had on her short tunic and sandals that laced to below the knee. A golden band held her hair back, and on a golden belt hung her silver dagger and a thin sword.

Rana replied, "No, my Lord. All has been quiet."

"Have you gotten Michael and his Angels involved?"

"Yes, we are working together. I must say I am enjoying working with Michael. It is the first time that we have."

"He is a strong and loyal Archangel, Rana. You can count on him."

She bowed, knowing the same thing could not be said about her, "Oh, yes, my Lord."

Calla walked over to the watery abyss. The waters were still and dark, as the eternal flame was still extinguished. She looked over at the place where they had found the tuft of hair and cringed. It had been almost nine days now. Calla did not know precisely how or what had happened, but she felt sure Mylia's hair had been on that rock. *But where was Mylia now?*

She turned to Rana, "Rana, thank you for guarding the mountain so well."

"Thank you, my Lord. I am honored."

Rana smiled. She had never felt entirely accepted by the Lords, not like Splendora, who was always the center of their attention. Calla's words made her feel important. "Thank you, my Lord."

They stood slightly apart, both looking out over the horizon at Holy Mountain far off in the distance. "Well, I have to go," Calla said.

Rana gently reached out her hand, touching Calla's forearm, and asked in a soft, whispered tone, "My Lord, may I ask you a question?"

Calla nodded, "Yes, go ahead."

Rana looked around to make sure no one else was listening and then leaned closer and asked, "Will the Angels ever be able to have children?"

Calla half-smiled, "It is not part of the plan, Rana. You will see. There is a marvelous plan."

Rana pretended not to be bothered, "How many children will Eve have, my Lord?"

"It is not clear, but it could be as many as ten, or even more."

"I see. Thank you, my Lord."

Calla smiled and left, but all the way down the path, she kept thinking about the comments made by the two female Angels, as well as the looks on some of their faces.

~ ~ ~ ~

Luminé paced at the office. Oxana had abandoned him. Splendora was abandoning him. Oxana accused him of having no friends, and he was beginning to believe her. Where were all his supporters now? He glanced out the window again at the courtyard. Four of his guards were standing in front of the pole where the proclamation still hung. The crowd outside reading the proclamation was growing. There had been a steady stream of them all day, and many were not leaving, but instead hanging around the courtyard in groups. Fights had broken out between Angels, who scoffed at the proclamation with those who took issue with their scoffing.

There was a knock at the door.

"Who is it?"

"Marcellus."

"Come in," Luminé said, as he sat down. He knew why Marcellus was there, to chide him for allowing everyone to congregate.

"Luminé, I wanted to see if you have anything specific you would like everyone to be doing right now."

"I don't follow you, Marcellus."

"Well, there is a lot of discontent out there today, Luminé. I thought it would be good to keep everyone busy."

"Do whatever you want. I can't be bothered with that right now."

"Are you okay, Luminé?"

Luminé snapped, "Of course, I am okay. I have more important things to figure out. Now go and do your duty!"

Marcellus nodded and left.

Luminé got ready to leave. He needed answers.

~ ~ ~ ~

When he found Rana at home in her Realm, she opened the door with a surprised look on her face. She was out of her uniform and wearing a light tan tunic and a beaded necklace and bracelets that perfectly complemented her golden skin. Her hair was up and tied back with a maroon ribbon. She asked in a concerned tone, "Luminé?"

"Hi, I was hoping to talk to you."

"Sure," she said, glancing outside for a moment, "Come in, Luminé."

Luminé stepped into her living room and waited for her to come in. He looked her up and down and said, "You're all dressed up."

"I have a friend coming over."

"Oh, I should leave," he said, gesturing if he should go.

"No, it's okay. He won't be here for a little bit. How are you?"

"Not good," he replied. "Are you good? With this news about the Humans?"

"I am… coming to grips with everything," she said in a non-committal tone. "Look, there's no changing it."

Luminé exhaled loudly; he had been so tense for so long. It was as if he was holding it all in.

Rana could clearly see how tense he was. "Luminé, try to relax. Everything is going to work out."

Luminé sighed again. Rana could see he was struggling, and she wished Samuel was not on his way over. "Luminé, I spoke with Calla today. She tried to assure me that everything is going to turn out very well for everyone." She paused and added, "You know, I asked her how many children Eve was going to have, and she told me maybe ten, perhaps more, even fifteen. That's a lot of Humans."

Luminé got up, "I can't listen to this. I'm sorry. I have to go think."

Rana took hold of him, "Luminé, please."

He tried to pull away, then stopped and faced her, "Rana, I appreciate your words. I just have to go work this out on my own."

She nodded and let him go. Her words rang through his mind, *perhaps more, even fifteen.* He had been right all along. They would become servants to the Humans.

~ ~ ~ ~

Sadie was recovering quickly. She planned on returning to her duty within a week or so. She was anxious to see Adam and Eve, especially Eve. She needed to thank them for alerting everyone. Eve had probably scared Legion away, and there was no telling how badly he would have hurt her had she not appeared. Sadie had already prepared a special thank you basket with some special nuts, fruits that only grew in Heaven, as well as two bracelets and a beaded necklace she knew Eve would enjoy having.

As evening descended, she sat down on the balcony to watch the sunset over the Heavenly Sea. It was a warm, balmy evening, and a refreshing breeze was blowing in steadily off the sea. It reminded Sadie of a night long ago, when on just such an evening, she and Marcellus had made love with her bedroom window wide open allowing the breeze to soothe their bodies.

She wished he were coming over tonight, but he had kept his distance during her healing. As the sun faded below the horizon, dusk descended, and soon after, it was dark.

From the nearby woods, eyes were peering at her. Legion had come to exact his revenge, to strike fear into the hearts of all Angels. He was not one to be crossed or challenged, especially by lowly Angels. He crept through the woods and walked up to the side of Sadie's house. He peered inside. She was sitting on the balcony with her feet up. Her eyes were closed, but he could tell she was not yet sleeping. A lamp was dimly lit next to her, and a letter was unfurled on the table next to the lamp.

He could go in now and easily surprise her, wounding her badly, worse than she was now, or he could go and get the Golden Sword and snuff her life out forever. He was not entirely sure of this, as he only suspected it. Mylia had died, yes, but whether it was from the waters of the abyss or the Golden Sword, or both, he was unclear.

Perhaps he could use Sadie as a guinea pig and test his theory. He had plenty of time. He decided to retrieve the Golden Sword and come back, so he crept away and flew toward the Dark Mountain.

He headed for Dark Mountain. When he arrived, he noticed his canoe had been moved. He saw lots of footprints also. Something was going on. A large number of people had gone in and out of there lately. But why? His disposal of Mylia had been secret. The Golden Sword had been carefully hidden away from the plateau. *Why would they be coming here?*

He took the canoe, quietly placed it in the water, then pushed it out, sending it to the other side. He then stepped back into the woods and waited. As soon as the canoe reached the opposite bank, two Angels came out of the woods with swords drawn. They looked all around, then called up the mountain to their commanders. Legion heard the call being relayed up the mountain path, from Angel to Angel. Within a little while, the calls stopped. Minutes later, Michael the Archangel, along with three other Angels, came out of the woods to look at the canoe and speak to the two Angels. They all looked across toward him, though they could not see him.

Michael shouted across in a booming voice, "Who goes there!"

Legion remained still.

Again, Michael said, "Who is over there?"

Legion knew they were fishing, so he stayed still. Michael and the others went back into the woods.

Legion cringed. *So, they are guarding Dark Mountain. Why did I leave the sword there!* He left, frustrated, and returned to the Earth. He would deal with Sadie another night.

Discontent

Yeshua and Adon rode their horses across the vast interior plains of the Land of the Lords to the edge of the Heavenly Sea and bolted into the sky at lands edge, flying with their horses to Luminé's realm. The sun had just risen, and both of their faces were focused, determined, as both realized a great crack was threatening to appear in the foundation of their plans. Halfway across the sea, it began to rain. Adon looked over at Yeshua, grimacing. They would never have been caught in the rain like this before the chaos. Now the elements were random and often harsh. They had the power to stop it, but they, along with Calla, had agreed to experience the world not only as their Angels did but also as the Humans did.

By the time they reached the 2nd Heavenly Realm, the rain had subsided. They landed on the road leading to Luminé's headquarters and slowly trotted towards it. Along the way, they saw hundreds of homes with Luminé's Angels inside or out, milling about, starting their days. Many were leaving, on their way to meet up with their units for their assigned duties. Most waved, but some waves were more forthright than others. Some of their faces bore smiles, others almost possessed looks of distrust.

Ahead they saw the vast headquarters. Luminé had spared little expense building the ten-foot-tall walls out of logs and the towers and parapets at every corner, taller than the walls, overlooking his realm.

They rode up the gate and dismounted as the guards came out. "Greetings, my Lords."

Adon offered a hearty reply, "Greetings, good Angels."

The guards smiled. Adon always had a way of making others around him feel good.

Adon asked, "Is Luminé here?"

The guard looked over to Luminé's quarters. "Yes, he is, but he gave orders yesterday that is he is not to be disturbed for any reason."

Yeshua looked at Adon and nodded, then said to the guard, "Please go tell him we are here."

The guard ran to the door and knocked. Luminé answered, and the guard informed him of his visitors. He looked over the guard's head and went back in. Moments later, he was walking out, tucking in his shirt, fixing his disheveled hair. He looked tired and worn out, with bags under his eyes. He smiled and said, "My Lords, to what do I owe this honor?"

Yeshua said, "We wanted to talk with you. We thought we could walk down to the sea, Luminé. Would that be okay?"

"Sure. Let's go."

They walked out of the compound gate and down the road, Adon on one side, Yeshua, on the other, with Luminé between them. They did not say much as they passed Angels at their houses and on the road. Eventually, they reached the sea and walked down onto the sand until they were far enough along to have privacy. Adon stopped them, "Well, this is as good of a place as any. Luminé, we wanted to talk with you. What is bothering you?"

Luminé looked out to sea, pondering how forthright he should be. He decided that he needed to be as honest as he could. "My Lords, honestly, I feel that we Angels are becoming less and less significant."

Yeshua shook his head, "Luminé, that's not true. We are all significant; we all have a role to play."

"What is the plan, anyway?"

Yeshua replied, "Luminé, we created the Human Race to grow and expand and fill Earth. The Angels, as those closest to us, were created to live forever with us, and to help us guide the Humans."

"It seems the Humans have the biggest role," said Luminé.

Adon dropped his head, disappointed in Luminé's attitude, and said, "Luminé, no role is bigger than another."

Luminé was not listening. He had been making calculations all morning. He needed to know something. "My Lord, how many years will a female child grow before she can have her own children?"

Yeshua said, "Luminé, that is not important."

"To me, it is," he replied.

Yeshua brow furrowed. He was growing angry that Luminé would not fall in line. Adon saw this and placed his hand on Yeshua's arm and answered Luminé, "About sixteen or eighteen years, Luminé. But there are many dynamics at work. Some will bear their first child much later, others, perhaps not at all. It will be slightly different for each of the females."

Luminé did not say anything. Their reply made his numbers more frightening.

Adon said, "Luminé, listen, please. We want you to be happy."

Luminé lowered his head, holding his tongue, refusing to look at Adon.

This angered Yeshua. Luminé had practically destroyed everything they had planned by his carelessness and had been given great mercy. Now, he was on the verge of rebellion; it seemed. Yeshua said, "Don't do anything stupid, Luminé. Like you did last time."

Adon shot a disapproving glance at Yeshua, then looked at Luminé to gauge his reaction, but Luminé did not look up. He kept looking down, turning his head slightly away, unable to hide the grimace on his face.

~ ~ ~ ~

Luminé spent the day fretting over his new calculations. The Human would completely dwarf the Angels in a matter of generations.

He needed to talk to someone. Rana was unsympathetic. Splendora would only get angry. He needed to speak with Oxana. She alone would listen to his concerns and advise him.

He waited until it was night and walked to the house. Her house was five miles down the coast. He walked along the coastal road, passing house after house, many with fires lit both outside and in. He kept al ow profile, speaking to no one. When he arrived, he knocked on the door, and within a minute, Oxana answered. She was dressed beautifully, and she just stared at him with sorrowful eyes. Luminé looked into her dark eyes, seeing again so much he had seen before, so much of what he needed right now. "Oxana, I was hoping we could talk."

"Come in," she said, her face trying not to show the elation she felt.

He walked into her modest-looking living room and sat on the couch in front of the window that looked out onto the night sky above the sea.

She sat across from him in a chair. "What is it, Luminé?"

"It is the Humans.

Luminé said, "Do you know that within ten generations, the Humans will number almost a hundred million."

"I know, I have been doing some math myself. Luminé, what does this mean?"

"It means that we are to be nothing more than their servants."

The plan Legion had told Oxana to implement was running through her head. She was divided as to whether it was the best thing for her and Luminé. But she could see that he was troubled, and she knew him better than anyone. This matter would never resolve itself in his mind. He would be tormented forever with this fact that the Humans would greatly surpass the Angels. So, she asked, "What can you do, Luminé?"

"That's just it. I am trapped. There is nothing I can do."

Oxana paused, thinking, knowing her words at this moment could determine her future. She said, coyly, "Did you ever think of starting your own kingdom."

"My own what?"

"Your own kingdom. If you are truly unhappy, the Lords might just give it to you."

Luminé chuckled, "My own kingdom. Do... do you really think they would?"

"I think you can do whatever you want, Luminé. You must know too that I belong to you, and all your secrets are safe with me."

He gazed into her seductive eyes and lowered his voice to just above a whisper, "Do you think I could lead a kingdom?"

Before she could answer, she felt a dark rush, the same feeling she had in the woods with Legion yesterday. It startled her for a moment, but she harnessed it, realizing it was part of her new powers. "Of course, Luminé, it is your natural destiny to be a great leader, and I will come with you. Many Angels admire you and look to you for guidance. Don't forget how many you inspired when you questioned the Lords last year during the great announcement." Oxana marveled at her own words, realizing though, they were not her own.

"That's crazy, Oxana." But as soon as he said it, he knew it was not so crazy. It was the Humans who would be the Lords' crowning achievement. What purpose did he have now? He refused to become a lowly servant for the rest of his life. He smiled, thinking of how many of the Angels loved him. He relished the thought of being in charge; it was natural to him.

She stood up and walked across the room to him, holding her hand out. He took it and stood, gazing into her eyes, as a wide smile slowly crept onto his face. Oxana hugged him tightly, absolutely overwhelmed at what seemed like an answer to her prayer. "Oh, Luminé, I have missed you."

He picked her up in his arms and walked her back into her bedroom, hastily laying laid her on the bed and removing her clothing, then his own. There was no time for anything except to reunite their bodies. Afterward, they laid in bed, staring at the ceiling, relishing their reunion.

Rana and Michael

It was one of the great mysteries in the Heavens, but no one could fly across to Dark Mountain. The waters needed to be traversed by swimming or in a boat. Rana got in one of the many canoes they now had at either shore and paddled across. When she arrived at the other side, one of her guards came out of the woods with a grim look on his face. It was Edward. "I'm afraid there's trouble," he said, as he glanced to the path, adding, "Up at the top."

"What trouble?"

"You better go see for yourself."

Rana gave him a cross look, wondering why he would not go into more detail, but it didn't matter. She would find out for herself. She started up the path. When she neared the top, she saw Michael standing in the middle of the stone plateau, standing between two guards, one hers, one his, who were in the middle of a loud argument. She ran up onto the plateau, and hastily walked over. "What's going on here?"

Michael turned, "Ah, Rana. I am glad you're here. One of your guards seems to have a LOUD complaint."

Rana turned to the guard, "What the problem?"

"The problem is, Michael's Angels are not taking their fair share of night shifts. They are leaving all the lousy shifts to us."

Rana turned to Michael. "Is this true?"

"It's only true in the eye of the beholder. My guards signed up for the shifts they wanted. The rest fell to your team. I can't help it if they don't like night shifts."

"No, no, no!" Rana said. "We have to redo the shifts."

"What if I don't want to redo them, Rana?"

"You have to."

"I'll tell you what. I'll arm wrestle you for it."

"What! No, we will not arm wrestle for it. You're... you're twice my size!" She did not know whether to be mad or amused.

"All right then. I'll flip you for it."

"Flip me for it? What are you talking about?"

"I mean, I will pick you up and flip you. If you land on your feet, you win."

Rana looked at him strangely and then burst out laughing. The guards also started laughing, and after a few moments, Michael started laughing. He smiled, glad he had gotten everyone to lighten up, and said, "All right, Rana. You win. We will redo the shifts."

Rana playfully slugged Michael in the arm, saying, "You're starting to grow on me, Michael."

Michael laughed; Rana was beginning to grow on him too.

A loud cry came from the direction of the backside of the mountain. Rana looked at Michael, and they ran over. They stood at the top, and Rana called down, "What is it?"

"We found something."

She and Michael started down. Two of their guards were standing just off the path, with one of them toying with something in the brush. He lifted it with his sword. It was a blood-soaked tunic.

Rana ran over and took it off the sword. She unfurled it, seeing it belonged to a female. She had been struck in the midsection and run through, as both sides were soaked with blood. She looked at Michael and said, "Mylia?"

The News

The Lords and the Archangels conducted an emergency meeting. The meeting had been requested by the Archangels themselves because of tensions being so high everywhere in the Heavens. All the efforts to re-establish peace and order following the Fall of Adam and Eve were suddenly in limbo. The news of the Humans being able to procreate, as well as the projections flying around, showing that the Humans would dwarf the Angels in mere generations, was unsettling to many. A good number of Angels were not reporting for duty. A good number of Host

Commanders were also not reporting, or not enforcing the dictates of the Archangels to keep order. A general lack of order was unfolding.

Yeshua opened the meeting by walking down from his Throne and standing in front of all the Archangels. He stood tall, with a serious look on his face, his lips held tight as he prepared to speak to them. He looked around at all seven of them, and asked, "I am alarmed that there so much dissension about this news? Are you doing your jobs as our emissaries? Are you telling those under your command of our plans?"

Gabriel said, "Lord Yeshua, perhaps we don't see the big picture."

"The big picture? I'll tell you about the big picture. It's very simple. Out of love, we gave life to all of you, Angels. Out of love, we gave the Humans and the animals life. Life was created for love, so love can grow. It's going to be going on for a very long time; that is the big picture. Love is the big picture."

Gabriel replied, raising his eyes, with a look of skepticism on his face, "My Lord, it just seems that so much has happened. It feels like, at least to me, that love is very far from everything right now."

Yeshua dropped his head in frustration, putting his hands on top of it, shaking it back and forth. He said, "Of course, Gabriel... you are exactly right. But it wasn't supposed to be like this!" He looked up into the air, pointing with the index fingers of both hands, shaking them, and said, "You will pay for this, Legion. You will pay for all of it."

No one said a word as Yeshua turned and went back to his Throne.

Adon waited a few moments to allow Yeshua's profound words to sink in, then asked, "How how many of the Angels are angry about the pronouncement?"

Splendora stepped forward, "Most of my Angels are content. I would say ten percent are not. I currently have only five of my one hundred commanders who seem disgruntled, and I am about to relieve them of duty."

Luminé said, "My Lords, I am afraid, over half of mine are upset. Every day there are gatherings in front of the proclamation, where new fights break out between those in support and those opposed."

Michael said, "About a fourth of mine are discontent, my Lord. This morning, we had to go after a group of Angels who abandoned their posts and left for the Olympus Islands. They have been found and are being disciplined."

Raphael said, "The same as Michael, my Lord, at least a fourth of mine are not showing up for duty, or performing their duties half-heartedly."

Gabriel said, "Less than a third are discontent, Lord Adon."

Rana lied, "I would also say only ten percent of mine are discontent."

Cirianna said, "About a fourth of mine are discontent."

Adon nodded, trying not to show alarm, but the numbers were worse than he feared and worse than Calla or Yeshua had imagined. He called the meeting to a close.

~ ~ ~ ~

As they were leaving, Luminé caught up to Splendora just as she walked down the stairs and headed to the jump-off point to fly home. He said, "Hey, can I talk with you?"

Splendora turned, "Here?"

"No, let's uh… let's just fly down to the valley, and we can take a walk."

They flew down to the lake and landed, and walked around the edge of it to a few large boulders where they could sit. Splendora asked, "What do you want to talk about?"

Luminé knew Splendora was not happy with the news about the Humans either. He felt sure she would accept what he was about to tell her. "Splendora, I was thinking…" he paused, knowing how utterly critical this was to his desire to love her.

"Thinking what?"

Luminé paused. He was thinking suddenly, it might be a mistake.

Splendora would not let him off the hook, not now, "What did you want to tell me."

Luminé calculated again, as he had all night, what her response might be. He needed her to understand. He needed her to approve, and more than anything, he needed her to come with him. He slowly said,

"If I ever left here, would you come with me?"

"Left here? Luminé, I am sorry. I don't understand. What are you talking about?"

"What if I had permission to start my own kingdom somewhere else? Would you come with me?"

Splendora stared at him with her mouth open for several long seconds. Then her face grew cross. This was absolutely the worst thing she had ever heard Luminé say. She raised her voice and snapped, "Luminé, are you crazy? That is impossible!" She started to turn away. Luminé reached out to stop her, but she yanked her arm away, stopping to get one more word in, "Don't Luminé. Do not even think of it!"

~ ~ ~ ~

Later, Luminé was in his office, stewing over Splendora's rejection earlier in the day when his secretary came in with an alarmed look on her face. "Luminé, you have an urgent message from the Throne Room."

Luminé put out his hand, "Give it to me."

"I'm sorry, Luminé. She says she has to deliver it in person."

"Fine, send her in."

A sharply dressed, athletic-looking female Angel walked in wearing the Throne Room Guard's blue and white uniform and stood at attention. "Greetings Luminé, I have a summons for you from the Lords."

"Summons? I thought it was a message."

"No, Luminé. It is a summons," she said as she stood straight and tall in front of his desk.

Luminé looked up from his chair behind the desk and said, "Leave it there on the desk."

"But, Luminé, you have to read…"

Luminé looked up with gritted teeth, "I said… leave it there on the desk!"

"Very well." The Angel said as she turned abruptly and left.

Luminé stared at it for a long moment, then reached out and grabbed it. He hastily unfurled it and read it slowly.

Luminé

You are hereby summoned to appear before the Lords at the Throne Room immediately.

By order of the Lords.

He went to his living quarters and showed it to Oxana.

Her eyes widened, "Why are you being summoned?"

"I don't know," he said. He suspected, though, that Splendora had reported their conversation.

Kingdom Come

It was late evening when he landed on the porch of the Throne Room. No one was there, and he stood alone at the entrance for a moment, thinking things through one more time. Before him stood the immense wooden doors, and behind them was the vast, opulent Throne Room. It was a sign of the Lords' power. Could he really leave all of this? When he felt ready, he walked up the steps and into the Throne Room. To his surprise, the Lords were already seated, silently waiting.

"Come forward, Luminé," said Calla in a quiet, confident tone.

Luminé walked up slowly and stood before them. He felt unsettled in almost every way, humiliated at being summoned, angry about the Humans, and nervous for what he was considering asking them. He asked, "Why have I been summoned?"

Yeshua replied, "Splendora spoke to us this afternoon. She said you had something to tell us."

"I see," he said. He needed more time to think everything through, but the truth was, he had not known just 'how' to ask the Lords. Here they were, asking him. It all felt right.

He stared at the floor for a few moments, gathering his thoughts, then looked up, "My Lords, you are aware of my great discontent. I have been trying to come to terms with all of this, but I cannot. If my entire existence is going to involve serving the Humans, then I would rather leave."

Yeshua stood up with an angry look on his face, "Leave? What are you talking about?"

Adon chimed in, "Luminé, your existence will not be serving the Humans. It will be serving us and leading the Angels of your realm."

Without looking at Adon, Luminé resolutely replied, "I would ask that my followers and I be given land, such as the Southern Realm, where we… where I… can start my own kingdom."

"That is ridiculous," said Yeshua angrily. He looked at Calla, whose face was frozen with her eyebrows pulled down, and her lips tightened. Her look conveyed both fear and anger. Adon simply stared at the floor with a defeated look on his face.

Yeshua said, "Luminé, you are not a Lord; you cannot have your own kingdom. This is the world we created, and this is the world you must live in."

Adon interrupted and said in an unusually firm tone, "Luminé, why can't you be happy with the life we have given you, in the world, we have given you?"

"I cannot, Lord Adon."

Yeshua then said, "Luminé, you got off the hook, unpunished last time, but this… this is too much."

Luminé looked up in anger, "Punished for disliking the Humans? Is that fair? Do we not have free will?"

Adon stood up and walked down the few steps and over to Luminé. He took Luminé by the hands and said, "Luminé, you have always been one of our most beloved Angels. Do you really wish to leave us?"

Before Luminé could answer, and knowing he would only disrespect them by his answer, Yeshua shouted, "No more Luminé, do not say any more. Go outside and wait for us."

Luminé hated when Yeshua rebuked him, and it was happening again, but he did not care this time because he had told them. He turned and walked back across the marble Throne Room floor, closing the large wooden doors behind him.

Yeshua could hardly contain himself. "I say, let him leave. Who will follow him anyway, a handful of troublemakers?"

Calla had been silent until now, but no longer, "Leaving is a grave offense against our love and kindness. What is worse, they will be completely susceptible to Legion. He will take advantage of this. He will surely master them and make him his slaves."

"Master them?" Adon said.

"Yes, master them!" said Calla loudly, "I told you this would happen!"

Yeshua interjected, "Hold it, we all know that Legion was going to have his impact, one way or another, the question now is, do we just let him leave?"

Adon slammed his fist against his armrest, "This is all happening too fast."

Calla said, "How many do you think will follow him?"

Adon said, "I can't imagine it would be that many. We may be talking less than ten percent of the Angels."

Calla said, "That is over 70,000 Angels, Adon. Do you think that many would want to leave?"

"Well, that does sound like a lot. Perhaps it will be less."

"Summon him now," said Calla.

~ ~ ~ ~

Oxana paced their living quarters anxiously, waiting for Luminé to return. Every few minutes, she stepped onto the terrace and looked to the west to see if he was coming. The sky was almost dark, with the faint glow of the sunset still lingering in the western sky. Finally, she saw him. He landed in the courtyard and came right up to his living quarters. Oxana rushed to the door to greet him, but he seemed troubled, not happy as she had anticipated. It must not have gone well. She was instantly worried that perhaps her suggestion, or rather, Legion's had backfired and would fall back on her head. She gently asked, What happened?"

Luminé tried to hide the growing divide inside him. The initial euphoria he felt at the Lords granting his request faded all the way home. He was concerned about the magnitude of such a move. Was he making a mistake? Seeing Oxana, though, momentarily bolstered him. "Everything went just as I had hoped. In fact, even better."

"What did they say?"

"They said I could have my own kingdom." No sooner had he said it than he began to worry he was giving up too much. He was giving up Heaven and the Lords. He was giving up the idea of loving Splendora.

"What! Oh, Luminé! That is... that is fantastic! Where are we going?"

The question stopped him, and for a long moment, almost derailed him. He had labored to be the leader of this 2nd Heavenly Realm, and now he was leaving it all behind.

Oxana watched his confidence diminish, and she, too, worried.

Luminé recovered and said, "We are being given the Southern Realm."

"Really? The whole Southern Realm?"

Luminé's smile was manufactured now, the conditions replayed in his mind. *Nothing will be provided any longer.*

"Luminé, are you okay?"

"Yes, yes. Call our Host Commanders together at once. I want everyone assembled tomorrow morning so I can make the announcement."

"Yes, Sir!" she said as she whisked around and headed for the door. She stopped, turning to ask, "Luminé, will I be your queen?"

"Of course, Oxana, of course," he said. But who would be his queen was the very last thing on his mind. He felt very divided.

~ ~ ~ ~

The following day, Luminé peered out the window at his 100 Host Commanders and the over 100,000 Angels under his command, assembled in formation in the sky above his headquarters' courtyard. He was beginning to have real doubts. Perhaps they would all laugh at him. Perhaps he would be ridiculed and have to back out. *Are they going to come with me?*

There was a knock at the door. He let go of the curtain and slowly walked to it, anxiously contemplating what he was about to do. *It's not too late to call it off.* He placed his hand on the knob and paused. *It's not too late.*

He opened the door. Oxana and Marcellus were standing in uniform, waiting to escort him to the courtyard. Oxana was dressed to the hilt with her collar up, accentuating her pulled up hair. She stood tall and confident with tall heeled boots. She proudly said, "Great Luminé. Everyone has assembled and is waiting for you."

Luminé looked at her and smiled, then he looked at Marcellus, who had no idea what was going on, and his fears came rushing back. His stomach lurched inside, but he caught himself and said, "Yes, I am ready."

Marcellus, who did not know what was to come, turned and led them at a quick pace down the hallway and down the stairs to the waiting stage that had been set up. Luminé marched up the steps, then stopped in the center at the wooden podium.

Luminé looked out and up, scanning the faces of his Angels. *There is still time.* He pretended to be looking down at some notes. *But this is what you fought for; this is what you've earned. The Lords already said yes!* He looked over at Oxana. With her black uniform and tall heels and hair up, she really did look like a queen, a dark queen. He began, "Host Commanders and Angels, I welcome you." *I used to add 'in the name of the Lords of Heaven.'*

He continued. "I have asked you all here today because, as many of you know, I, along with a great many other Angels, are not happy with the way things are going with the Humans. Specifically that they will be able to reproduce, and their Race will greatly expand, as ours will not. It is my opinion that we are destined to become inferior creatures. I have decided I cannot live under such conditions any longer."

Luminé watched the mixed reaction of the crowd. He noticed some slowly beginning to nod their cautious approval. Other eyes grew wider, expressing a look of bewilderment. The majority were looking right and left at each other, trying to see if others felt as they did. But others only stood unmoved, still standing at attention in the wind, not having heard enough to react yet.

He raised his hands for everyone to quiet down and said, "Because of all of this, I have decided to leave the Heavens. Yesterday I was given permission to start my own kingdom in the Southern Realm."

A gasp went up. Luminé raised his hands high, "Silence, please!"

Quiet returned, but not like before. This was not the anticipatory quiet prior to the announcement. It was a foreboding quiet like no one was willing to speak. Luminé continued, "Those of you who follow me there, will be allowed to own your own land, like the Humans do on earth, and build your own wealth as the Humans can. The entire Southern Realm has been given to me and to all of you who choose to follow me."

Chaos ensued, and everyone broke ranks. The announcement suddenly threw a wedge into the allegiances of everyone. Luminé nervously watched their reactions, and he raised his hand into the air, signaling for everyone to quiet down, but no one listened. Marcellus shouted out over the noise of the crowd. "Everyone, quiet down. Let Luminé finish!"

Luminé smiled and looked over at Marcellus, expecting his usual look of loyal allegiance, but instead, Marcellus was glaring at him with an angry frown on his face.

He turned back to the crowd. "We will be leaving in one week. Let everyone know. This invitation is extended not just to you but to every Angel in all of Heaven's realms.

Marcellus stepped off the other side of the podium. He did not wait for Luminé. Instead, he waded through the sea of commanders and joined some of his closest friends who had gathered to decide whether they would stay or go.

Wildfire

The news spread like wildfire. In a matter of an hour, Heaven was being turned upside down.

Splendora was flying to a meeting at the Throne Room. She had been ordered to bring her most trusted Host Commanders. As they neared the land of Holy Mountain, they saw a group of Angels flying in jagged lines, whooping and hollering, darting playfully in all directions.

"Who are those Angels, Arcano?"

"I don't know, but I will find out." Arcano raced ahead to catch up with them. "Stop," said Arcano to the group of Angels. "Where are all of you going?"

Sparkis, with his red hair strewn in every direction by the wind and his eyes and mouth wide open, smiled widely and replied for the group, "Haven't you heard the news?"

"What news?" Arcano asked, just as Splendora and the others caught up with them.

Sparkis said, with a look of surprise on his face, "What news? Where have you guys been? One of the greatest announcements in the history of the Heavens has just been made."

Splendora snapped at him, "Tell us now. What is the news?"

"Luminé's great announcement!" Sparkis boasted. "He has been granted his own Kingdom in the Southern Realm by the Lords. Anyone in all of Heaven who wishes to go with him must decide within the week."

Splendora's mouth fell open, and her mind drifted far away. Luminé had done it again, but this time it was worse than ever. Arcano saw her, and he jumped in. He demanded to know. "When did you hear this? How do you know?"

"I was there," Sparkis said. "I just relayed the information to my friends in your realm. They took a vote and disbanded their unit."

"What do you mean 'took a vote'? There can be no vote without Splendora." Arcano drew his sword, "Sparkis, take your lies out of our realm, and as for the rest of you, get back to your units now."

The Angels looked at Arcano, "We have no more units. Everything has been disbanded. Units don't exist anymore. We are leaving Arcano."

Splendora shouted, "Are you all crazy?"

Sparkis defiantly responded, "Sorry, Splendora, the Lords of Heaven have decreed that we can do this."

"But why?" she cried out.

"Because we, like Luminé, are all tired of these Humans and their special treatment."

She raced up to him, pressing her face against his, then grabbing his shirt, lifting him above her. "Watch your tongue, Angel. You speak with respect to me."

"Yes, Splendora," Sparkis said, knowing she was about to rearrange his face.

Splendora suddenly realized she should not be treating another Angel with anger like this. She slowly let go of Sparkis and backed away.

"Fine. All of you go. Go wherever you were going. Do whatever you like. But I will tell you right now you are all making a huge mistake."

Splendora turned to her companions. "And will you be leaving me too? Are you going to follow Luminé?"

Though no one said a word, Splendora could see by the look in their eyes that some of them were suddenly considering it.

~ ~ ~ ~

The week held the same excitement as when the Angels were first created. Everywhere, everyone was talking about nothing except who was going and was staying. All semblance of order in the Heavens completely disintegrated.

Luminé and Oxana were busily packing and keeping a tally of whom and how many were coming. By the 3rd day, 168,000 confirmations had come in. More were rolling in every minute. At the end of the 3rd day, Luminé asked, "Did any of the Archangels decide to come?"

Oxana dropped the tally sheet on the couch. "No, Luminé. None are coming! In fact, I am being told they are all angry with you, especially that know-it-all Splendora."

Luminé whirled around, "Don't talk about her like that, Oxana. She has always been a good friend to me."

"Oh, really? If she is such a good friend, why is she trying to convince the other Angels not to join us?"

Luminé said, "Splendora has a right to her own opinion, just like you do. There is still time for her to change her mind."

"What are you talking about, change her mind? She is against you, Luminé, don't you understand?" The sudden insecurity Oxana felt scared the hell out of her.

"She is not against me!" *But if she does change her mind, you will be doing a very different job,* he thought.

~ ~ ~ ~

Calla stormed into Adon's quarters at the back of the Throne Room, "This is a complete disaster! Call it off, call it all off!"

Adon knew she was right. Things were spinning way out of control. He never imagined a complete collapse of the entire framework they had set up. "Calla, I'm sorry."

"I don't want to hear, sorry!" she shouted. "What about Adam and Eve and their children and their children's children? What does the future hold for them now?" She picked up a vase and threw it across the room at Adon, barely missing him, then stormed out his door, shouting, "We have to do something!"

"Where are you going?" he shouted.

"To see Yeshua."

Splendora and Luminé

On the 5th night following the announcement, 220,000 Angels and Host Commanders had signed up to leave with Luminé. Luminé felt the pressure mounting. There was still time to call it all off.

Leaving Splendora was the thing that haunted him. He could not fathom how he had made the decision, knowing she was not coming. He needed to speak with her.

He got up from the living room chair and said, "I have to go do some thinking. I will be out late."

Oxana's eyes lit up. She knew exactly where he was going. "Luminé, please don't doubt what is happening. That many Angels can't be wrong. This is your destiny."

"Look, I have to get away and think."

"Where are you going?"

"I don't know."

Luminé left and flew straight to Splendora's home. He knocked on the door, and suddenly she whisked the door open, holding her sword in her hand, and stared at him. "What do you want?"

"Splendora, I have to talk to you." He looked at the sword, "Put down that sword. I need your help. Please."

Seeing her made him suddenly realize how self-absorbed he had been. Maybe he was making a terrible mistake, perhaps the worst of his life.

She turned and put her sword down, "Come in."

Luminé followed her into her living room. She turned to face him with arms folded, waiting. Luminé said, "Splendora!" "Don't Splendora me! You have torn apart the entire Heavens!" She shook her head and looked out the window, then turned back, "Nothing will ever be the same! Don't you see?"

She threw her hands up, "I thought you said you loved me. Didn't you tell me this? Didn't you?" Her face was tired, tired of trying and pleading with him to relieve her of her pain finally.

"Yes, I did say that. I do love you, Splendora." His voice trailed off. They both stood looking at the floor, neither one knowing what to say. The silence between them became deafening. Splendora knew it was now or never. She looked as sincerely as she could into his eyes, "Why don't you call it off?"

"What did you say?"

Splendora tried to speak with a tone to convey the deep love she felt for him, "Why don't you call it off?"

"Why… why should I?" he said, not meaning it, but it was the only thing he could say.

She gave him a fixed look and took a step closer to him, "Because of everything good that will be forever lost. Because of the very foundations of the Heavens, that need to be restored." She paused, looking at this one she had loved since the beginning, hoping that he would open his eyes to see her. She said, lastly, in a trailing voice, "Because of me."

Luminé searched her eyes, seeing something more profound than he had ever seen. He had been so confused for so long. Only when he was around her could he see clearly, and now, he saw it all clearly. This was a mistake, and it was not too late to change it. "I will call it off," he said, as he stepped forward and took her by the hand, "because I love you."

Splendora stepped closer, her eyes locked in a loving embrace with his, and took him by the hands, leaned forward, and kissed him.

Luminé stayed with her kiss, then pulled back, not letting his eyes move from hers for even a moment, then put his hands around her backside, holding her firmly, kissing her slowly, passionately. Years and years of pent up desire were melting into this one kiss. Splendora said, "I love you, Luminé, I have always loved you."

"At last, I have you," Luminé said, as he took her by the hand and led her into her room. They faced each other and undressed. Luminé sat on the bed and pulled her next to him, standing, holding her tenderly, feeling her skin against his cheek, kissing her, kissing her breasts. They held each other for a long time, then lowered themselves onto the bed, loving each other like it was their first day and their last day.

An hour later, they lay awake, saying nothing, knowing that what had to be done still had to be done. He turned to look at the ceiling again, feeling a peace he had never felt, and drifted off to sleep.

~ ~ ~ ~

Oxana was up all night, worried what Luminé was going to do. Early the next morning, she sent a message to Luminé but received no response. She knew he was with Splendora and feared he would back out. She had failed, and now, it would be over for her. There was only one thing left to do. She raced to the Earth, to the forest where Legion was. He was waiting for her.

"I sensed you needed me, Oxana."

Oxana explained everything and asked, "What should I do?"

"Luminé has one weakness. Gather everyone together who has signed up to leave and do exactly as I say."

~ ~ ~ ~

Luminé and Splendora made breakfast together. Two messenger birds arrived with messages from Oxana during the meal, urging him to come back, but he ignored them. Splendora urged him to go speak to the Lords, but he told her he wanted to spend time with her first. After breakfast, he left, telling her he would go to shore, freshen up, and then go and see the Lords. He would come back as soon as he was finished.

He left and flew toward Holy Mountain. He wanted to go back to his place, to the rock where he carved his promise so long ago. He needed to think because he was making the biggest decision of his life.

Rana

Rana stood on the edge of the cliff, overlooking the sea. She came to this place often to think, but she was running out of time.

It was Luminé. It was always Luminé. The truth was, she felt exactly the same way as he did about the Humans and their ability to reproduce life. Luminé at least dared to do something about it, shouldn't she?

She needed to talk with someone she trusted. She took off to go talk with Gabriel. He would know what she should do. She flew to his realm and walked right up to the steps. His office door was open, and she walked in to find him sitting at his desk, looking out the window.

"Gabriel?"

He turned, "Rana?"

"Where is everyone?" she asked.

"Everyone? You're it. Come in." He motioned for her to enter and led the way into his living room. Gabriel looked relaxed, wearing pants and a light blue shirt and wore dark brown sandals. He held a book in his hands and had obviously been reading.

"It's a real mess. I can't believe Luminé has done this."

"Yes, I know. I'm sorry, Gabriel."

He interrupted, "Anyway, with everyone having to decide on staying or leaving, I thought it best to suspend all protocol. This way, everyone could have time off to figure things out. I told them all to go home and make their decision."

Rana said, "It's a big decision, and certainly one that has to be considered carefully."

She stopped, saying nothing else. Gabriel heard loud and clear the reason for her visit now. He could see the same confusion he had seen in countless Angel's faces since the announcement. He motioned for her to sit down.

Rana asked him, "Gabriel, I don't know what to do."

"I will try to help. What's on your mind?"

"What's on my mind?" She jumped up off the couch and walked to the balcony. "What's on everyone's mind. It's Luminé! It's the Southern Realm. It's the Humans. It's everything!"

Gabriel quietly listened. His worst fears were now confirmed. Rana would be making a terrible mistake to go. Any of the Angels would, but as an Archangel, for her, it would be an even greater loss. He asked forthrightly, "Rana, are you thinking of going with him?"

Hearing it from someone else stopped her momentarily. *It sounded absurd, or did it?*

"I don't know! That's the problem! Would it be wrong if I did? The Lords said we could go freely! They said we would be given our own land there and many say it will be very wonderful. Isn't that worth thinking about?"

"But it's not about those things at all, Rana. Is it?"

"No, it's not."

"It's about Luminé, isn't it?"

She began to frown, "Yes, it is. I don't know what it is, Gabriel. I just love him… he was my first lover."

Gabriel listened, then stood, "Rana, listen to me carefully. The answer is no. Do you hear me? No! You cannot do this, and you cannot even think about it!"

She looked at him with a deep sadness in her eyes because he had not convinced her. She stood up, half smiling, "Thank you, Gabriel."

She hugged him, turned, and left. She knew she'd never see him again.

Luminé! Luminé!

Oxana had one card to play, and Legion had helped her decide how to play it. She gathered her friends Sansa, Holly, and eight more of the most stunning Angels who were leaving Heaven, and had them dress in their most stunning outfits. They met in her office.

Oxana said, "I need you to leave at once and intercept Luminé. My scout tells me he will be heading to Holy Mountain very soon for a meeting. You must get to him, and bring him here. You will do whatever is in your power to persuade him to come here, just for a short time, because I have a special gift for him. Tell him, afterwards, he can return to wherever he was going."

"But what is the gift?" asked Sansa.

"You will see, now go. Do not fail me. You will all be well rewarded by me in the new kingdom."

At once, they left.

~ ~ ~ ~

They found Lumine in the skies several miles away from Holy Mountain. Sansa led the pack of vixens as they surrounded him. Sansa said, "Greetings, Great Luminé."

Lumine stopped, smiling, and shook his head. "What sort of game is this?" he asked.

Sansa smiled at him for a moment, then said, "Luminé, Oxana sent us here to capture you. She said, before you speak to anyone, she needs to give you a special gift from all of your followers."

"A gift?" He knew there was no gift. "I don't have time..."

"Girls?" Sansa said, and at once they all zoomed in and took hold of Lumine's arms.

Lumine laughed loudly, "Oh, this is a predicament." He loved the attention, and loved the beautiful beings holding him.

"And if I don't want to go? You know, I can thrust all of you off me in a moment if I wanted to."

Holly interrupted him, "Luminé, please, you need to just come with us. It won't take long, and we will get in a lot of trouble if you don't come."

"Yes," Sansa said winking. "Just come with us. You can leave as soon as she gives your gift."

Luminé's face tightened, as he glanced toward the distant Holy Mountain. He had time, and he perhaps he owed Oxana an explanation at the very least. She deserved as much. "All right, I will come with you."

They all flew with him, surrounding him, away from Holy Mountain, out over the Heavenly Sea, toward the 2nd Heavenly Realm. Then, all at once, they stopped. Sansa said, "We have strict orders to blindfold you the rest of the way, Luminé."

"I am not going to be…"

Sansa flew behind him, pressing herself against him, "Now, Luminé. This won't hurt a bit. Let us do as she asked."

"Okay, fine, blindfold me, but let's hurry."

They put the blindfold on him and led him through the chilly night to the wooded area behind his headquarters and in through the back door. They walked him down the familiar hall and opened what he knew was his office door. They stepped in and left him standing in the middle of the room. Sansa took off the blind, and they left. Luminé found himself face to face with Oxana.

She was dressed in an exquisite short red mini dress. Her hair was up, in a way, he had never seen before. No matter what he felt for Splendora, Luminé could not deny the strong, sexy, and powerful looking female Angel standing before him. The curtains in front of his second-story balcony, which overlooked the courtyard, were drawn closed behind her.

"Great Luminé," she bowed and eyed him carefully with a sexy smile. Keeping her glance and smile fixed on his face. She turned and said, "Your loyal subjects await you." She snapped her fingers, and two Angels who had been standing outside on the balcony quickly drew the curtains back. Oxana took Luminé by the hand and stepped out onto the balcony with him. Thousands upon thousands of lights suddenly appeared, and to his amazement, over 200,000 Angels were standing at attention, all dressed in their finest battle uniforms.

Luminé looked at Oxana, so excited. She raised their joined hands up into the sky as the crowd went crazy, cheering wildly. It was even louder than the cheers he had heard at the Olympus Games. Luminé was getting light-headed, feeling the pressure of what he had promised Splendora.

Oxana saw the indecision creeping over his face. She knew this was the moment of truth. She had to make her move. She raised her other hand into the air, egging the crowd on, and shouted, "Luminé! Luminé!"

At once, the crowd began chanting, "Luminé! Luminé! Luminé! Luminé!" and pumping their fists into the air.

Shaken out of his stupor, Luminé heard their cries. He listened to the roar of voices calling him forth. *I am a king. I am their king! I don't need the Lords anymore. I have a kingdom!*

Oxana waved at the immense crowd, and Luminé's newly designated 235 Host Commanders flew to the front of the massive crowd of Angels. She shouted out, "Host Commanders, divide your Angels into their command units tonight." They all saluted and floated back into the ranks. Luminé looked on with immense satisfaction, then gave the final command himself. "All of you, assemble in battle formation on the eastern shore tomorrow before dawn."

A sinister smile of deep dark satisfaction came over his face. He turned to Oxana and let his smile become even more confident. Then he stepped forward and thrust their joined hands to the sky even higher and out towards the crowd. Everyone went crazy with delight, shouting louder now, "Luminé! Luminé! Luminé! Luminé!"

Crucible

Splendora woke without worry for the first time in what seemed like ages. Her love for Luminé was finally about to be realized. Nothing else mattered. The day was just dawning over the horizon, so she opened her windows, stretching out her arms as the morning sun bathed her face. A new day was dawning, a new day of hope and love. She showered, dressed, and set about making the needed plans to restore her dismantled realm. She thought to herself, *What a mess everything is. It's going to take time to put it all back together, but it will be worth it.*

Her mind returned to Luminé. She was proud of him for having the courage to call off his plans for their sake. During the night, she had vowed that she would be 'all in' with Luminé and no longer aloof and apart from him. There was only one more problem that had to be addressed. Oxana had to go immediately, and while she was unsure how this would ultimately transpire, Splendora was sure of one thing, she would face it head-on, even as soon as today.

~ ~ ~ ~

Luminé opened his eyes wide, feeling the weight of the world, pressing them closed again. The confusion he had felt for so very long was back in full force. He had no idea what was right or wrong, and he did not understand how his faculties had become so clouded. It was as if some dark cloud had drifted into his mind long ago, and it was getting darker and foggier. He took several deep breaths, trying to calm his racing heart. There was still time. It was not too late. Oxana did not matter. None of his supposed followers mattered. He could turn his back on them all right now, and he would find new followers, new 'assistants.' He closed his eyes for a few moments, slowing his breaths even more now, bringing himself to the decision.

"Luminé?"

He didn't want to see her now. He looked up. Oxana was at the door of his room. "Luminé, everyone is ready. We await your presence."

"Oxana... I..." he stopped. She looked so radiant, so strong, so incredibly sexy and smart. She had been so much to him, and she had been right about so much too. He asked, "Oxana, am I doing the right thing?"

"Luminé, 235,000 Angels cannot be wrong about you, and neither can I."

He glanced out the window at the sun, now completely lifted above the horizon. He said, "I need time to get ready."

"Don't take long, Luminé. Everyone has been waiting for over an hour."

"I don't care about that, Oxana. I need some time."

Oxana nodded slowly, then smiled. She turned away with a worried look. She could see the collapse of all her plans etched on his face. She did not have time to worry. Not now. She needed to show strength. It would be what Luminé needed. It would be what the rest of them needed to see if she were to ascend this day to her rightful place.

Darkening skies and growing storm clouds rolled in from the East, settling above the heads of over 235,000 Angels gathered at the shore of Lumine's 2nd Heavenly Realm. The Angels were waiting for their leader, Lumine, to come and lead them away to their new homeland.

Today was the most exciting day in many of these Angel's lives. None of them ever imagined leaving the Heavens, but all felt justified in their doing so. Most were discontented at the special privileges the Humans had been given, that of being able to create new life by having babies, but it was more than discontent that ruled this day. Following Lumine, the greatest of the Archangels, to a new world was a thrilling adventure, one that promised to be filled with wonder and excitement.

It had all happened so fast. Only ten days earlier, the announcement had been made that they were free to leave. No one imagined that a third of the Angels would go, but here they all were, anxiously waiting with great anticipation.

The scene at the beach was escalating in tenor, and nearing a fever pitch. The time was near, imminent, and Angels jostled with each other, laughing, talking excitedly, speaking of what they would do when they arrived at Lumine's new kingdom. One thing they all agreed on. They would be finally free of the dominination of the Archangels and Host Commanders they were leaving behind. In their new land they would be ruled by Lumine, the greatest and most daring of all the Archangels. They would welcome his rule.

~ ~ ~ ~

Oxana lifted her head high and walked out of her quarters and into the headquarter's compound of Lumine's 2nd Heavenly Realm. She was dressed in an exquisite skin tight gold and black uniform with a silver colored belt holding her sword sheath.

Today was the day she had dreamed of for years, and nothing was going to stop her rise to power. She drew in a deep breath, savoring the feeling of exhilaration, then turned to the hundred Angels, stationed on the walls of the compound, holding large maroon-colored banners. They were stationed on the wall so they would be visible to those on the beach. Soon they would wave those banners, sending the message to the mass of Angels on the beach that it was time to to set the great day in motion. The drummers and trumpeters she had organized were also there on the beach, at the front, waiting for their cue to launch the departure with pomp and fanfare. Oxana planned it all this way, to ensure all would feel the elation she felt, that Lumine's new kingdom awaited them.

It would be a different kingdom, not one saddled by Heaven's silly rules, nor structured in a way that the Humans were of first concern. No, this would be their own kingdom, one in which they could do whatever they pleased.

It was almost time for Lumine to emerge from their living quarters. With a gleam in her eye, she raised her arm high above her head, holding it there for all to see, then waved. All at once, the hundred Angels stationed on the walls stood tall, raising the massive maroon-colored banners high into the air, and began joyfully waving them to and fro, sending the first signal to all on the beach get ready.

She watched the spectacle, the listened to the immense roar from the beach. It sent shivers up her spine, and she knew they would now assemble in tight formations, readying themselves for her and Lumine to join them, waiting for Lumine's to conduct his review of their lines. It would be his last act in the Heavens before leaving for their new realm.

Oxana turned and looked at the large arched entryway of the headquarters where Lumine would stride out any moment, ready to embrace his destiny. She glanced up at the faint sun behind the clouds to gauge the time, nervously chewing the inside of her cheek.

He was taking too long.

The moments were beginning to feel like hours, and her heart beat quickened noticeably in her chest, as inevitable apprehension set in.

She glanced around, half smiling at all who were waiting inside the compound, knowing there was no way she could show even an flicker of her growing concern.

Several minutes passed with no sign of him. She glanced up again at the location of the sun barely visible through the darkening skies. Was this an omen? Was this a sign that it was to all be stopped, that the Angels would lose their will? Was Lumine having second thoughts? It would be the end for her. She would be relegated back into obscurity, back to being nothing more than a lowly Angel. She would face Legion's wrath too, the punishment for failure.

Her teeth clenched tightly, stopping a look of concern from breaking through her stoic smile. She decided to do the only thing she could do. She whispered a prayer, though strangely it did not feel like a prayer, that Lumine would not turn his back on his new Kingdom.

Then, she waited.

They all waited.

~ ~ ~ ~

Splendora walked over to her living room window and glanced out at the eastern morning sun. It had been up for over an hour already, and she wondered when she would hear from Luminé. He had said he would be going to speak with the Lords, and with something of this importance, she imagined he was either there, or on his way back, to deliver the news to her personally.

Dismissing her fears, she tried convincing herself that he must be delayed for some extraordinary reason. *Maybe it is taking him a long time to talk to the Lords.*

She poured herself some coffee and tried to relax, but it was impossible. The worry was mounting. She left her living quarters and went over to her office. The compound was empty, except for a few guards who Splendora would not let abandon their duties. She went inside and stood behind her desk, too nervous to sit down. Suddenly she heard someone running down the hallway, and moments later, Arcano rushed in, "They are assembled on the beach Splendora."

Without looking up at him, she slowly asked, "Who is assembled and where?"

Arcano was surprised that she had even asked. Everyone knew what was supposed to happen today. He replied slowly, "Luminé and his 235,000 followers!"

She looked up, "Are you sure? Are you sure Luminé was with them?"

"Well, no, not yet. Oxana and the leaders are outside the headquarters waiting for him to come out."

Splendora said nothing.

Arcano then said, "Rana is there too. On the beach with several of her commanders. It looks like they are going too."

"What!" Splendora stood up quickly. She turned to the window, looking out at the rising sun in the direction of the 2nd Realm. She asked, "Arcano, I need to know. How long have they been waiting outside for him?"

"A while!" he said.

She clutched her hand tightly. Everything inside her was screaming. She bolted from behind her desk, saying, "Come with me!"

"Where are we going?"

"I have to stop him!"

"But... but they are already waiting for him outside..."

"I don't care! Are you coming or not?"

"Yes."

The Angel Sagas are continued in Book 3 of the After Life Series, Judgment.

Part 2 of Rebellion
The After Life Journey of Duncan follows.

Part 2

The After Life Journey of Duncan
Forward

With the rise in cases of Autism across the world, Duncan's story hits right at heart. Many of us know of someone or have a friend or family member who has an autistic child who is at the severe end of the spectrum. It is a hard road for these families, but a loving road, founded on the unshakeable bond called family love.

I know someone like Duncan, and I hope this story reflects the hope I have for that person. My story is meant to capture the interior life that may exist in such an innocent person. It is also my hope that this life is merely a forerunner to a wonderful eternal existence, free from the bonds put on us by our life here.

Note to Reader   Duncan's story, like all the After Life Journeys, is also available separately. It is called Duncan: An Autistic Boy's Struggle and Triumph.

Chapter One

Tracy put her daughter's upside-down hairbrush to her lips and belted out the words, "Sweeeeet Caroline... Ba, Ba, Baaa... Good times never seemed so good... So Good! So Good! So Good!"

She whisked the hairbrush into her other hand, closing her eyes, extending her other hand to the imaginary crowd, "I've been inclined... Ba, Ba, Baaa... to believe they never would."

She danced her way down the upstairs hallway to her son's room, humming the next part of the song only because she didn't remember the exact words.

It was one of those sunny fall days when everything in the world felt right, and Tracy was on top of the world today. She and her husband had loved each other that morning before he left for work. Her daughter was getting ready to graduate in a month, and her son Duncan had just gone to sleep downstairs after a hearty lunch.

It was 1 p.m., and she planned to gather her children's sheets, wash them, and hang them out in the fresh breeze on what was turning out to be an unanticipated glorious day.

Suddenly, the sound of screeching tires riveted through the air, followed by silence. She froze for one agonizing moment, as a feeling of dread seized her and worked its way through her body. "God, please, please," she uttered, as she turned and bolted out of the room.

30 years earlier...

Mr. John Davis turned onto his street and glanced over at the thirteen-year-old girl seated next to him. He understood why she didn't want to make eye contact. He smiled and said, "Tracy, are you ready to meet our family?"

Tracy half-smiled back and gave a hurried nod, contemplating the road ahead. Inside she was shaking like a leaf, scared just like all the other times, but she could handle it because anything was better than going back to the County Home. She wished she could skip past all the introductions and 'beginnings' and get a month or two down the road to the part where she would find out if she were going to stay or not. Too many times, the answer had been 'no.' Even so, Tracy held onto hope. This was her fifth trip to a new foster family in the last four years.

As they pulled into the drive, and the moment neared, she quietly prayed that this time might be different. They parked, got out of the car, and John Davis led Tracy up the walk. Tracy swallowed hard as he opened the front door and ushered her inside. She stepped into the foyer and saw a beautiful woman and two children all standing in the living room, smiling at her.

John made the introduction, "Everyone, this is Tracy."

Ellen Davis stepped forward, "Hi, Tracy, welcome."

Tracy nodded, proffering a fake smile, hiding the nervousness she suddenly could not shake. Perhaps it all seemed too perfect, and the Davis family looked too perfect.

Ellen stepped forward and gently asked, "Can I give you a hug?"

Tracy nodded.

Ellen warmly embraced her, then said, "Tracy, please consider our home, your home. We want you to be comfortable here."

Tracy replied in a soft voice, "Thank you… Mrs…. Davis."

Ellen turned toward her children, "Tracy, this is Suzy, and she's 11, and this is Alan, he is 8."

Both children stepped forward and shook Tracy's hand. Suzy looked jubilant, her face holding a wide unmovable smile. Tracy was glad to see a girl close to her age. A small inkling of hope crossed her mind, but she knew not to trust it. She remembered all the past disappointments. She had been through this routine many times before.

Ellen said, "Suzy, take Tracy upstairs and show her where her room is, and remember dinner will be in an hour."

Suzy wasted no time and grabbed Tracy by the hand and excitedly ran toward the stairs, pulling her along. Tracy turned momentarily and said, "Thank you." Tracy had been taught the importance of courtesy from one of the nuns who visited the County Home.

Ellen said, "You're welcome, Tracy."

Suzy reached the top of the steps and stopped at the first bedroom on the right, proudly saying, "Here's your room! It's right next to mine."

Tracy peaked inside. As Suzy hurriedly asked, "Do you like it? I helped mom fix it up," Tracy's face lit up with excitement.

But Tracy didn't reply, only looked around, marveling at every aspect of it. It was painted a sunny yellow with sheer white curtains on the windows and light blue drapes. On the bed was a coverlet that was imprinted with roses in yellow, pink, and blue colors. It was the most beautiful room she had ever seen, and she could not believe it was hers.

Suzy asked again, "Well... do you like it?"

"Yes, I do, thank you."

"Do you want me to help you unpack?"

"No that's okay. I'll do it myself, but thank you."

"Okay then, I'll see you downstairs for dinner." Suzy turned and ran back down the steps, just as excited as on her way up.

Tracy closed the door halfway and began to unpack. First and foremost, out of her suitcase came her most prized possession, her stuffed tiger 'Jerry.' Her dad had given her Jerry as her birthday present when she was 6: A few months later, her dad had died unexpectedly in his sleep. Jerry was the only thing left of her family, and he knew his job was to stand guard and protect her.

Tracy continued unpacking and exploring her room, still wondering if she was in some kind of dream. An hour later, she heard Mrs. Davis call up, and within another minute, Suzy appeared at Tracy's door, still as excited as before, "Are you ready for dinner?"

"Oh, yes, I'm hungry."

"Well, follow me."

Suzy ran down the steps. Tracy hurried behind her, politely running down the stairs, and walked into the dining room for the first time. It was a cozy room with a large table in the center. The table was adorned with a royal blue table cloth, matching dishes, and surrounded by five elegant chairs.

Ellen walked in from the kitchen and said, "Tracy, you sit over there by Suzy."

John and Alan came in next and sat down. Ellen went to the kitchen, then returned moments later carrying a small tray holding a platter of roast beef and side dishes of corn and carrots. She set them down, then went back in and returned with a bowl of mashed potatoes, a gravy boat, and a basket of rolls. Tracy was so excited as the meal would be the best she had had in ages.

After everyone was seated, John said, "Shall we thank the Lord?"

Everyone joined hands, and John began, "Heavenly Father, thank you for providing for us, as you always do. And we especially thank you for bringing Tracy here to our home. Now together, we say?"

Everyone joined in, "Bless us O Lord in these thy gifts which we are about to receive, from thy bounty, through Christ our Lord. Amen."

Tracy knew the prayer, and she followed along in a soft voice. She had never been welcomed to a foster home so warmly, and it thrilled her, but part of her knew how things went. The warm and fuzzy beginning eventually waned and led to her having to leave. Still, the Davis family was truly special. Maybe this time, things would be different.

~ ~ ~ ~

That night when everyone was asleep, Tracy lurched up in her bed, shaking from another nightmare. It was the same nightmare she always had, especially at times when she was under stress. Suddenly facing another foster family was definitely one of those times.

In her dream, she is 7 years old, and her mother is taking her to a park filled with children, swings, and all kinds of things to play with. In the dream, her mom asks Tracy to sit on the bench and tells her she will be right back. Tracy sits on the bench for a long time, but her mom does not return. Tracy gets up, panicked, and runs all over the park looking for her mom. At one point, she gets too close to a pond, far away from the play area, and that is when an older couple stops her. They start to question her, and Tracy begins to cry and tells them she is looking for her mom. She tells them her mom is coming right back.

The dream is always the same, but it isn't a dream. Long ago, her mother did leave her in the park, and she never returned. The police later discovered her mother had rented a home near the park months earlier under an assumed name. They would never locate her, and Tracy became a ward of the state.

Tracy lay awake, looking at the full moon illuminating the large tree outside her window. She cried quietly, pressing her face into her pillow. She learned to cry this way in the County Home so the other children would not hear her. Her tears dried up, and she thought back to the kind old nun who used to visit her there.

Sister Gertrude had told her that if she asked God for anything and honestly believed, He would give it to her. However, Sister Gertrude also said that answers to some prayers could take a long time to come true. Tracy never forgot those words, and she did pray almost every night, asking God to give her a normal life. She wanted to get married and become a mom and have lots of children, and she always vowed she would never leave them.

Tracy reached over for her tiger Jerry and pulled him close before falling back asleep.

Chapter Two

Two Years Later

Tracy's time with the Davis family were the most beautiful years she could ever remember. Her days were filled with joy and happiness, and being part of the Davis household gave her a new outlook on life. But deep inside, she worried. She was getting older, and she knew the time would come when she would have to leave. Foster homes were not meant to be forever.

One evening the whole family was sitting at the dinner table. Everyone was unusually quiet. At one point, Ellen said, "Tracy, Mr. Davis and I, and Suzy and Alan have been talking."

Tracy's heart stopped. Here was the moment she had been dreading. She looked up, "Yes, what is it?"

Ellen half-smiled, "Well, as I said, we have been talking together, and we were wondering if you would be willing..." Ellen paused, and wiped a tear from the corner of her eye, then started over, "We were wondering if we could adopt you so that you would become our daughter and be part of our family."

Tracy closed her eyes. The long, painful years of feeling unwanted, the years of being held close, then pushed away, were suddenly thrust back to the forefront. She lowered her head as tears began forming in her eyes. The truth was she was afraid, afraid it was not for real, afraid of failing.

Ellen got up and knelt next to her, hugging her, "I am sorry Tracy, did I upset you?"

Tracy closed her eyes tighter, trying to stop the tears, and managed to say, "No... you didn't." But it was all she could say.

Ellen looked over at John, and he asked, "Tracy, is that a yes?"

Tracy paused for a moment, then looked up through tear-stained eyes and began nodding, trying to stop herself from crying, finally saying, "Yes... I would like that very much."

Ellen pulled her close and hugged her tightly, and they both started crying. Suzy and Alan jumped up and ran around the table to hug Tracy, one on each side, bringing an end to the tears, bringing the needed laughter and joy.

After everyone celebrated, they all sat back down and began to eat. John and Ellen looked at each other, and then Ellen asked, "Tracy, from now on, we want you to call us Mom and Dad?"

"Yes, I will, Mrs. Davis... uhh... I mean, Mom."

Within a week, the adoption papers were drawn up and signed. Tracy now began her life as an official member of the Davis family.

Five Years Later

Under the Davis home's stability, Tracy became an excellent student, and after high school, she was accepted to The Ohio State University in the International Affairs Department. The first couple of years at Ohio State, passed very quickly. Belonging to the larger school community meant a great deal to her, and she loved the atmosphere and the excitement of campus life.

On an unusually warm Indian Summer afternoon, Tracy finished her chemistry lab class and walked out of the building. She paused at the top of the steps and looked out at the campus grounds. *What an amazing day,* she thought. Below her in the open area between the buildings, hundreds of students were outside enjoying the day. She walked down the sidewalk toward a bench and sat down near some guys playing frisbee.

She recognized one of them, thinking to herself, *Boy, he's cute. Where do I know him from?* The young man was tall and tan and had a great smile, and at that very moment, he was jumping up into the air to snag the frisbee. He laughed as he landed, turned, and fired the frisbee back at his friends. *Oh, I know, he was in Algebra class with me.*

The four young men continued their game, narrowly missing nearby students. Tracy glanced up periodically as she was studying her notes for her next class. At one point, when she looked up, she noticed the young man was looking right at her, smiling.

The game ended, and they all picked up their belongings, heading in different directions for their next class. Tracy got back to her studies but then noticed that he was walking toward her. She felt her heart begin to race, and she looked back down at her notes.

The young man stopped right in front of her and said, "Hi, didn't we have a class together last semester?"

Tracy looked up, feigning surprise, "Oh, hi… I'm not sure."

The young man said, "Algebra, last semester?"

Tracy shielded the sun from her eyes, "Oh yes, I remember."

"By the way, I'm Kevin."

"Hi, Kevin, I'm Tracy."

He asked, "Can I sit down?"

"Sure," said Tracy. She was thrilled and couldn't help but smile.

Kevin asked, "So, what are you reading?

"Oh, I'm reading about the Middle East for one of my International Affairs classes. That's my major."

Tracy then asked, "What are you majoring in?"

"I'm a marketing major."

"Well, that sounds interesting."

"I like it, and I have an internship coming up."

"That sounds nice."

"Yes, it helps to get into the real world."

The sun shined brightly on them as they sat in silence for a moment. Kevin then asked, "Would you like to go have some pizza together sometime?"

"Yea, sure, I would."

"Okay, how tomorrow at lunchtime?"

"Yes, that works."

"Okay then, I'll meet you here at say noon, we can walk over together."

"Alright," said Tracy, "I'll see you then."

~ ~ ~ ~

Tracy and Kevin dated for the remainder of college, during which time they fell deeply in love. They were married soon after graduation. Tracy's parents gave her away in a beautiful ceremony at the old Episcopal Chapel on campus. They bought a house in the suburbs of Columbus, joined the neighborhood church, and began their life together. They were so happy and so in love that they felt God was smiling down on them.

Chapter Three

One Year Later

It did not take long for the young couple to find they were expecting their first child. The time of Tracy's pregnancy went quickly, and on a cloudy morning in late October, Tracy and Kevin woke up at 4 a.m. in the morning. Tracy's water had broken.

They nervously rushed into the car and raced to the emergency room. An orderly took her back to a room, and within minutes a doctor came in. "Okay, we are going to take you right upstairs to the maternity ward."

Tracy asked, "Am I going to have the baby?"

The doctor smiled, "Yes, your water broke, and that means that your little baby is on its way into the world. Don't worry, though everything will be just fine."

An orderly came and helped Tracy into the wheelchair and wheeled her through the long hospital corridors, with Kevin in tow, to a large elevator that took them up to a bustling maternity ward.

Four hours later, Tracy lay on the delivery room table, exhausted, as the nurse carefully placed the bundled-up baby boy onto her chest. Tracy began to cry tears of joy, saying, "Thank you, God."

Kevin leaned over and kissed her as Tracy uttered her first words to her new baby, "Hello there. You're so beautiful."

She looked up at Kevin, with hopeful eyes, as he placed his tear-stained cheek against hers, and they kissed and together gazed upon the face of their newborn son.

They had discussed several 'boy' names but had not yet settled on one. Kevin asked Tracy, "What would you like to name him, honey?"

"Duncan," Tracy whispered.

Kevin peered into the boy's eyes and said, "Hello Duncan, I'm your dad."

~ ~ ~ ~

A fantastic year of change ensued, filled with the myriad of things a young family with a new child encounter. Their home was now point-central for all their parents and siblings. Hope for the future became the touchstone of life together. Tracy's life-long dream of having a normal life was unfolding before her very eyes.

When Duncan was a few months shy of two, Tracy felt it was time for her to get started toward her career goals. She put together her resume and began applying for jobs with local international firms. She was excited to enter the workforce and trusted she would find a job where she could keep life in balance.

On a particularly pleasant morning in June, her mother Ellen stopped over to visit. She and Tracy shared coffee while Duncan sat quietly in his booster seat at the kitchen table. As they talked, Duncan mumbled something, banged his fist, and knocked his bowl of baby cereal off the table, splattering it all over the floor.

Tracy tried in vain to catch the bowl, exclaiming, "Oh Duncan." She smiled and went to the counter to grab some paper towels to clean up the mess.

Ellen watched as Duncan did not follow his mother's cleaning up as any toddler would, but blankly stared off into the distance. Ellen hesitated and then asked. "Tracy, have you noticed anything unusual about Duncan?"

"No, not really, why?" she asked as she stopped wiping the floor and looked up at her mother.

"Well... what I mean is, have you had him checked at the doctor recently?"

"Oh yes," answered Tracy, pretending there was no issue. Her fears, though, of recent weeks suddenly resurfaced. She said, "We were at the pediatrician a few months ago, and Duncan is up to date on everything. The doctor said he is perfectly healthy. Why are you asking mom?"

"I don't know. For a moment, he just seemed to be not acting normally. I'm not sure. It's probably nothing. But maybe you should let the doctor re-evaluate him." Ellen paused, then added, "He doesn't seem to be paying attention. Has he said any other words yet?"

Tracy's heart quietly plummeted into her already tightening stomach. "Not really, but he's still young. It's different for every child."

"Well, listen, just get him checked out."

"I will, Mom, but I'm sure it's nothing. I have an appointment in about three weeks. I can mention it then."

Tracy had lied to her mom. She *had* noticed signs for the last few weeks that something was wrong. Duncan was not responding to his name, and he hardly ever smiled. She was secretly hoping that she was imagining things and thought a little time would erase all her fears.

That afternoon, as Duncan napped, Tracy sank into her couch, desperately afraid, knowing she had to make the call. She picked up the phone and dialed her pediatrician, and made an appointment for the following afternoon.

~ ~ ~ ~

The following day was gloomy. The sun had all but disappeared, and threatening rain clouds were rolling in from the east. Kevin went to work as usual, but today he arranged to leave work early to go to the appointment. He picked up Tracy and Duncan, and they drove to the office of Duncan's pediatrician, Dr. Sam Fawzy.

They sat in the waiting room for a short time until they were ushered into the exam room. After a few preliminary questions from the nurse, the nurse left, saying, "Dr. Fawzy will be in shortly."

Tracy sat nervously in the chair, holding Duncan in her lap. Kevin stood across from her, leaning against the wall of the cramped exam room. Neither said a word. Both were apprehensive at what they might find out. After 10 minutes of anxious waiting, Dr. Fawzy walked in. "Good afternoon, and how is Duncan doing?"

Tracy felt the weight of the world on her. She wanted to say to him that everything was fine, though she knew it wasn't. She began, "Well, doctor, he is fine... but it just seems, sometimes he's not..." She wiped her moistening eyes quickly, hoping the doctor would not notice, and said, "Sometimes, it seems he's not paying attention."

"I see. Let me check a few things." Dr. Fawzy raised Duncan's shirt and placed his stethoscope, listening, and asked, "Is he eating normally?"

"Yes," replied Kevin.

"Has he been sick at all?"

Tracy replied, "No, not in a while, doctor."

"All right, hold him comfortably in your lap Tracy. I'm going to do a few screenings."

Dr. Fawzy took out a penlight from his shirt pocket, "Hi Duncan, see my light?" Dr. Fawzy moved it around at a few angles, flashing it into Duncan's eyes. He put the light in his pocket and gently snapped his fingers a few times, near and away from Duncan's field of vision. He took a deep breath and repeated his actions again. When he finished, he said, "Duncan is not really responding as he should. I think we should let a specialist check him."

Tracy's heart fell to the floor. She looked down, searching, then looked up quickly, asking, "What do you think it is?"

"I cannot be sure," said Dr. Fawzy, "Duncan may just be having an off day. These screening tests are nothing more than that."

"But I don't understand. What kind of specialist do you want us to see?" asked Tracy.

"A doctor who specializes in Autism."

"Autism?" Tracy asked, surprised, yet she was not so alarmed. She knew someone whose child was autistic. Tracy did not completely understand, but she knew he was low on what was called the spectrum, and he lived a normal life. Tracy felt a great sense of relief, imagining Duncan might have a similar condition.

Chapter Four

Within a week, Duncan visited the specialist for diagnostic testing. After an hour, the doctor delivered the news to Kevin and Tracy. Duncan was autistic, and there was a strong possibility of it being very high on the spectrum.

Kevin and Tracy's beautiful world suddenly turned entirely upside down. They walked out of the doctor's office on a sunny afternoon, carrying Duncan in their arms, and before they made it to their car, it started to rain.

They buckled Duncan in and started for home, neither of them saying a word. Tracy sat in the passenger seat, staring blankly into the afternoon rush hour as the rain pelted the windshield. The numbness reached all the way back to her uneasy feelings of childhood. *All I ever wanted was a normal family.* Only the mindless rhythm of the wiper blades kept her from going over the edge.

Kevin could see Tracy was devastated, and he tried to hold his own emotions in check for her sake, but his world was rocked to the core as well.

Over the next several weeks, Tracy felt intense grief, and she held it privately in her heart. She had never told Kevin of her desire to have a normal family, and it just did not feel it was time now, either.

Kevin adjusted more easily and accepted the news. He had come rom a large family who had seen its share of suffering. Kevin knew full well that life had its difficulties. He knew the only way to deal with them was to pick yourself up, trust in God, and move forward.

Tracy had strong faith too, but she was not willing to accept Duncan's condition. She prayed harder and silently every day, seeking a miracle, just as Sr. Gertrude had told her to pray for whatever she needed.

Over the ensuing months, as other toddlers Duncan's age were busy talking away and beginning to socialize more easily with other children, Duncan showed little improvement. Instead, his condition only became more apparent. His form of Autism was, indeed, very severe.

As the next year progressed, Duncan's condition progressed, and it became apparent he had other issues as well. His head began to shake for no reason, and his blank stares into the distance now became his normal gaze. He could not speak at all, and it soon became apparent that it was possible he never would.

Tracy would not accept that his condition was permanent, though. She kept seeking medical advice from specialists and praying for a miracle cure for her son.

Two Years Later

"You're going to have another baby," said Tracy's family doctor. She had suspected she was pregnant, but now it was confirmed. She closed her eyes for a moment, with a myriad of emotions running through her mind. She was already overwhelmed as a stay-at-home mom with a special-needs child. Her plans of trying to start a career were now completely on hold. This news of another child on the way scared her some, as she feared it might all become too much for her. But that was not all that was bothering her.

She drove home quietly, thinking, then called Kevin to tell him the good news. That night after they got Duncan to bed, they celebrated by having a glass of wine and ordering some pizza. They went to be early and made love long into the night.

Over the next few days, Tracy wrestled with her fears and finally decided she needed to talk to Kevin. After Duncan was in bed for the night, she sat down in the living room with Kevin. "Kevin, I have to talk to you about something that is bothering me."

"Sure, honey. What is it?"

"What if this baby has Autism too? What are we going to do?"

"If he or she does, we'll get through it. We will accept whatever child God sends, no matter what."

"I know that, of course, but I'm afraid. I... I don't know if I will be able to handle it."

Kevin pulled her close, "It will be okay, Tracy, no matter what happens, we'll work together, and we are going to get someone to help during the day when the baby comes."

Tracy sighed, "I think that is a good idea… I'm mentally exhausted, Kevin."

Kevin held her tightly for a long time. He was also concerned, and as he held her, he silently said a prayer that their second child would be healthy, mentally, and physically.

After nine long months, the worrisome pregnancy gave way to the birth of a baby girl. They named her Sarah Ellen after both mothers. The new baby brought a newfound level of joy to Kevin and Tracy. Along with this joy came a new level of daily demands. Caring for Duncan, along with a newborn, immersed the family in a chaotic world, but one blessed by love and life's little joys.

Kevin and Tracy embraced these days, spending their time focused on their children. Like so many parents of a special needs child, hard work was the order of each day, along with establishing a routine for Duncan so he would feel safe.

Now the anxious early years of waiting to see if Sarah had any symptoms of Autism passed without incident.

Both grandmothers helped out a few times a week, but they were busy, and at times the help seemed sporadic. Kevin wanted to bring in a caregiver for Duncan, to offer more steady assistance. One evening, when Duncan and Sarah were in bed, he talked it over with Tracy.

"Tracy, I think we need to hire someone to help you more consistently."

"No, Kevin. We can't afford it for one."

"Listen, we can afford it. I thought we would find someone just a few hours a day. You can be here, or, if you need to, you can go to the store, or just take a break."

"Kevin, I don't think it is a good idea. Duncan needs very special attention, all day long. Someone else won't understand that. I… I just don't think he will be taken care of."

Neither said a word for several long moments. Tracy asked, "Can you come home earlier?"

Kevin grimaced. The economy was not doing great, and his company was already talking about having to lay people off. Right now, he felt strongly he had to do all he could to hold onto his job and to their health benefits. "I don't, I can't right now, Tracy. Things are shaky over there."

"Look, I will be fine. Our moms are doing enough, and I will try to rest more or relax some when they are here."

Kevin nodded, he took her into his arms and hugged her tightly. "The kids are lucky to have you."

She looked up into his eyes, "They're lucky to have you too." She kissed him warmly and said, "Let's turn in early tonight. I miss you."

Kevin smiled, nodding, "I miss you too."

~ ~ ~ ~

By the time Duncan turned 5, Tracy had found herself becoming angry at God. Her dream world that she so desperately and faithfully prayed for most of her life seemed shattered. Just as, long ago, her real mom shattered her dreams by abandoning her in the park.

Tracy would often lay awake for hours, silently crying out to God for help, still clinging in the back of her mind to Sister Gertrude's formula, which said, 'you must believe.' Tracy wanted to believe, but increasingly, the 'you must believe' part of Sister Gertrude's formula seemed futile. She had done her part by faithfully praying since she was a young girl, but as far as she was concerned, God had not done his. One day, she abandoned all hope of believing, and her prayers changed to begging God to heal Duncan.

Chapter Five

By the age of six, Duncan's interior life had become a constant battle of feeling overwhelmed. His senses were out of sync, and everything around him hit him with extraordinary force. He heard everything, saw everything, smelled everything, and all of it, when combined, often became too much for his mind to handle. His hypersensitivity made the world hostile many times a day. The only respite he had from all of this was the solace of his home life's order and routine elements.

Tracy instinctively knew this and tried her best to provide that environment. Sarah's demands, only being 4 years old, and the demands of modern life meant Tracy could not be completely consistent. This would not matter to a normal child, but Duncan desperately needed this consistency.

Duncan was starting to grow taller and stronger, and this was causing difficulties of its own. His ability to communicate verbally or in any written form did not exist at all, and his non-verbal communication was severely stunted. It was rare that either of his parents would ever know what he wanted, and very frequently, his needs were misinterpreted, causing him deep frustration, which he was beginning to show through tirades no one could interpret.

Duncan understood it all, he was aware of everything, and he knew that no one knew this. Deep inside his mind, he knew what he wanted or needed, and he knew what his parents wanted or might be trying to convey. The constant frenzy of his mind stopped any of it from forming into any coherent words or actions.

Duncan also possessed a high degree of emotional intelligence. As the oldest, he was keenly aware of the emotions of his parents, especially his mom. Duncan understood her words and felt her feelings. He also felt the unconditional love she had for him and for his sister Sarah. He had no way to show her that he knew.

During the long hours of the day, Duncan silently witnessed Tracy's moments of happiness, and also frustration, and even despair often caused by his actions. There were days when he would see her break down and cry, and though he wanted to comfort her, his mind was too immersed in chaos to do anything.

He understood his actions were causing both of his parents' stress. It made him feel sad, and he wanted to tell them he was sorry, but there was no way. No one realized the severity of his emotional suffering, as everyone just assumed that this was the way he was, and they incorrectly assumed that he was content in his disabled state.

There were other moments, plenty of them, happy moments of family joy. Duncan perceived these too, and the excitement they would bring were not easy for him to handle either, often sending him into a frenzy. But they were happy nonetheless, and the entire family was united in their shared mission of helping each other and Duncan through life.

~ ~ ~ ~ ~

On early Thursday morning, Tracy's mother Ellen, called to say she was sick and would not be able to watch the children while Tracy went grocery shopping. Tracy tried her mother-in-law, but she was not home, so she decided to go to the store, taking Duncan and Sarah with her.

Tracy preferred to go alone, but once in a while, she took them along when no one was available to watch them. Duncan was always harder to handle at the grocery store, but Tracy had learned how to make it work. She imagined that Duncan enjoyed getting out of the house.

From Duncan's point of view, the smells, the noises, the bright lights, the faces of strangers... all these were very difficult for him. On the other hand, he did enjoy being outside and going to a new place besides his house.

When Tracy arrived, Duncan was already on edge. She thought about going back home but decided that she would pick up just a few necessities and return home since they had already made it inside the store.

Duncan's trial began as they passed the fresh food counters along the back wall of the store. The strong smells of the seafood counter sickened him. Sarah was also not herself today and was whining and pleading with her mom to hold her hand, which Tracy could not do, because she was holding Duncan's hand.

Duncan's mind was beginning to chant, *Too loud. Too loud.*

Tracy did not know, only hearing his usual unintelligible mumbling. She whisked through the store, holding onto her goal of getting only a few things and getting home.

When they got to the checkout line, an older lady in front of them was wearing perfume so strong that Duncan felt like vomiting. His mind began to chant, *Feel Sick. Feel sick.* He jumped up and down, trying to get Tracy's attention. His mind was screaming. *Get out. Get out.* All Tracy could see or hear was his normal nervousness and mumbling. "It's okay, Duncan, we are going home soon."

Tracy quickly unloaded her cart, and the clerk began scanning the items. "Beep." "Beep." "Beep." "Beep."

Duncan put his hands on his head. His mind was overloaded. *Stop! Stop! Get out!* He wanted to cover his ears, but with little motor skills, he could not. He jumped up and down and looked behind him toward the front door. His mind was screaming now, *No! No! Out! Get Out!* The register kept roaring, "Beep." "Beep." "Beep." "Beep." Duncan suddenly panicked, shouting out loud, "Ouuhhh... ouuhhh... ouuhhh." He unintentionally pushed Sarah down in his effort to race out of the store. Sarah fell and began to cry loudly, inflaming the chaos of the moment.

Tracy screamed, "Duncan!" as she tried in vain to grasp him, but Sarah screamed only louder, and Tracy had suddenly lost all control of her two children.

"Duncan!" Tracy yelled again as she ran through the front end of the store after him. One of the clerks saw him running for the door and realized Tracy was trying to stop him and stepped in Duncan's way. Duncan stopped and started screaming, "Aaahhhhh! Aahhhhhh!" His mind screaming inside, *Get out! Get out!*

He broke free from the lady and ran to the automatic door. When the door would not open, because it was the entry door and not the exit, Duncan threw himself down in frustration, rolling on the ground.

Tracy reached him and picked him up, holding him tightly, whispering, "It's okay, Duncan. It's okay." Duncan kept moaning.

The manager came running over and assisted Tracy. He had their few groceries brought out to the car by one of the clerks. He helped Tracy, Duncan, and Sarah outside and made sure they were all safely in their car. Tracy said, "Thank you. Oh my gosh, I forgot to pay!"

"Don't worry a bit about that. These are on us today. You go home and rest with your family."

"I should pay you," Tracy said.

"I won't hear another word about it. We'll see you next week."

"Thank you," Tracy said as she nodded, and the manager closed the door.

Tracy waited until the manager made it into the store, put her head down and began to cry, Sarah started to cry too, and Duncan was making sounds no one understood except him.

Soon, in the isolation of the car, Duncan finally began to quiet down. His mom's tears broke his heart. *Stop mommy. Stop. I sorry! I sorry!* He wanted so bad to tell her, but all he could do was mumble and stare out the window of the van.

Tracy now knew that she needed more help from her family and friends if only to get groceries. Duncan needed to be left at home. Today proved it.

Chapter Six

The next year brought news of the couple expecting another baby, and nine months later, the family welcomed their third child, a boy named Zachary.

The first two years held the same anxiousness they felt with Sarah, wondering if the child would be autistic, but it passed, and gradually a sense of relief settled in for Tracy and Kevin. Another child's adjustment was harder because of Duncan's particular needs, but Tracy held herself together as best she could. She was learning how to be strong. But her habit of often trying to do it all herself continued, and she did not accept help as often as she should.

One day when Duncan was 10, everything changed. Tracy's resilience had reached a tipping point. She was alone in the kitchen cooking when Duncan threw his dish across the room and ran away from the table. Tracy yelled. "Duncan! Why did you do that?" Sarah started to cry, and Zachary, who was already fidgeting in the playpen for his bottle, became startled, and he too started to cry.

Tracy turned to pick up Zachary, but Sarah only screamed louder, wanting attention too. At that moment, something in her mind shut down.

Her heart raced, her mind went blank, and her breathing slowed. She was not even aware she had snapped, and she robotically turned off the stove and walked down the hall toward the front door. Without saying a word, she sat down on the stairs' bottom step that led to the upstairs bedrooms. She held her head in her hands and cried.

Over the next hour or so, the phone rang several times, it was Kevin. He was calling from work. Duncan would answer and would quickly hang up. Finally, after several tries, Sarah picked up.

Kevin asked anxiously, "Honey, where's mommy?"

"Mommy is on the steps, daddy."

"Go get her, sweetheart?"

"She said to call back, daddy."

Kevin hung up, and a half-hour later tried again. Sarah picked up the phone again, and Kevin could hear Zachary crying in the background. "Sarah, tell mommy I need to talk to her."

"She's crying, daddy."

"Where is Duncan?"

"He's in the kitchen."

Kevin had heard enough. He knew something was very wrong. He told his boss he had an emergency at home and left, driving home as quickly as he could through the afternoon rush hour. He parked in the drive and ran up to the front door. He opened the door and saw Tracy sitting frozen on the steps, her eyes reddened from hours of crying. She had a look on her face that scared him, she just stared forward into nothingness.

"Tracy, what's wrong. Tracy! Tracy, what happened?"

There was no response.

He ran down the hall, as Sarah came running around the corner to greet him. He picked her up and walked into the kitchen and family room area. Duncan was sitting in front of the TV, bobbing up and down, with food all over the living room floor and all over his face and hair. Zachary was screaming in his playpen.

Kevin saw that the clothing from the basket he had folded before he left for work was strewn over the house in every direction. Pots and pans, and anything else Sarah and Duncan could get into, were also strewn everywhere. Kevin sighed and thanked God they were at least safe.

He picked up the baby and ran back to Tracy, kneeling beside her, "Tracy! Are you okay? Tracy?"

He couldn't get her to talk. She just stared straight ahead. Kevin called 911 and then called her parents, Ellen and John, who came right over. An ambulance arrived and evaluated Tracy. She looked okay physically but appeared to be in a catatonic state, so they took her to the hospital.

Kevin followed the ambulance as best he could. Tears were flowing down his face, as all he could see in his mind was Tracy's blank stare. The ER doctors concluded Tracy was experiencing a mental breakdown, so they admitted her to the psychiatric unit for evaluation and care.

As they rolled her out of the ER room toward the psych unit, she looked at Kevin with no response other than tears rolling down her face.

~ ~ ~ ~

After five days in the hospital, Tracy had stabilized to a large degree. Kevin was there with her, waiting for Dr. Craig Ryan, the Psychiatrist assigned to her, to come in. They were supposed to speak with him today about the next steps for her recovery.

The doctor walked in and asked, "Good morning, Tracy. How are you today?"

"I'm okay, I guess."

Dr. Ryan asked, "How do you feel about going home?"

She looked out the window with despair on her face, "I don't know if I can handle it."

Kevin sat down on the edge of the bed and put his arm around her.

Tracy looked over at him, "I don't think I'm ready, Kevin, I'm afraid of what's going to happen."

Kevin nodded, rubbing her back. "That's okay with me, Tracy. You can stay here." He looked up at the doctor to see if he agreed.

Dr. Ryan was nodding subtly, as he had not made up his mind. "Kevin, can you arrange for Tracy to continue her bed rest at home, say for a week or two? This way, she can be back home with the family, but without any responsibility."

"Yes, I am sure I can. The whole family has pulled together."

Dr. Ryan turned to Tracy. "Tracy, how does that sound to you?"

Tracy's eyes showed she was scared some, but she slowly nodded and said, "I think that I would like that."

Dr. Ryan then said, "Well, Tracy, stay here one more night, and if you feel well tomorrow morning, Kevin can pick you up after lunch. How does that sound?"

"That sounds good to me," Tracy said.

Kevin stood up and walked Dr. Ryan to the door, then returned and said goodbye to Tracy.

The next day, he ushered her out of the hospital, and they drove home. Tracy walked in, hugged each of the children, and went directly upstairs to her room. The feelings of anxiety she feared she would have upon arriving home came sweeping in. She got under the covers and went to sleep, glad to be home but very worried she would be unable to cope with the reality that was waiting for her downstairs.

Over the next week, Kevin took vacation time and stayed home. He and Tracy's mother pitched in, and they all took turns watching the children and making sure Tracy had everything she needed.

Throughout each day, Kevin would periodically walk up the stairs to check on her. Tracy laid curled up in a fetal position most of the time, staring blankly out the window. Every time he would ask, "Tracy, are you okay? Do you need anything, honey?" There was usually no response, but sometimes, she would softly say, "I need to rest after several uncomfortable minutes."

That was always the end of the conversation.

Kevin began to worry that Tracy would never pull out. He started making plans in his head to have someone take care of the kids each day when he returned to work.

Chapter Seven

It was Saturday afternoon, the fifth day since she had arrived back home, and in Tracy's mind, things were becoming clearer. The fork in the road seemed evident. Her despair that God would never help Duncan now turned to a siege, a siege demanding action. Her silent, tear-filled prayer became *God, either heal Duncan or take me out of this world because I can't handle it. I cannot return to the way things were.*

This went on for several days, with Tracy sitting up on her bed praying, reading, and periodically staring out the window, hoping to get an answer to her silent request.

It was Saturday in the very early evening, and the sun shined brightly into the window, brighter than usual, lighting up the entire room. Everything grew unusually quiet, and Tracy felt herself drifting into the silence. An overwhelming sense of peace and love flooded her entire being. The warmth she felt was unexplainable, yet she knew it was God; she could sense his presence.

She closed her eyes, letting the tears of long pent-up anguish flow, basking in the warm feeling for a long time. Then afraid to open her eyes and risk breaking the trance, she held her eyes tightly closed and spoke into the stillness. "Oh, God… I wanted a normal, healthy family… you… you know that is all I ever wanted. Please, please heal Duncan." Tears were cascading down her cheeks, years of unfulfilled hope pressing up from deep within her. She lowered her head, shaking it, then shouted in anger into the air, "Why did you let this happen to me?"

It was quiet for a moment. Then she heard the words echo in her mind as clear as day, "Because he *needed* someone like you."

Tracy held her breath, pondering what she had heard. She let out a deep breath, then burst into tears. It was not the answer she wanted, but it was an answer she could grab hold of.

She began to weep, tears of exhaustion, tears of so many years of frustration, then lifted her head and continued basking in the light, asking for strength, asking for understanding. Something real was happening between her and Heaven. An exchange was taking place. She was letting go, and courage was pouring in. She let out all the tears that were left inside and drifted off. When she opened her eyes, it was dusk.

~ ~ ~ ~

Tracy got up from bed, showered, and dressed appropriately for the first time since her breakdown. She quietly made her bed, threw her clothes down the laundry chute, and went downstairs. Kevin was in the living room sitting on the couch with Sarah, holding Zachary. Duncan sat on the floor in front of them, bouncing up and down, watching TV. Kevin turned his head, "Tracy?"

She smiled and nodded, unsure what to even say.

Kevin put Zachary down and ran over to embrace her, holding her tightly, letting her rest her head on his shoulder, "Tracy, are you okay?"

She looked into his loving eyes. "Yes, I am. I'm going to be okay."

Kevin hugged her again tightly, as Sarah ran up, crying out, "Mommy, Mommy."

Tracy bent down and picked her up, hugging her tightly. "I've missed you, honey. Mommy is okay now." Tracy carried her into the living room and set her on the couch, where Zachary was waiting. She hugged Zachary, then held him close, kissing him. She set him on the couch next to Sarah and bent down in front of Duncan. She helped him to stand and hugged him tightly. "I love you, Duncan."

Duncan began jumping up and down, turning around as he did, muttering "Maaa… Mmmmaaa…"

Kevin announced, "I'm ordering pizza, and we are celebrating!" Sarah started to clap, and Duncan, sensing the mood, began jumping even more.

Tracy took Duncan by the hand and sat down on the couch with the other children while Kevin called in for pizza. She now understood that Duncan desperately needed her. Sara and Zachary did too. But more importantly, she now understood that Duncan's life was a gift, not a burden. A tear rolled out of her eye as she realized that somehow, she needed him just as much as he needed her. It was part of her calling in life, and she now fully accepted Duncan's condition and would never question God again.

Until now, she had been reluctant to join a support group, but she did the research and went to a group. She ended up meeting and making wonderful friends. Friends who understood her plight. Years of graced living followed, surrounded by people who realized what her family was going through.

Chapter Eight

When Duncan was 14, his parents became friends with the McReynolds family, who they had met at their church. They had a daughter who was Duncan's age named Annie. Annie was only two years older than Sarah, so Annie and Sarah usually spent time together when they visited.

From the moment Duncan met Annie, he developed a crush on her, yet he did not understand it. Every time Annie came over, Duncan wanted to be around her. He was strangely calmer when she was over, not a lot, but enough for Tracy and Kevin to notice.

One Saturday in the late afternoon, the McReynolds came over for a cookout. Kevin and Mr. McReynolds went out back to talk, while Tracy and Mrs. McReynolds stayed in the kitchen to fix a salad. Sarah took Annie out to the yard to play, and they began swinging on the swing set.

Duncan followed them around as best he could, trying to be near to Annie. At one point, he tried grabbing Annie's hand and shaking it up and down, smiling, muttering unintelligible words. Sarah protested, "Duncan, let Annie swing on the swing set!"

Annie replied, "It's okay, Sarah." She smiled at him, "Hi Duncan!"

Duncan tugged at her hand, muttering something, so Annie asked, "Duncan, do you want to show me something?"

Duncan turned, pulled her by the hand, and led Annie into the house with Sarah following them. When he got inside and stood in front of his mom and Mrs. Reynolds, he did not know what to do, so he started excitedly jumping up and down.

Tracy smiled, "Duncan, go outside with Annie and swing on the swing set."

Duncan paused, then grabbed Annie's hand again, jumping up and down, smiling at her. Mrs. McReynolds said, "He's so cute."

Annie said, "Let's go, Duncan." This time, she led him by the hand outside.

Duncan felt immense joy that he could not convey. The fact she was spending time with him and leading him outside meant the world to him. Before long, everyone was called to dinner.

As they were seated around the table, Duncan began to feel incredibly nervous, bobbing up and down in his chair, spewing unintelligible sounds. He got up and ran around the table, grabbing Annie's hand, muttering more unintelligible sounds.

Tracy knew he wanted to go outside, so she said, "Duncan, sit back down, honey. You can go outside after dinner." She got up and released his hand from Annie's and brought him back to his seat.

After a few quiet moments, Mr. McReynolds began telling a story. During the story, he became quite animated and started to laugh loudly. Before long, everyone was roaring with laughter at the funny story, everyone except Duncan. The laughter only served to put his already nervous emotions over the edge. He screamed and threw his plate of food into the air, immediately silencing everyone. He kept yelling, but he was embarrassed at having done so in front of Annie in his mind.

Tracy excused herself and took him upstairs, leaving everyone to finish dinner without them.

It was a sad moment for Duncan, one which he could not talk to anyone about. That night, all he remembered was the look on Annie's horrified face. He laid in his bed, mumbling and hardly slept the entire night.

The McReynolds understood entirely and were not in any way, upset. The families remained close friends, but Duncan was now afraid to be around Annie, and when they did visit, he kept to himself as much as he was able.

Another few years passed, and physically, Duncan was fast becoming a man. At 18 years old, he stood 5'10" and weighed 150 pounds. Tracy could no longer handle him or help him the way she used to. He was powerful now and very quick.

Duncan understood that he was beginning to do dangerous things, his parent's reactions to him confirmed it, but he could not help himself. Some mornings, while sitting eating breakfast, he would feel the impulse to get up and run. Kevin's mother noticed this on several occasions, and one day she decided they needed to talk, so she called Kevin on his cell phone.

"Hello?" said Kevin.

"Kevin, this is mom."

"Hi, mom, what's happening?"

"I wanted to speak with you and Tracy. Can I come over tonight?"

"Sure, come over after dinner."

"Okay, I'll see you then."

Kevin's mother came over, and the three sat in the dining room. She began, "I don't know how to say this, but I am worried about Duncan. Yesterday when I was watching him, he ran out into the street."

Kevin lowered his glance. This was not the first time he had heard something like this. Tracy said, "Kevin, we need to put locks high up on the doors."

Kevin shook his head, "I don't think that will work."

His mother said, "I don't like to say this, but perhaps Duncan would be safer in a home."

Tracy replied, "A home? No way!"

"But Tracy, it may be the safest place for him."

"Safe or not, I don't care. Duncan won't be taken care of properly in a home. No. He stays here with us."

Tracy got up and went into the kitchen, she felt it would be like putting her son into prison, and she refused to even consider it.

Kevin thanked his mom for her concern and idea, and the subject never came up again.

Chapter Nine

Four months after his 18th birthday, a young female Angel hovered outside Duncan's bedroom on a warm summer night. She looked inside and tapped on the window to wake him.

Duncan heard the tapping, opened his eyes, and quickly sat up. He heard the tapping again, so he got out of bed and lumbered over to the window. It was a bright moonlit night, and Duncan leaned closer and peered out into the darkness. Suddenly he found himself face to face with a beautiful young female.

The Angel smiled and waved. Duncan smiled back and began bouncing up and down as she reached down and raised the window. Duncan watched her climb inside. He took a step back, making room for her to step into the room.

"Hi, Duncan," she said cheerfully.

Duncan immediately felt she was the most beautiful being he had ever seen, but he was puzzled as to how a young woman could fly up to his window. However, he sensed her goodness and knew she posed no threat to him. He tilted his head, smiled, and stepped backward further, sitting back down on his bed, mumbling and gently bouncing up and down.

"Duncan, my name is Linda. I am one of Heaven's holy Angels, from the 4th Heavenly Realm, governed by the Great Archangel Raphael. And... I am your new Guardian Angel. The Lords of Heaven sent me to bring you a message." She walked over to him and slowly waved her hand above his head.

Duncan suddenly felt the noises around him grow quieter, and his ever-whirling thoughts slowed down. He began to mutter again and bounce on his bed.

Linda reached out and grasped his hand, and Duncan felt the energy. He looked into her eyes with his mind suddenly stiller than he had ever remembered.

She squeezed his hand and said, "Go ahead, Duncan."

Duncan began to try to form words, "Li... uh... uh... aahhhhh!" He stopped and looked down in frustration, but Linda squeezed his hand harder, "It's okay, Duncan, try again."

He looked up, "Li... Li... Li... Lin... Linda... Linda!" He began to smile. "Linda, I... I... am able to... speak."

Linda grasped his hand tightly and put her hand on top of his forehead again, this time whispering a prayer. She smiled and said, "Duncan, you will be able to speak while I am in your presence."

Duncan opened his mouth and began to utter words, which were not foreign to his mind, but which were foreign to his ears. It was the first time he heard his voice make clear sounds. "Linda? Are you... really an Angel?"

"Yes, why? Don't I look like an Angel?"

"You do," said Duncan. "I mean, I am... surprised... that you are here."

Linda laughed, "Most people are surprised the first time they see an Angel. So don't worry, you're not alone."

Linda was 5'4", slender, with green eyes and reddish, brown shoulder-length hair. She had been assigned to him only a short time earlier because Duncan's other Guardian Angel had been called away on an important mission. Up until now, she had only watched over Duncan from afar. Tonight was the first time she had heard his 'real voice,' and in hearing it, she could feel Duncan's immense goodness. It felt beautiful to her.

Neither said a word for a few moments, then Linda announced, "Oh, Duncan, I am your new Guardian Angel. I've only been watching over you for a couple of years. Your former Angel, well, he had to be reassigned."

"Reassigned? How come?"

"Oh, it's a long story, trouble with the dark side I am afraid."

Duncan nodded, he did not question her answer, and this surprised her. He said, "I've sensed your presence before, but I did not understand it."

"Really?" said Linda, even more surprised.

They were both silent for a while. Linda felt the specialness of the moment.

Something was pressing on Duncan's mind. He said, "Linda, no one understands me. My parents seem to... but they get frustrated a lot. What can I do? Will God cure me; will he allow me to be normal?"

Linda sat down next to him and turned to face him. "Duncan, when your parents conceived you, even though you would experience difficulty in life, the Lords of Heaven saw how beautiful your heart was. They decided way back then that you will be one of the Eternal Messengers of God's Love. You are one of the rare people who gets chosen for this."

Duncan took a deep breath. The years of feeling unimportant, the years of feeling like a burden to his family, fell away in one shining moment. He suddenly felt like his life had meaning. "But what is an Eternal Messenger?"

"I can't tell you everything now. I am only allowed to tell you the news. But, Duncan, it means that you are part of their plan to stop the actions of the Dark Side."

Duncan's face grew serious, as if he understood. This caught Linda by surprise also. She expected him to have a hundred questions, but he didn't have any. She grasped his hands, peering closely into his eyes, "Duncan, your heart is radiantly beautiful. I can feel it. The days of this life seem long, but they will pass quickly, and in the Eternal World, you will be a special beacon of light for others."

They sat in silence for a few moments. Duncan sighed, "Linda, there is something I have to tell you. Sometimes I have dreams, very dark dreams."

"What do you mean?" she asked, "Why do you say dark?"

"I see dark clouds rushing forward toward a mountain, but it seems like the mountain has something to do with Heaven."

Linda thought for a moment, and she began to get worried. "I will tell my superiors, Duncan. It may have to do with the fact you are to become an Eternal Messenger."

Again, they sat in silence for several moments. Linda's kindness and beauty reminded him of Annie. He still thought about Annie every day and every night. He wondered ever since then if he would ever feel that way for someone again.

Linda patted him on the knee and stood up, saying, "Duncan, I have to go now."

Duncan quickly stood up too, and gently grasped her hands, "Linda, don't leave, not right now. I want to talk with you for a little while longer."

"I will come back, Duncan. Be strong, young man."

"Bye, Linda," he said.

She climbed out the window, turned back for a moment to smile at him, then left.

Duncan watched her fly into the sky. A tear ran down his face. There was something about her he couldn't let go of. Her kindness and her beauty struck him as nothing else ever had struck him. He went to his bed and sat down. His mind began to grow frantic again, the noise his chaotic mind resurfaced, and he began to mutter unintelligible sounds again. But it didn't bother him anymore. He laid down, staring at the ceiling, smiling.

~ ~ ~ ~

In the next room, the sound of voices woke Tracy. She got up, hastily threw on her robe, and quickly walked down the hall to Duncan's room. She was sure she had just heard someone talking. She opened the door and turned on the light, "Duncan, are you okay? Is there someone in your room?"

Tracy looked around. An eerie feeling instantly came over her. She was sure now she had heard a woman's voice, and she was sure she had heard Duncan say, "Good-bye, Linda." Tracy walked over to the bed and glanced at the window, noticing it was slightly open. She looked down at Duncan, who was lying in his bed wide-awake. He motioned for her to come closer, and as she leaned closer, he reached up and gave her a warm hug.

"Duncan, honey, did you say something? Was someone here?"

Duncan nodded as if he could read her mind, which completely caught Tracy by surprise. He never communicated with any such clarity. She hugged him tightly, "Oh Duncan."

Duncan held his mother for a moment, then rolled over and fell asleep. Tracy put the cover over him, then walked over and turned off the light. She sat in the darkness at the foot of his bed, quietly thinking, gazing at the moonlight shining in through the open window. She sensed a warm presence in the room, something she had not sensed in a long time, not since she felt God's presence in her own room after coming home from the hospital so many years earlier.

Chapter Ten

The Dark Angel Sylvia flew into the southern shore of Luminare to the Dark Lord Legion's home. She landed and walked inside. He was waiting for her on the balcony overlooking the Sea. He turned, "What did you want?"

"I have found him, Lord Legion."

"Found who?"

"The Eternal Messenger destined to play an important role in the coming war."

"How do you know it is him?" Legion asked as he scanned her legs up and down.

"I was at Raphael's Headquarters. I listened outside the window after his new Guardian Angel was assigned."

"Very well. Where is he?"

"He lives in Columbus, Ohio, in America, Lord Legion."

"Good. Keep an eye on him. We need to be sure, then, we need to get him over onto this side of the divide."

"Yes, Lord Legion."

Legion smiled, "Now go into my room and wait for me."

~ ~ ~ ~

When Duncan was 19 years old, he woke from an intense dream with sweat beads rolling down his forehead on a hot summer night. He had dreams like this frequently over the last year, but this one shook him to the core. He knew that he needed to talk to Linda, so he went to his window and cried out in his mind, "Linda, Linda, please come."

He had not seen her since the night in his room over a year earlier. He cried out again, but this time to the Lords, "Lords of Heaven, please allow Linda to come to me this night!"

Suddenly a tiny bright light appeared just outside the window. Duncan stared with great hope as it flickered and then slowly grew larger. A moment later, Linda's face looked in the window, smiling and waving at him. She lifted the window open and stepped in. Duncan instinctively stepped backward and began bouncing on the edge of his bed, muttering unintelligible sounds. Linda walked over to his side and placed her hands on his head, saying a prayer to unlock his speech.

Duncan let out a deep sigh as he felt the frenzy of his mind grow quiet. His spiraling thoughts slowed and became clear. Duncan closed his eyes, drawing in a deep breath, as a tear fell down his face. "Linda, I'm so glad you came. I've missed you."

"Duncan, I've missed you too, but I've been watching over you." It surprised her how happy she was to see him and speak with him. Something about Duncan stayed with her. Even though she had numerous other clients, Duncan was on her mind almost every day since the night she visited him. Linda said, "My Host Commander said you requested I come."

"Yes," said Duncan wide-eyed, "You said my dreams last time were important. Well they have been becoming clearer and clearer to me."

"Really? Tell me about them, Duncan?"

"Tonight's was the most vivid. It scared me."

"Tell me about it, Duncan."

Duncan turned toward her and closed his eyes, remembering as he spoke, "I saw a dark figure in a dark hooded cape. He stood on top of a throne room that was on top of a large mountain. Three thrones were sitting empty in the throne room. This dark figure raised a scepter over his head and laughed with a roar that shook the entire world."

"Duncan, that sounds very..."

Duncan interrupted her, "Wait, there's something else."

"I'm sorry, go on." Linda was on the edge of her seat. She already knew this must have to do with Legion.

Duncan continued, "After he roared, dark clouds moved in from every direction and millions and millions of hideous-looking people, and Angels with very dark wings surrounded the mountain. I then saw Seven Angels in a circle, all dressed in white with their swords drawn, surrounding three people they seemed to be protecting."

Linda's alarm bells were going off. She knew exactly who all the characters he was referring to were. The thought of this happening at the Throne Room scared her. She grasped his hand tighter, "Duncan, I am glad you called me. I will relay this message to my superiors."

Duncan held fast to her hands. "Linda, don't leave yet. Stay just a little while. I want to talk with you for a little while longer."

Linda felt emotional. She was happy to see him too. "I can stay a little while."

Duncan took her hand, and they sat on the edge of the bed, looking out into the moonlight, neither speaking a word, both just happy to see the other.

Duncan asked. "How are you?"

"I am… doing well," she said, "Being a Guardian Angel is a lot of work! But then I meet… someone like you… and it all becomes easier."

"Will I be able to see you again?"

Linda smiled and grasped both his hands. "Yes… but I don't know when. I'm new at this, and… as far I know, it's not that often we get to reveal ourselves. I mean, you are kind of the only person I have revealed myself to." She lowered her head, "But when you feel my presence, know that I am near, watching over you."

Duncan loved her, and the joy he felt was overwhelming him. He just smiled, not knowing what to do. After a while, Linda said, "I must go." She grasped his hands and helped him stand, "Bye Duncan."

"Linda, please stay a little longer."

Linda nodded. She didn't want to leave either. There was something about his wisdom, his presence that drew her. She put her arm around him and hugged him in a warm embrace. "Duncan, you are a special young man. I'll stay for a little while longer."

They both sat back down and sat in silence. After several long quiet minutes, Duncan reached over and warmly kissed Linda on the cheek, with neither of them talking.

Linda's eyes opened wide, in shock. She didn't know what to say, but she knew what she was feeling. They sat still for a while longer, both quietly smiling, both aware of the special moment they just participated in. After a few minutes, Linda slowly got up and said, "I must go now, Duncan."

Duncan stood up again, "Can't you stay for a while?"

She leaned forward and whispered into his ear, "Duncan, I will see you again. Let your heart and mind be at peace now." She reached up and gently kissed him on the cheek, saying, "Remember this night, and remember this kiss."

Duncan watched her step backward toward the window and climb out. She gave one last wave before turning and leaving. Overwhelmed with joy and sudden hope for his future, he walked to the window, leaned out, and said into the night sky, "Goodbye, Linda."

The kiss had awakened something inside of him. It conveyed a feeling of true love, which he had always longed for but never imagined experiencing. He closed the window and laid down in his bed. Within a few moments, his mind began to slowly grow frenzied again. He tried to speak, but his ability had vanished. He was not sad, though; his mind and heart were on fire for the Angel, who just unlocked hope for his future. He smiled and closed his eyes to remember Linda and this beautiful night.

He knew he would not see her for a long time, but he could bear it because he loved her, and he somehow knew that she loved him too.

Chapter Eleven

Seven months later, on a warm Indian Summer Tuesday in October, Kevin left for work as usual after making breakfast for the family, and Tracy had just gotten the other children off to school. Duncan had just turned 20. Tracy gave Duncan his breakfast, set him up in front of the television, and popped in one of his DVD's to keep him busy until his tutor arrived. This was the morning ritual that they did almost every day.

Tracy walked out onto the back patio just as the breeze gently rippled its way through the colored leaves of the backyard trees. She paused to marvel at the beauty of the day and closed her eyes, taking in the fresh air, thanking God for their lives and her family. Today, Tracy did not have a care in the world. Fall was her favorite time of the year. For some reason, it always made her feel strong.

It was a perfect day for airing things out, so she decided to wash the blankets and sheets and hang them outside to dry. She carefully closed the front door and locked it as she always did when she left the main floor. She went in and checked on Duncan one more time. He was watching his DVD, bouncing up down on the couch, mumbling to himself. She walked over and kissed him, then went upstairs to the master bedroom to begin collecting the blankets and sheets.

Outside the window, an inflated red ball rolled across the lawn. Duncan jumped up and ran for the window, staring out at the ball, still being driven by the wind onto the neighbor's yard across the street. He mumbled something and ran down the hall towards the front door. He reached up and unlocked the deadbolt and went out.

Tracy was upstairs singing her best version of Sweet Caroline by Neil Diamond as she changed the sheets on the family beds. Suddenly, the sound of screeching tires riveted through the air, followed by silence. She froze for one agonizing moment, as a feeling of dread seized her and worked its way through her.

She closed her eyes for a second and prayed, then bolted out of the room. As she reached the top of the stairs, she could see the front door wide open. She flew down the stairs, leaping over the last three steps, and raced out. Halfway down the driveway, she stopped, put her hands on either side of her mouth, and screamed, "Duncan!"

She ran towards the car with a woman driver sitting stunned and motionless, with her hands still gripping the steering wheel. Tracy feared the worst, and as soon she got closer, she saw him. It was Duncan lying face down in the street, ten feet in front of a car. Tracy stopped, holding her hand over her mouth, then raced to him. She knelt over him, sobbing, screaming, "Duncan, please, Duncan... Duncan! Oh my God, help us!"

She rolled him over only to see blood run out of the side of his mouth. "Duncan... oh, my God... help us... please, somebody, call an ambulance." She felt for his pulse. He still had one. He was still breathing.

Duncan opened his eyes. He felt the searing pain all over his body, but he also felt his Angel Linda's presence. He could not see her, but he knew she was near, and he knew he would be okay. He looked up into his mother's face and made sure his eyes met hers.

Tracy had never seen such an expression on his face before. It was a look of peace. It was as if he was trying to tell her that everything was going to be okay.

Tracy knew he was seriously injured, "What hurts honey? Duncan?" She tried to prop his head up a little higher, "Duncan, hold on, keep breathing." She looked around with a frightened look on her face as now a crowd had gathered, and the sound of approaching sirens became louder.

Linda had arrived shortly after Duncan was hit by the car. She knew there was nothing she could do; it was his time. A tear rolled down her cheek as she turned away, only able to hope it was not too painful for him. She prayed for his speech to unlock once more, then watched intently as Tracy and Duncan share their last moments on earth.

Duncan grasped his mother's hand, then squeezed it tightly. He looked at her, then closed his eyes. "No, wait, Duncan, hold on! Hold on!" She put her ear near his mouth, listening to see if he was breathing, suddenly she froze, as she clearly heard him whisper, "Mom, I love you. I will... see you... in Heaven."

Duncan took his last breath and fell lifeless into his weeping mother's arms. She held his limp body tightly, rocking him, sobbing, letting years of worry unfold until the arriving paramedics gently pried him loose. They tried to revive him, but it was in vain. So, they covered his body and lifted it onto the gurney.

Linda felt profound sorrow but also a sense of peace as she saw Duncan speak to Tracy his final words of reassurance. The moment he died, she hung her head, quietly thanking God she had been given the gift of knowing Duncan, of being his Guardian Angel.

Tracy wailed as the paramedics gently moved him away from her and loaded his body into the ambulance. She collapsed in the street, and all her neighbors rushed to help her, picking her up and helping her toward her house. The drivers gave the neighbors the name of the hospital they were going to, and the ambulance quietly drove away.

Linda watched the sad scene unfold and then saw Tracy's Guardian Angel approaching from the sky. She landed, surveyed the scene, and turned to Linda, saying, "I'm sorry he had to suffer like that, but he is at peace now."

"Yes, thank you," Linda said as she wiped the tears from her eyes. "He's an extraordinary young man."

"I know you really cared about him."

"Yes, I really do, I'm just so sad he had to suffer, but it was his time." Linda realized Duncan's life would now take on a new purpose, that of being an Eternal Messenger.

"Are you going to be okay?"

"Yes, go help, Tracy. I have to go and get ready for Duncan to wake up in the eternal world."

~ ~ ~ ~

Tracy's neighbors took her inside her home and called Kevin. Some of them went over to the school to bring Sarah and Zachary home. A half-hour later, Kevin arrived home, and he and Tracy held each other tightly, crying for the longest time. A lifetime of hardship, love, and hope had just ended in a way they never wanted.

They kissed each other, holding their tear-stained cheeks together as they did the day Duncan was born, then turned to comfort Sarah and Zachary. The wider family was called, and they, friends and neighbors would all spend the next several days grieving, and making the arrangements for Duncan's funeral, and laying him to eternal rest.

~ ~ ~ ~

In the Heavens, the bells in all the Church towers of all seven Heavenly Realms rang at once for several minutes. It signaled to everyone that an Eternal Messenger arrived. This occurrence happened almost every week, but no one tired of it, especially in these days, when rumors abounded everywhere that the Dark Forces were planning on attacking the Heavens again.

The bells gave everyone hope and courage to face what might come and reminded everyone in Heaven that no matter the threat of darkness, the Lord's plan would triumph in the end.

Chapter Twelve

On the rim of the Grand Valley of the 4th Heavenly Realm, in a secluded section of tall spruce pine trees, Duncan's heavenly body laid perfectly still in a soft bed of pine needles. The sky was deep blue today, and a breeze blew through the forest, ruffling the pine needles in a wave. His eyes stirred behind his closed eyelids as he took his first breath and took in the smell of fresh pine.

Keeping his eyes shut, he felt the life-giving breeze hitting his face. His mind drifted to the accident, and he saw again the image of his mom's worried face looking at him, and he recounted his words to her, words that would console her until they met again. He kept his eyes closed, slightly opening them for brief moments, not wishing in any way to disturb the peace he felt as he began to wonder, *Am I in Heaven?*

Next to him, Linda was kneeling perfectly with a look of love on her face. She gazed at him quietly, not wishing to wake him, yet anxious to welcome him to Heaven. As he stirred, she softly brushed his hair with her hand and whispered, "Duncan, wake up. Duncan, your sleep is over."

Duncan instantly knew who it was. Before even opening his eyes, a broad smile came over his face, and he called out, "Linda!"

Linda laughed out loud, beaming, as she leaned over and gazed into his eyes. "I've been waiting for you, young man."

"Linda, I've thought about you every day since the night you first visited me."

Linda smiled and bowed her head, "I have thought about you ever since then to Duncan." She blushed. She couldn't believe how much joy she felt. It was like never before.

Duncan suddenly looked concerned, "Linda, what about my Mom and Dad?"

"They are grieving Duncan, but they will get through."

A tear rolled down his cheek, "I was able to speak with my Mom right before I died."

"I know I saw it."

Neither said a word, then Linda helped Duncan up. He wasted no time embracing her warmly. It was the most beautiful moment of his life. He knew now he was healed forever, but more importantly, he was with Linda. He was no longer the autistic youth Linda first met. He was a strong 20-year-old man in his prime, and yet there was no boundary between his old life and his new life at this moment; everything suddenly felt eternal.

The moment was just as special for Linda. Like all Angels, she had been alive since the beginning of time. However, she was not one of the most accomplished Angels. She spent a great deal of time working lower-level jobs and had not worked with any Humans until she was assigned to Duncan. She never imagined falling in love, and indeed, her emotions had been turned upside down of late because of it, yet she felt beautiful, and she knew it was right.

She took Duncan by the hand, "Let's walk for a while."

They began to walk through the pine forest. Duncan looked around at the beauty of the new world he now lived in, a world with hope, a world with freedom, a world that would never be taken away.

He asked, "Where is everyone?"

"Oh, there are lots of us here. We are just out in the countryside of the 4th Heavenly Realm.

"How many Heavenly Realms are there?"

"Seven. They're all similar, yet different in their own way. But no one would trade one for the other. As a citizen of Heaven, you may travel freely to any of them. It's just that everyone has a home in one or the other." She added, "Each one is commanded by one of the Archangels."

"I see. That's neat."

"Yes, it is," said Linda. The Archangel Raphael is in charge of the 4th Heavenly Realm. He is my boss. Well, he is actually the big boss. I have a Host Commander over me. He reports to Raphael directly."

"Wow, no kidding."

Linda laughed, and looked him wide-eyed, and said in a funny tone, "You're not kidding, no kidding! They all take things very seriously." She laughed, "I try not to."

Duncan chuckled. He loved the way she talked. They walked a little further, and Duncan asked, "Will I ever be able to see my mother?"

"Yes," Linda said. "There is a special place in the Great City of every Heavenly Realm. It's called a viewing room, and when we get to the city, I will take you there. You'll be able to see your family, and you will also be able to send messages of love directly to their hearts."

"Really, wow! I would like that."

They walked for a while longer, exiting the forest, and walking along a path at the rim of the canyon that overlooked a beautiful river gorge below. Linda looked up at the sun and said, "Well, it looks like it's time to go now."

"Where are we going?"

"I have been ordered to take you to the Great City to begin your assignment as an Eternal Messenger."

Duncan protested, "No, no, I don't want to go now. I want to spend time with you."

"Duncan, I am not supposed to 'spend time' with you right now. I have orders straight from the Archangel Raphael."

"Linda, I'm sorry, but I have been waiting to see you every night for a long time. Eternal Messenger or not, I need to spend time with you."

Linda grasped her chin, "Hmmm. Let me think… I better go right to the top." She signaled with her finger to wait a moment and then raised her eyes to the sky and uttered a silent prayer. Her face illuminated for a moment, and a peaceful smile descended onto it.

"Duncan, the Lords, are considering my request. We will wait until we find out what their answer is."

They continued walking through the forest. At one point, Linda said, "You know Duncan, I was not supposed to kiss you that night so long ago. I was only supposed to deliver a message to you. I don't really know what happened but I... well... I guess you could say... that I didn't follow the rules. There! I said it!"

Duncan looked over, trying to keep a straight face, then burst out laughing. Linda slapped him on the shoulder and started laughing too. Just then, a cardinal flew down and landed on Linda's shoulder. Linda held out her finger, allowing the bird to jump onto it, then took the small rolled-up message from its claw. She unrolled it and anxiously began to read.

"What does it say?"

"It says... we can spend a few days together."

"Yes!" said Duncan, thrusting his fist into the air!

Linda lifted the cardinal into the air, then playfully said, "Let's see if you can keep up with me." She started running down the path that led into the valley.

Duncan ran after her, feeling the exhilaration of running with all his senses. In his old life, he could only lumber along, but now he was agile and athletic, running full speed down a hill with the wind blowing in his face, giving him a feeling of freedom he had never before felt.

As they reached the bottom of the hill, Linda turned to see how close he was and then leaped up into the sky, calling out, "Follow me, Duncan."

Duncan leaped into the air after her, and to his amazement, he began to fly. "Whooooohooooo!" he yelled as he soared higher and higher above the valley floor.

Linda flew across the river, then swooped down, flying low over the river with Duncan right behind her. She then flew up out of the valley, stretched her arms out like a hawk, and began to circle in a wide arc, signifying that the chase was over. Duncan followed her lead, and they circled in the sky, taking in a warm breeze.

After a while, Linda pointed to a distant stream, "C'mon, let's go cool our feet!"

She darted down, and Duncan followed. They landed on the grassy plain next to a mountain stream. Linda walked into the knee-high water, pulling her white robe up so as not to allow it to get wet. She looked back and caught Duncan admiring her legs. She laughed out loud and turned, kicking some water up onto the shore, shouting, "C'mon in."

Duncan backed up, then ran forward, landing feet first into the water, instantly slipping on the mossy streambed, going completely under.

Linda waded over, laughing, "Duncan, are you all right?"

"I don't know," he said as he reached up to his hand, so she could help him up. As soon as she grasped it, he pulled her down.

"Duncan!" she screamed as she fell face-first into the water with a splash. They both laughed hysterically as they helped each other up and climbed up on the bank.

It was a fun-filled time for them both. They laid back in the warm grass, drying off and talking.

Duncan rolled over onto his elbow, leaned over, and stared into her eyes. He watched her sigh, then leaned closer and kissed her. As he pulled away, he saw the expression of love on Linda's face and knew it was right.

Linda, though, knew it was not the time for them, so she jumped up, "Let's go, we have a lot to see."

"Do we have to?" Duncan asked.

"Yes, let's go."

~ ~ ~ ~

They spent the rest of the day journeying deep into the Grand Valley on the most epic adventure of Duncan's life. They made their way into more populated areas, and met countless people, enjoyed exquisite foods, and saw stunning natural wonders. All the while, they both knew that they were falling in love with each other.

That night, as they sat by a fire, Duncan felt sad. He knew their time was growing short, and he could not imagine life without her.

The next morning, as the sun burst over the horizon, Linda felt the sun on her face. She opened her eyes and saw Duncan gazing at her.

"Good morning Duncan."

"Good morning."

"Today, we go to the Great City of the 4th Heavenly Realm."

"Wow. What's it like?"

"It's very special. Let's not waste a moment."

Chapter Thirteen

Within a short time, they turned onto a road that led through a forest, and suddenly it opened into the Great City of the 4th Heavenly Realm.

In every direction, there were thousands of people, and yet it did not seem crowded. There was joy and hopefulness in the air. Lovers were strolling around; some people were in cafés eating, coffee shops were filled with people relaxing and sharing stories about their old life. Nature was all around, beautiful pathways and streams winding their way around everything, weaving in and out of all the buildings.

After over an hour of strolling through the city, Linda pointed, "We're here. This is the main Administration Center."

"Administration center? Really? In Heaven?"

"Oh yes," said Linda. "People think Heaven runs by itself, but it's no different than Earth. There is lots of work to be done, and everyone has some type of job."

They ran up the broad entrance steps, and Linda pointed to the stairs, "Follow me, it's on the 5th floor." They started to climb the five stories of stairs. As they reached the fourth floor, Duncan asked, "Don't they have elevators?"

"Oh, yes, I never thought of that. Do you want to grab the elevator?"

"Well, not now. We only have one flight left." They both laughed.

When they reached the fifth floor Duncan was amazed, "Linda, this is the most beautiful place I've ever seen."

"Isn't it amazing? Believe it or not, it's only 400 years old."

"That's a long time."

"Not by Heaven's standards. This facility was designed by Michelangelo himself, shortly after he arrived here."

"Michelangelo is here?"

"Yes, he lives here in the 4th Heavenly Realm."

"Wow."

A man was sitting at a desk in the center. He looked up, "May I help you?"

"We would like a viewing room, please."

"Sign here," the attendant said as he pointed to an X, she made on the next line. "You may have room 17."

They went into the room, and Duncan sat down as Linda punched in some codes. Suddenly on the screen, Duncan saw Sara and Zachary sitting on their swing set in the backyard. Sara said to her younger brother, "I miss him."

"Me too," said Zachary. "He would be following us around the yard right now."

Sara began to cry. Duncan stepped forward to the screen, "Sara, I'm okay. I'm okay." Sara kept softly crying, but she paused for a moment and closed her eyes.

"Does she hear me?" Duncan asked.

"Not exactly, but she senses your feelings."

Suddenly Duncan's father Kevin came out of the house. He was in his work clothes and looked like he just got home. Sara ran to him and threw her arms around him. Kevin said, "I know Sara. I miss him too."

Duncan shouted toward the screen, "Dad... I'm okay." Kevin held Sara tightly, looking out into the distance.

Duncan's tears were running down his face. "Where's my mom?"

Linda punched another code, and the screen suddenly showed Tracy, laying on her bed, crying. It reminded Duncan of how she had been when she came home from the hospital after her breakdown years earlier. "Oh, mom... please don't cry."

Duncan touched his hands on the screen, his own tears practically melding with hers, and said, "Mom, I love you. You were the best, but I made it mom, I made it. I'm no longer... I mean, I am well. I can talk."

Just then, the evening sun slowly crept through Tracy's window, hitting her right in the face. She turned to bask in it, as she had done so long ago, and stopped crying. She got up and walked to the window, then dropped to her knees. She was quiet for a while, but it was clear she was finding peace.

Duncan smiled as he looked over at Linda. "She heard me."

"Yes, she did. Your message was given to her."

"Is it time for me to leave?"

"Yes, they are waiting for you."

Duncan stepped forward, took Linda by the hand, and pulled her close. He kissed her gently for several long moments. They then embraced tightly, knowing it would be a long while before they saw each other. This was their private goodbye.

"Where are we going?"

"To the headquarters of the Archangel Raphael."

Chapter Fourteen

Linda and Duncan flew along the coastline, heading north. Within a half-hour, a majestic castle, built on the side of a cliff, jutting out over the sea appeared.

"There it is," Linda said.

"It is magnificent."

"Who are we meeting here?"

"We are meeting the Archangel Raphael. All Eternal Messengers report directly to him, at least the ones belonging to the 4th Heavenly Realm."

They landed at the front gate and waited for the people and Angels in front of them to pass through. When it was their turn, the Angel guard asked, "May I help you?"

"We are here to see Archangel Raphael."

"Go on through."

They walked over to the main entrance and headed up the central staircase. At the top, an Angel, sitting at a desk, looked up. "May I help you?"

"Yes, I am Linda. I work in Raphael's command. I brought one of our Eternal Messengers to begin his assignment."

The lady looked down at her desk, picked up a clipboard, and asked, "Duncan?"

Linda smiled and nodded, "Yes, this is Duncan."

"Welcome to the 4th Heavenly Realm, Duncan."

"Thank you. I am glad to be here."

"One minute." She turned and walked over to a large oak door, gently opening it, and peering inside, saying something, then turned back, "You may both go in."

As Duncan stepped into the office, he saw a magnificent looking Angel seated behind his desk, with pen in hand. Raphael stood, and Duncan stepped forward to grasp his hand, looking eye to eye with him.

"Welcome, Duncan, welcome. I've heard a lot about you. And welcome back, Linda. You took a long time to get back here. Your Host Commander thought you were lost."

Linda looked down, "Sorry about that. I had orders from all the way at the top."

"Yes, I know, I was consulted."

"Oh, I see," said Linda.

"Sit down, both of you, please."

Raphael called outside his office to his secretary, "Mandy?"

In a moment his secretary came in. "Yes, sir?"

"Please send for Duncan's guide."

"I already did sir. She is waiting outside."

"Well, in that case, show her in." A moment later, a woman with short brown hair, and brown eyes, wearing a knee-high tan tunic with brown sandals, walked in. She stood at attention, then bowed. "Greetings to you, great Raphael."

"Greetings, Sonya. This is Duncan, and this is his Guardian Angel, Linda."

Sonya turned to face them and extended her hand toward Duncan. As soon as he grasped her hand, he immediately felt a draw of his power. He felt the darkness creeping toward him, along with her extended hand. He glanced into her eyes and saw turmoil, and more importantly, he saw evil. He knew instantly she belonged to the other side.

He held her hand momentarily, watching her face.

She too felt something, as her eyes signaled alarm, or worry, that somehow his goodness challenged her at the very core. "It's nice to meet you, Duncan," she said, nodding and looking away.

She then extended her hand to Linda and said, "It's nice to meet you, Linda."

Linda had observed the interaction between her and Duncan. It had not gotten past her that something strange had occurred. But what? Linda smiled, "It's nice to meet you too."

They all then turned to face Raphael. "Duncan, Sonya will be your guide. You are being assigned to the 3rd Land of Reform."

Duncan immediately raised his hand. "Sir, what is the 3rd Land of Reform?"

"Good question, Duncan. I heard you were smart. There are 4 Lands of Reform. They were created for people who missed the mark, but ultimately, did not deserve to go to Hell. There are four separate Lands of Reform. 1st, 2nd, 3rd, and 4th. The 4th Land of Reform, is where the worst offenders go. These people, are on thin ice, you might say. The 3rd Land of Reform, is 40 miles away, over the open sea, and that is where you will be working. If a person does not go straight to Heaven, or straight to Hell, they start in one of the Lands of Reform, and work their way up. Is all that clear?" Raphael asked.

"Clear as a bell, sir," replied Duncan.

"Good," Raphael said,. "Your first stop will be to meet the governor and get more details about the situation on the ground down there. It's not the lowest Land of Reform, but it's a tough place, and there are some tough characters down there, not all of them with an eye toward Heaven."

"I see," said Duncan, nodding.

"Sonya knows the lay of the land, and of all the areas, including the trouble spots. She began her journey in the 4th Land of Reform long, long, ago, and made her way to Heaven. Now, she aids us in our mission to thwart the efforts of the Dark Forces to seduce the people there away from their goal."

"Their goal?" asked Duncan.

"Their goal of getting to Heaven. It's the reason the 4 Lands of Reform exist to give people second chances. But there are forces at work against us, spies and agents, all promising a brighter future to those who will follow them. That's where you come in."

"I see," replied Duncan.

Linda had been eyeing Sonya and asked, "So Sonya, tell us about yourself. When did you live? Where did you die?"

"I lived in Russia during the time when Napoleon's army invaded. I was watching one of the battles from afar when a bullet found me."

"Napoleon, that was a long time ago."

"Yes, it was."

"And you ended up in the 4th Land of Reform. How come?"

Raphael was not happy that Linda was questioning her. Sonya had paid her dues and did not owe anyone an explanation. He glanced at Linda, but she would not relent.

Sonya said, "It's a long story, but I killed someone... actually... three people."

"I see,'" said Linda. "And how long before you made it into Heaven?"

"A long time."

"How long?"

"67 years."

Linda shook her head, "That's a long time. I'm puzzled."

Raphael interrupted, "Look, Linda, we are acquainted enough at this point."

Sonya interrupted him, "No, it's alright, I want to answer. It's because I resented my captors."

"Captors!" Linda replied.

"Yes, captors. They were Angels, not unlike you, Linda, and they thought they were better than me, just because I was a peasant, accused of...." She stopped.

"Accused of what?" Linda quickly asked, "Murder? Or was there more?"

Raphael stood abruptly, scolding Linda, "That's enough!"

An immediate silence fell on the room. Raphael said in an authoritative tone, "Sonya, you will accompany Duncan from here to the 3rd Land of Reform."

Duncan raised his hand, and said in a determined voice, "Raphael, may I have a word with Linada?"

Raphael looked at him, surprised at his commanding tone. He replied, "Yes, you may, but keep it brief."

Duncan walked over and opened the door, then turned, signaling that Raphael and Sonya should leave and wait outside.

"In my office?" Raphael asked, suprised.

"Yes, please. It will only take a minute."

Sonya walked out, followed by Raphael.

As soon as Duncan closed the door, Linda said, "Duncan, I don't like her. There is something about her that bothers me."

Duncan knew Linda's instincts were correct, but he also saw the conflict in Sonya. He had an inkling he could win her back from the Dark Side. He took Linda by the hand and said, "Listen, I'll be careful, Linda, but I think everything is going to be fine. I don't want you to worry."

"Duncan, it is a dangerous place. You have to be careful."

"I will, but that is not why I wanted to talk with you," he said.

"What is it?" she asked, her eyes wide with concern.

"I'm going to miss you, a lot," he said, as he stepped closer, taking her hands, gazing down into her eyes. "Will you visit me?" he asked.

"No, Angels are not allowed to enter the Land of Reform without special permission, and they don't grant permission for social reasons. So, I'm afraid," she wiped a small tear from her eyes, "I'm afraid it will be a while."

Duncan frowned for a moment. He had not expected to have to say goodbye right now. But nothing bothered him. He was in love with her, and he felt stronger and more confident than he had ever felt in his life.

He pulled her close and kissed her. Linda accepted his kiss and pulled him close, holding him tight as she kissed him back.

Then, they parted, and Linda turned and left.

Duncan is continued in the last 3 books of the After Life Series

The Angel Sagas are continued in Book 3 of the Series, Judgment.

Click Here to View on Amazon.

Thank you for Reading

**Help this sad Wittle puppy smile
by posting a Weview.**

Review on Amazon

Follow me on Amazon

Join my Newsletter & Get Starry Night Free
Here or at **dpconway.com**

A Magical Short Story You'll Never Forget

Also by D. P. Conway

And much more to come

Acknowledgments

Mary and Colleen, thank you for your excellent ideas and first-class editing. Having both of you carefully and tirelessly team up to shape and refine this book has made it as much yours as it is mine.

For Elizabeth Dawson, aka Megan Franciscus. Megan you were there at the beginning to help me craft the foundational ideas and stories that became the heart of this book series. Thank you.

For Marisa, your love and encouragement, made it possible for me to write this series. Thanks for letting me spend all these years refining this series. I love you more than these words can say... *Cara Mia, Io ti amo. Solo tu femmina.*

For Carla Reid, who with her strength and flare inspired the Archangel Splendora. Carla, the joy I receive from your wonderful friendship can never be measured.

For Sadie Sutton, who inspired the Angel Sadie. Sadie, you really must be an Angel, because meeting you changed me forever. Always... my friend.

For Ed Markovich, King Edward, thank you for the years of your edits, ideas, and counsel.

For Reda Nelson, our long-time associate, who helped keep the ball rolling, and moving through seven long, difficult years.

Also, thanks to Jocelyn Caradang, Rosie Queen, Peggy Stewart, Mary Greene, Angela Rabbitts, Annette Joseph, Bridget Mae Conway, Patrick Conway, and Christopher Conway (who thought of Legion), Ann Dewerth, and all 50 or so test readers over the last five years.

And to Caroline Knecht, who really brought this story to its final form by doing some awesome developmental editing. Wow.

Special Thanks to Beta Readers Katie Schantz, Peggy Stewart, Collette Murray, Courtney McKirgan, and Sara Cornwell. Thanks also to Larry, Tanja, AJ, and the wonderful team at Books Go Social

Copyright & Publication

Daylights Publishing
5498 Dorothy Drive Suite 3:16
Cleveland, OH 44070

www.dpconway.com
www.daylightspublishing.com

"Rebellion" is a work of fiction. All incidents, images, dialogue, and all characters, except for some well-known public figures, are products of the author's imagination and are not to be construed as real. Where real-life historical persons, images or places appear, the situations, incidents, and dialogues concerning those persons are entirely fictional and are not intended to depict actual events or to change the altogether fictional nature of the work. In all other respects, any resemblance to actual persons, living or deceased, events, institutions or locales is entirely coincidental.

Photo sources and credits are listed at www.dpconway.com

Cover: Nate Myers, Maura Wise, Colleen Conway Cooper
Contributing Story Editor: Elizabeth Dawson
Developmental Editor: Mary Egan, Colleen Conway Cooper
Editor: Connie Swenson
Final Developmental Editor: Caroline Knecht

Made in the USA
Monee, IL
18 November 2020

48297994R00146